The
Railway
Murders

ALSO BY J. R. ELLIS

The Railway Murders

A YORKSHIRE MURDER MYSTERY

J.R. ELLIS

THOMAS & MERCER

Text copyright © 2022 by J. R. Ellis
All rights reserved.

Published by Thomas & Mercer, Seattle

www.apub.com

Amazon, the Amazon logo, and Thomas & Mercer are trademarks of Amazon.com, Inc., or its affiliates.

ISBN-13: 9781542031363
ISBN-10: 1542031362

Cover design by @blacksheep-uk.com

Printed in the United States of America

The
Railway
Murders

Prologue

Murder on the Orient Express, 1934, by Agatha Christie is probably the most famous railway mystery story of all time. It has inspired a number of film and television versions. Famous actors playing the part of Hercule Poirot in these adaptations include Albert Finney, David Suchet and Kenneth Branagh.

It was very early on a sunny Wednesday morning at the beginning of June. The dawn chorus of birdsong could be heard in the peaceful rural scene around the Wharfedale Bridge Inn in Lower Wharfedale. The sun shone through the branches of the large oak and sycamore trees that grew around the inn. Nearby, the River Wharfe ran under the medieval bridge that gave the inn its name. Some mallards were paddling in the shallows with their large brood of fluffy ducklings. A dipper stood on a mossy stone in the middle of the river and the iridescent blue of a kingfisher flashed by.

There was little sign of any human activity yet, and the road was quiet. In one of the curtained bedrooms of the inn, a woman got out of bed leaving the man beside her still asleep. She pulled on a dressing gown and quietly left the room, closing the door carefully behind her. As she moved silently down the corridor, the door to another room briefly opened and shut again, but she didn't notice.

By the time the man was finally woken up by the strong sunlight that had made its way around the side of the curtains, there was the sound of traffic going past the hotel, doors opening and closing and voices inside and outside the building. He pulled himself up in the bed, noticing that his partner had left. He rubbed his eyes and smiled before wincing. He had the devil of a headache, and his mouth was like a birdcage bottom, as the saying went. It had been a good night: we were carousing to the second cock, he thought, quoting *Macbeth* to himself. And not only carousing. He glanced at the empty side of the bed again.

Daniel Hayward was in his early fifties, an actor who had made many appearances in films and TV series over a thirty-year career. These days, in addition to his famously dissolute lifestyle, he had developed the disaffected air of the fairly well-known actor who has never quite made it to the very top, but believes he deserved to. He often considered his current roles beneath him, feeling that he was too often typecast as the supporting character who could be pleasant or nasty; a familiar face playing parts in family and historical dramas.

He hauled himself heavily out of bed – he'd put on weight in recent times, mainly due to his drinking – and padded over to the bathroom. He winced again partly due to the headache, but also as he thought of the day ahead. He was in Wharfedale along with other actors and a film crew to shoot some scenes of a film called *Take Courage*, a somewhat sentimental story set in Edwardian times about a young woman who is ejected from her family home when it is inherited by a nasty uncle and has to make her way in the world alone. Unsurprisingly she eventually finds love.

What a load of crap! he thought to himself. Of course, he was playing the relatively minor role of the evil uncle; exactly his kind of part, at least according to producers and audiences who wouldn't appreciate range if it hit them in the face. Today's scene was where the evil uncle arrives at the station and is met by his solicitor and servants from the manor. If only the locomotive would explode as it stopped at the station, obliterating the sweet heroine and the rest of the family. Then his character, Montagu Lloyd, could inherit the property and not have to worry about any of them. End of story, and then all the cast could go home! Somehow, he knew that the director Gerard Blake would not take the same view even if Hayward dared to suggest such a thing.

He filled the bath and lowered his heavy frame into the water, trying hard not to splash it over the side. He sighed as the warm water covered him. It was a moment of bliss, but it didn't make him any more sanguine about the day ahead.

The dining room at the Wharfedale Bridge was a large oak-panelled room with a stag's head over the fireplace. Three of the principal actors were just finishing breakfast. Anna Whiteman, an up-and-coming actor in her mid-thirties, was playing the lead role of Victoria Branwell, the disinherited niece. She was wearing wide-legged linen trousers and a sleeveless top. The elderly white-haired Christopher North, eccentrically dressed in a red checked shirt, yellow waistcoat and blue trousers with red braces, was playing the family solicitor Edward Wilding. North was also a well-established character actor with a wealth of experience. Sheila Jenkins, in her early forties, wearing designer jeans, was in the role of the house-keeper Mrs Wilson. Other members of the cast had remained in London as they were not involved in the Yorkshire location scenes.

'Oh! Here he is at last,' cried North. 'Last man standing last night was it, old boy? You were still going strong when I went off to bed.' His tone was subtly cold and mocking.

Hayward had dressed hastily in jeans and a white shirt that strained over his belly. His untidy hair and pale look testified to his hangover.

'Something like that. God! I could use a coffee. Good morning, ladies.' Whiteman and Jenkins returned the greeting without enthusiasm. Hayward sat down at the table and a waiter took his order. Hayward declined anything to eat, but sipped orange juice until his coffee arrived. 'Where's Gerry then?'

'He's not here yet,' said Whiteman. 'But he'll want to get moving as soon as he gets back.' Blake had spent the night visiting a friend in Leeds.

Hayward ran his hand through his famously thick black hair which was now streaked with grey. 'Bloody hell. All day in this heat sweating it out in Edwardian costume, coming and going on a train while Gerry does five hundred takes before he's satisfied.' Blake was a notoriously demanding director, far too much of a perfectionist for Hayward. 'Anyway.' Hayward leered at Whiteman. 'At least you'll be there, Anna. It'll be worth getting out of the train for you waiting on the platform.'

Whiteman smiled as if she were sorry for Hayward, and shook her head slightly. She was not going to engage in anything flirtatious with this old roué, and she was relieved to see Gerard Blake coming into the room. 'Ah, here's Gerry. He'll want us to get moving. It's after nine o'clock.'

The waiter arrived with Hayward's coffee.

'Hi guys,' called Blake in a breezy manner. He was thin and wiry with a neatly trimmed beard and a bald head. He was wearing the arty uniform of black T-shirt and jeans. 'Are we ready to roll?'

They all stood up except Hayward. They knew that time was limited for the outdoor shoots and if they got behind with the schedule and had to stay for longer in Yorkshire, the budget for the film would start to increase, putting the whole thing at risk.

'We'll follow you down, Gerry,' said Jenkins. 'They'll be ready for us in wardrobe now.'

4

'I agree about the costumes,' said Whiteman to Jenkins as they walked out of the building. 'It's roasting in that woollen skirt.'

'Are you coming?' called Blake to Hayward, who waved a hand.

'Give me a few minutes. I just need to drink this coffee and bring myself round.'

For a second Blake's face seemed to blaze with something like hatred. 'Don't be long. You're in the second scene.'

Everyone but Hayward left the building to get into their cars to drive the short distance to the railway. The two women went together in one car and North drove with Blake. The countryside around was in its early summer glory. White May blossom still covered the hawthorn hedges and the trees shimmered in the bright, fresh greenness of their new leaves. Blake was too preoccupied with Hayward and the day's filming to notice the beauty around him.

'What's wrong with him?' Blake asked North with whom he'd worked a number of times, and had come to regard as a kind of mentor.

'He was drinking quite heavily last night,' replied North.

'Was he?' Blake's car scrunched down the gravel of the hotel drive. The director shook his head. 'I've really had it with him. He's so unreliable. He holds things up all the time. To be honest I didn't want him in the part, but Henrietta persuaded me.' Henrietta Fawkes was the film's producer.

'Don't worry; he'll make it through. He always does.' Privately, however, North was thinking about his own experience of Hayward's unreliability.

'I hope you're right,' growled Blake.

In the other car, the two women were also discussing Hayward. Sheila Jenkins was driving. 'Does he bother you?' she asked the younger actor, remembering Hayward's comments.

'He's the kind of man you steer clear of, otherwise you know you'll get groped,' replied Whiteman. 'I've encountered him before.

Don't worry, I can look after myself. I'll be glad when these scenes are finished. His character virtually drops out of the storyline then, and good riddance.'

'Good. Don't let him get to you. I've known him a long time and he's not to be trusted. His type are still a problem. The industry isn't as bad as it used to be in the days of the "casting couch", but you have to stay clear-headed and strong. It's still tough for women. And the younger you are the worse it is.'

'I know, I've had my fair share of harassment from men.'

'I'm sure you have. There's still a long way to go. We're still being paid less than the men, aren't we?' said Jenkins.

'Yes,' said Whiteman. 'But at least it's recognised as an issue now. My generation are going to fight as hard as yours did, and we'll make even more progress.'

Jenkins slowed the car down, flicking the indicator. 'That's good to hear. Anyway, we're here,' she said.

Their car left the main road and entered Oldthwaite station car park, moving quickly past a small banner that someone had put up, which read: 'Stop The Filming Now'.

Blake's car was already parked near the main building. The Wharfedale Railway was in a beautiful section of the dale. Like so many of England's vintage steam railways, it ran on a line revived by enthusiasts after it had been closed by the Beeching cuts of the 1960s. In summer, tourists came in great numbers with their children to ride on the trains pulled by a steam engine, and the entertainment continued in winter with Santa Specials. But at present the line was closed to visitors, temporarily taken over by the film crew.

Oldthwaite, a typical small branch-line station, had already been restored to its Edwardian heyday complete with signage and contemporary adverts, flower beds, hanging baskets and staff in period uniforms. It was the perfect setting for the filming of railway scenes from that era and had already featured in a number of historical films. Today the Edwardian authenticity was augmented by the fact that most of the people on the platform, apart from members of the film crew, were extras wearing period clothes. A train stood in the station pulled by a black tank engine that was giving off some steam from a piston. There were three vintage carriages, beautifully restored with four compartments in each. There was no corridor, just a door on both sides of each compartment.

'It looks like everything's ready and they're just waiting for us,' said Jenkins as the actors headed for the wardrobe department, which was housed in portable cabins near the station entrance.

Back at the hotel, Hayward was still in the dining room, smiling as he received and answered texts. He got up lazily from the table, yawning as he made his way out of the hotel and then walked up the lane to the station. As he did so he wondered if, having been to wardrobe and got his costume on, he would have time for a quick drink before filming.

Blake arrived on the platform where he was greeted by a woman with long blonde hair and dark glasses. This was his wife, Frances, who had stayed overnight in the hotel. As it was such a beautiful morning, she'd had breakfast early before deciding to walk over to the station via a lovely riverside path.

'Hi, darling,' she said. 'How was it with Ian in Leeds?'

'Fine,' he replied rather coolly, making no attempt to embrace her. 'I'll see you for lunch; must get on now.'

'OK,' she said, surprised and disturbed by his dismissive tone.

Frances Cooper was an actor herself, but not in this film. She had travelled with Blake to the location as she was currently between roles and fancied a break in the countryside. Today she had decided to come and watch the action for a while. She sat on a bench set back from the platform, where she had a good view of what was going on.

Blake went to plan the day's shoot. As the train was ready, he would have liked to start with the scene where Hayward's character arrived, but as Hayward had still not turned up, he decided to begin with conversations on the platform between the characters played by North and Whiteman before the train reached the station.

Filming of these scenes went well, but eventually they reached a point where Hayward's presence was necessary for the arrival scene. Extras in costume could be seen sitting in some of the carriages and many were looking bored. They'd been waiting for some time for the action with the train to start. Blake looked around in exasperation.

'Where the hell is he?' Blake said, slamming his copy of the script on to a small table he'd set up on the platform.

An extra, wearing a suit with a watch chain, said, 'I've just seen him in the bar.'

'What?!' Blake marched over to the old station buffet which now housed a modern café and bar. Sure enough, Hayward – who was at least wearing his Edwardian costume, a heavy Edwardian sack suit with baggy trousers and a Derby hat – was sitting at one of the tables, drinking a gin and tonic. There was a pretty young woman in costume with him. Blake made a supreme effort to control his temper and decided to try pleading and flattery with the recalcitrant actor.

'Look, Dan, for God's sake can we please make a start? This is a key scene when your character returns from London to inherit the Yorkshire estate. Everyone's worked really hard to get the period effects just right. People love these Edwardian station scenes, and we need a really strong performance from you. I know you can do it really well.'

Hayward slouched in his seat, his hat at a rakish angle, and gave Blake a sour look. 'All in good time, Gerry; a man's got to do something to take his mind off the tedium of playing with trains in the back of beyond.' He glanced at the woman, who smiled back at him.

Blake's patience was wearing thin. 'That doesn't mean spending half the morning drinking and then falling asleep in the late afternoon. We're already behind with our schedule. I've told you, we've got to wrap these outdoor scenes soon and get back to the studio.'

Hayward sighed, gulped down the rest of his gin, and hauled himself to his feet.

'You'd better follow us, my dear,' he said to the woman. 'You're in the crowd on the platform, aren't you?'

She nodded and followed them out of the bar.

'Anyway,' said Blake, 'here you are back in your home territory. You come from round here, don't you? I thought all Yorkshire people were proud of their county?'

'I left a long time ago,' sneered Hayward, in that plummy accent that had long ago erased any trace of his native Yorkshire. 'And I've no desire to return.' He winked at the young woman, who moved off to join the crowd on the platform.

'Right!' announced Blake. 'We're ready to roll! On you get, Dan.'

Hayward opened the slam-door of the compartment reserved for him, and climbed inside. There was no one else present, and he sat by the window. All he had to do was look out as the train entered the station before stepping down on to the platform, where he would be met by members of his family. Then, after a brief conversation, he would be taken off by horse and trap to the fictional Bolton Gill Manor.

'OK,' said Blake, and the railway staff took over. A whistle was blown by a guard sporting an impressive Edwardian moustache. This was answered by a shrill blast from the engine that, with a

9

loud chuffing noise, started to push the carriages backwards down the line to a starting position some distance away, so they could be filmed steaming through the countryside and arriving at the station. The train disappeared down a short tunnel, quite close to the station.

A mile down the track, a crew with a camera mounted on a van were ready to start filming. A section of road ran parallel to the line. They saw the train arrive in position and, after a short pause and a signal from the filming crew, it headed off back towards the station. The van moved off at a similar speed and filming began.

The cameraman monitoring the pictures was pleased. They were getting some good shots of the engine spouting steam as it chugged through the gorgeous countryside. But then he looked at Hayward's compartment and saw that something was wrong. The curtains were drawn, which was not supposed to happen in this scene. There was meant to be a brief close-up shot of Hayward looking out of the window. He would have to report this to the director. At this point the train was lost to view as it entered the tunnel again.

As the train came out of the tunnel and into view, everyone on the station prepared for action. A brief interchange between two family members was shot and then the train passed along the platform and came to a halt. Doors opened and passengers started to alight. But Hayward did not appear. Blake saw that the curtains were drawn in his compartment.

'Damn!' he cried. 'Cut! That's ruined the whole shot! What the bloody hell is he up to now? Surely he's not fallen asleep!' Blake twisted the handle and wrenched the door of the compartment open. 'What the hell are you . . . ?' He was stopped in his tracks by the sight of Hayward slumped in the corner of the bench seat.

His eyes were open but sightless and his hat had fallen on to the floor. He had a bullet wound to the head and the seat was soaking in blood. Blake drew back, cried out and a number of people ran over to the compartment.

But there was nothing they could do. Neither Hayward, nor consequently his character in the film who was supposedly returning to claim his inheritance, had arrived at Oldthwaite station alive.

One

Alfred Hitchcock's The Lady Vanishes, 1938, was his pen-ultimate British film before he departed for Hollywood. Set mostly on a train travelling through Europe, it is a tense and dramatic railway mystery starring Margaret Lockwood and Michael Redgrave. It also introduced the comic characters of Charters and Caldicott who became popular in films of the 1940s.

Yes, that must be a willow warbler, thought Detective Chief Inspector Jim Oldroyd as he raised his binoculars and tried to spot the bird in the tree, having heard its song a few moments earlier. He was off duty and was taking the opportunity to do a bit of birdwatching and nesting in the woods around Birk Crag not far from his flat in Harrogate, which overlooked the large green space known as the Stray. He was dressed in a walking jacket, cargo pants and lightweight walking boots and was carrying a small rucksack.

He was not a super-keen birder, but he always liked to spend some time in spring and early summer in the woods enjoying the wildflowers and spotting birds in the nesting season. His father had taught him where to look for nests and he enjoyed the challenge of finding miniature wonders like the dome of a tiny wrens' nest, so well hidden you could be a few feet away and still not know it was there. Of course, he never took any eggs away from the nest. He just loved the challenge of finding them. His partner Deborah had encouraged him to go into the woods and pursue his interests. She was on a long-term mission to get Oldroyd to spend less time on work issues, and find his own mental space.

It was a beautiful day and he'd brought some sandwiches with him. He would eat these later sitting on a grassy bank looking over the rolling countryside towards Lower Nidderdale. It was all enough to make him sigh with pleasure. He thought he had just located the warbler when his phone went off.

'Damn!' he exclaimed as quietly as he could, but not quietly enough to prevent the shy bird from flying off. Why hadn't he put his phone on silent for a while? He let go of the binoculars, which hung around his neck, and looked at his phone. Skipton police station; what the hell did they want?

He answered the call. 'Jim Oldroyd speaking,' he said rather irritably.

'Hello, Jim, it's Bob Craven.' Oldroyd was surprised and pleased despite the interruption to his day. Craven had been a detective inspector at Skipton station for a long time and they'd worked together so often over the years that Craven still addressed his colleague by his first name, although Oldroyd was now a rank above him.

'Bob? Well, and how are you? I don't think I've seen you since that pothole business. It's been too long.' As Oldroyd spoke, his pleasure at hearing from Craven was tempered with foreboding; this was going to be about work and his peaceful day was probably about to end.

'I agree, Jim. I'm fine, and I'm sorry to disturb you. I rang Harrogate HQ and they said you were off duty, but something unusual has cropped up and I'd really like your help.'

'Oh?' Oldroyd was intrigued. If his day was going to be spoiled, at least it should be for something worthwhile.

'Yes. An actor has been murdered on the set of a film being shot at the Wharfedale Railway; Oldthwaite station to be exact. I'm sure you know it.'

'I do. I've ridden on it many times, especially when the kids were little.'

'Right, well he was found shot dead this morning in a railway carriage which had just come into the station – you know, it was a scene in the film. He was supposed to get out, but he didn't. When they opened the door of the compartment, he was dead inside, shot in the head. No sign of a gun so it couldn't be suicide, but no sign of any struggle either.'

'I see.'

'We were called in, Jim, but I can't make any sense of it. Lots of people testified that it was definitely the victim who went into the compartment and that there was no one else in there with him. Apparently the train was moving pretty much all the time he was in there, so I don't see how anybody could have got in and we've checked for hiding places. Anyway there's a lot more to it, but I wondered if you could come over and give me a hand, Jim? I thought of you straight away; it's a mystery, the kind of thing that's right up your street.'

Despite the disappointment of having his day in the countryside interrupted, Oldroyd was indeed interested. There was nothing he liked more than the challenge of seemingly impossible crimes, and he'd earned himself quite a reputation for solving them.

'OK Bob, just give me time to get myself sorted out and I'll be there. I would normally clear something like this with Superintendent Walker, but he's on leave. He's gone to his caravan at Scarborough, so I'm free to make my own decisions. Has Tim Groves been over?' Groves was a forensic pathologist who had worked with Oldroyd on many cases.

'Not yet Jim, he's on another case. I'm expecting him soon.'

'Tell him to hang on until I arrive; he's always interesting to talk to. Also, I'm right out near Birk Crag so it's going to take me a bit of time to get there.'

'OK, Jim.'

Oldroyd ended the call. The warbler had gone. 'OK, well I'll have to come again to see you,' he said, shaking his binoculars towards where the bird had been. He set off walking up the hill and decided there was no point going back to get changed; it would all take too long. Also, if Deborah was home he didn't fancy telling her that he'd sacrificed his birdwatching to take on a case when he was supposed to be relaxing.

He decided to ring one of the detective sergeants who usually worked with him on difficult cases and get them to pick him up. Those two sergeants were Andy Carter, who had joined the West Riding force from the London Met a few years ago, and Stephanie Johnson, who had been born and raised in Yorkshire. They were both in their early thirties, and had been in a relationship for some time.

It was Steph who answered his call to the office at Harrogate HQ. 'Good afternoon, sir, I thought you were having a day off today?'

'Well, I was, but Bob Craven from the Skipton station has just called. He wants me to come in on a murder case at Oldthwaite on the railway. Are either you or Andy available to come over?'

'Andy's out with Inspector Harvey interviewing people on that fraud case, but I could come.'

'Good, well no need to clear it with DCS Walker, as he's on holiday.'

'Right, sir.'

'So get a car and pick me up at the entrance to Harlow Carr Gardens. I've been walking in the woods near there.'

Steph laughed. 'Are you going over to Oldthwaite in your walking gear then, sir?'

'Yes. Complete with binoculars, rucksack and walking boots. Nobody will say anything; they wouldn't dare.'

'Right sir, I'll see you shortly,' she replied, laughing again as she ended the call. Yes! she said to herself and punched the air. Work had been rather slow-moving recently and being on a case with DCI Oldroyd was always lively and interesting. This time she had beaten her partner Andy to the job. He wouldn't be pleased – there was a friendly competition between the pair for Oldroyd's attention – but maybe he would be needed, too, if things became complicated.

At Oldthwaite station the contrived Edwardian atmosphere had been brutally disrupted. Police officers with crackling radios were standing on the platform and blue and white incident tape surrounded the door into the compartment where Daniel Hayward had been found. Looking at the murder scene from a distance and talking in subdued voices were actors still in costume, which gave the whole scene a bizarre feeling in its mix of old and modern. The driver was standing on the platform near his engine looking down towards the carriage and talking to a guard. All the volunteers were wearing Edwardian uniforms, and the station had been extensively refurbished over the years in the style of that period. There was considerable public interest in what had happened, and a cordon had been erected around the station. Inspector Craven had organised his men to take statements from the witnesses, and he was now watching Tim Groves who had just arrived and was examining the body which had been laid out on the platform by the carriage.

Craven had lived all his life in the Dales area and had relatives who were in farming. He was sturdily built, red-faced and looked like a farmer himself. He was a very competent detective who was especially skilled in dealing with Dales folk in remote villages, but he knew his limitations when it came to a puzzle like this.

'I'm expecting Jim Oldroyd soon,' he said to Groves. 'I'll need his help with this one. It's a bit out of the ordinary; like that business at Jingling Pot a few years back.'

'Oh yes, I remember that,' replied Groves as he prodded and poked around. 'The body had been preserved by the cold down in those caves and by the absence of bacteria; very interesting. I don't see many corpses like that.'

'No, it was an unusual case and—'

'Are you the officer in charge?'

Craven turned to see a smartly dressed woman.

'Yes.'

'I'm Janice Green, general manager of the Wharfedale Railway. I just wanted to say what a terrible thing to have happened and that you can count on our full cooperation.' She spoke in a confident, businesslike manner.

'Good.' Craven was quite surprised. He hadn't expected an efficient, professional person like this to be in charge until he remembered that the railway was a business, probably with a large turnover, and therefore had to be properly and professionally managed.

'We also need to deal with the media response, so as to minimise any damage to the railway. Do you mind me asking what your procedures will be concerning the media?'

Craven was taken aback; he hadn't had the opportunity to even think about such matters. She was well ahead of him.

'We won't be speaking to the press today,' he said. 'When we're fully informed about what happened we'll be calling a press conference. If anyone contacts you, say the minimum and don't mention any names.'

'Very good. I'll liaise with you. And please ask if you need anything. There are a number of our volunteers on duty.' She turned and her stilettos clicked as she walked briskly down the platform.

As he watched her move away, Craven saw a police car turn into the car park. 'Oh! I think they're here,' he said to Groves. 'He's bringing one of his detective sergeants with him; that will be a useful extra hand.'

Sure enough, Oldroyd got out of the car and was joined by a DS whom Craven recognised as Stephanie Johnson. It wasn't long before his old friend and colleague was striding down the platform towards them, but he struck a strange figure; he was wearing walking boots, waterproof trousers and jacket and looked more like a national park warden than a detective inspector.

Oldroyd beamed at Craven. 'Bob! Good to see you!' They shook hands and Craven laughed.

'Good to see you, too, Jim. Did I interrupt you on a walk?'

'Yes, I was doing a spot of birdwatching but don't bother about it. There was no time to go back and change. I wanted to get straight over here. My appetite was whetted; you know how I like a good challenge. You remember Sergeant Johnson?'

Craven and Steph exchanged greetings.

'Oh, Tim! I hadn't noticed it was you down there!' exclaimed Oldroyd, as he spotted Tim Groves crouched next to the body.

'Not to worry, Jim,' Groves said. 'I prefer to remain inconspicuous. I wouldn't want to be in the limelight like you, dealing with the press and stuff like that.'

Oldroyd laughed and then looked down at Hayward. 'What do you make of it then?'

Groves stood up, his lanky frame towering above the three detectives.

'Well, there's no mystery from my point of view: gunshot wound to the side of the head which would have caused death immediately. We know the rough time of death, as he was seen getting into the carriage very much alive. I'll confirm things when I do the post-mortem. The only problem I have is knowing what type of gun would have been used in Edwardian times.'

Oldroyd laughed. He always enjoyed Groves' dry wit. The forensic pathologist had told him years ago that having a sense of humour was essential in the job he did.

'Not much more I can do at the moment,' Groves said as he started to pack up.

'So tell me about the circumstances again, Bob,' Oldroyd said, turning back to Craven.

'OK.' Craven consulted his notes. 'The company is called Clear Sky and they're making a film called *Take Courage* set in Edwardian England. They're here to film some scenes at the station. The victim's name is Daniel Hayward.'

'Oh yes, I've seen him in one or two things on the telly.'

'Yes, he's quite well known. Anyway, in this scene, the character he plays arrives at the station and is met by other people. The train came down the line about a mile and got to the station. Then Hayward was supposed to get out, but he didn't. The curtains were drawn across the door. The director, Gerard Blake, opened the compartment and found Hayward dead, sitting by the door. No one else was seen getting in or out of that compartment and this is a vintage carriage; there is no corridor, so you can only move between compartments when the train stops.'

'OK, I'm with you.'

'We've checked for hiding places, but there's nowhere that appears immediately obvious. Have a look for yourself.'

Before they could enter the compartment, Groves intervened. 'I'll be off, then. The ambulance is ready to take the body away.' He looked at the door thoughtfully. 'There is just one thing. The victim was sitting on the left of the door with the right-hand side of his head facing the window, but the bullet wound is on the left-hand side of his head which strongly suggests he was shot from inside the compartment.'

'You're right,' replied Oldroyd. 'I'd already just about eliminated a pot shot from outside the train because that would have shattered the glass in the door or window, and if the curtains were pulled across no sniper would see anything, anyway.'

'Yes . . . Anyway, goodbye for now. Sorry the film's been disrupted. I presume that murder on the train was not part of the script.' Groves chuckled and strode off down the platform carrying his bag and his jacket, as the afternoon was warm.

'Let's have a look at the train then,' said Oldroyd. 'Come on, Steph, let's see what you think of the murder scene.'

'OK, sir,' said Steph who had been listening and thinking while Craven and Groves were explaining things. She always enjoyed the challenges Oldroyd set during an investigation.

They clambered carefully into the ornate compartment through the wooden door. The interior was beautifully constructed of polished wood, with richly upholstered sprung bench seats. Above the seats were large picture panels, three on each side. One contained a painting of a somewhat idealised rural landscape, with a train steaming along and happy travellers waving from the windows. Others had advertisements for various products and local attractions all in the ornate style of the time. Above these were metal-framed luggage racks with netting to hold the bags. On the left side, the rack was full of large, old-fashioned cases.

Oldroyd tried the door at the opposite side. It was locked. They had a quick look under the seats and up to the ceiling and then returned to the platform.

'Sir, I assume you've looked in those cases on the rack?' asked Steph.

'Yes, we've had them down,' replied Craven. 'They're all empty. I presume they're there to create a period feel.'

'Why is the other door locked?' asked Oldroyd. 'Surely that would be a health and safety issue for the production company? Anybody in that compartment should have been able to get out at both sides.'

'I'm on to that, Jim. The guard responsible apologised. Apparently, the lock is faulty and the door can't be opened. It should have been repaired. It's quite important because, by chance, it seems to rule out anyone getting into the compartment from the other side.'

Oldroyd frowned. 'I see. That would have been a possibility. If that door wasn't jammed, someone could have had a key, got in at that side, shot the victim and left, locking the door behind them.'

'They would have had to do all that without being seen, sir,' observed Steph.

'True, so it's not really likely, but this means we really are stumped.'

'It's another locked room mystery, sir, like the one we investigated at Redmire Hall.'

'It's looking like it, Steph. Or at least . . . it's a locked carriage mystery. Let's have a look at some of the other compartments.'

'We've already had a quick inspection,' said Craven. 'There's nothing unusual in any of them; they all look the same.'

There were six compartments in the carriage, all very similar, with the same colourful panels, luggage racks with period cases and upholstered seats.

'And you say no one was seen around that compartment or going in at any point?' asked Oldroyd.

'No. We've got to speak to the people including a camera crew who were out watching the train and filming it as it approached the station. We'll see if anyone saw anything. I've gathered the main witnesses in the waiting room and there's an office next to it which I thought we could use as our incident room.'

'Good.'

As they walked across, Oldroyd turned to look down the spotless platform and at the restored and brightly painted station buildings. What a brutal thing to happen in such a lovingly cared for and dinky little place where people came to enjoy themselves, the older ones to indulge in a little nostalgia. Murders on railways were common in films and fiction but this place was more redolent of the gentle atmosphere of *Thomas the Tank Engine* and *The Railway Children*.

The waiting room was silent except for a few whispered conversations. It was furnished in period style, with framed railway posters on the walls, and a small stove and a gas light, though the latter was not functioning. People, many of them still in costume, were sitting around the sides of the room on the benches, some tense and rigid, while others were slumped and apparently in shock.

In the latter category was Gerard Blake. He sat with his head in his hands, supported by his wife Frances on one side, and Anna Whiteman on the other.

Oldroyd introduced himself, and Steph and Craven invited Blake into the office which had been vacated by the railway staff. Inside there were some chairs and a table in the centre of the room that were probably used for meetings. Around the edge of the room were some PCs that seemed incongruous in the Edwardian building. A huge Edwardian-style hand-drawn map of the railway covered one wall.

'I know you've already made a statement,' began Oldroyd. 'But we would just like to go through it again. It was you who found the body.'

'Yes,' replied Blake with some effort, as if speaking was hard. 'He was supposed to open the door and get out on to the platform but he didn't, so I pulled the door open and . . . and there he was.'

'Did you notice anything unusual when he got into that compartment, or when you first opened it when it had returned?'

'No. The compartment was definitely empty when he got in and everything was as we planned it. But when the train got back to the station, the curtain inside was drawn across the door and the window which it was not supposed to be. I was obviously so shocked when I opened the door and saw his . . . his body that I didn't notice anything in the compartment. I feel particularly bad because I thought he was messing about, and I was angry. And then it turned out he was dead.' He shut his eyes and grimaced.

'Why was he alone in there?'

'It's easier when we're filming a scene like that. Other people in the compartment can get in the way. We use the extras to populate other parts of the carriage, look out of the windows, get off at the station and stuff like that. It means we've always got space around the main character for filming purposes.'

'I see.'

'We understand that you and he were not getting on well before this happened,' said Craven.

Blake sighed. 'I can't deny that. Dan was a pain in the arse. He didn't want to be here, basically, and he was late for everything.'

'Would you have preferred someone else in the role?' asked Oldroyd.

Blake looked at him, realising the possible implication. 'Yes, to be honest. But it was a bit too late for that. We've already shot a number of scenes with him in.'

'Was his behaviour at all strange recently?' continued Craven.

'I wouldn't say so. He was his usual vain, self-centred and unco-operative self. He considered the parts he was getting on TV and in films to be beneath him. I think he overestimated his talent.'

'Did he have any enemies?' asked Oldroyd.

'Quite a few I would imagine, given the rivalry in this profession . . . and the way he treated women. But I couldn't name any particular individuals.'

'Couldn't or won't?' asked Oldroyd abruptly.

'Look, Chief Inspector, I've heard dozens of people say negative things about him and about other actors too, but no one who's threatened to harm him, at least not when I was present.'

'Tell us what happened this morning, leading up to the events here.'

Blake shrugged. 'I stayed in Leeds last night. I was taking the opportunity to see a friend while I'm up here. I got up early and was back at the hotel where I'm staying with the main actors for nine.'

'Is that the Wharfedale Bridge?' asked Craven.

'Yes. When I got there, everyone was ready to leave, except Hayward who'd only just come down. I told him to get a move on, and then gave Christopher North a lift over here. Sheila Jenkins and Anna Whiteman came down in Sheila's car. They went to wardrobe, and I came on to the platform to sort things out for the tech team.'

'When did Hayward get to the station?' asked Oldroyd.

'Not until much later. At least we thought he hadn't. Turns out he got here, put his costume on and went to the bar. Didn't even tell me he'd arrived. I was furious when I found out and went to get him. He saw I was in no mood to argue and followed me out. There was an actor sitting with him, I think, a young woman. Bloody typical of him. He'd rather spend his time trying to seduce someone like that than get on with his job for which he was being handsomely paid.' Craven made a note of this.

'Your wife is with you, isn't she?' he asked.

Blake looked awkward as if he didn't want to talk about his wife. 'Yes, Frances Cooper. She's an actor, but she's between jobs just now. She came up for a bit of a break, staying at the hotel with me. It's turned out to be something traumatic instead.'

'It looks like we may have a number of suspects,' said Oldroyd after Blake had left the room. 'It often happens when the victim has had a colourful past, as seems to be the case here.' He turned to the other two detectives. 'Steph, I want you to join Bob's team and see where we're up to with statements from all the people who witnessed what happened on the platform. Check them and see if anyone reported anything unusual. Then speak to the other people who were on the train.'

'Right, sir. I've got it,' Steph said, as she left the office.

'The next people I think we should speak to are the crew who were filming the train as it went through the fields. I want to know exactly what they saw.'

'I think you're right, Jim,' Craven said. 'I told them to wait by their van in the car park. I'll fetch them in.'

Two men and a woman dressed casually in jeans and T-shirts followed Craven silently into the office and sat down. Craven did the introductions and Oldroyd began the questioning.

'OK, well you know that Daniel Hayward's been shot and he's dead, but no one's been apprehended yet. The compartment where he was shot was empty and it's clear that the shooting happened on the train either while it was reversing out into the surrounding countryside or when it was returning to the station. This means that, unless a member of the public comes forward who might have witnessed something from a field or a path, you were the only people who could have seen what happened.'

The crew looked at each other and the woman spoke. 'We've talked about what we saw, Chief Inspector, and we all agree. The train reversed to a point called Far Moss Hill where we were waiting on the road nearby. It stopped briefly and as soon as we signalled we were ready to film, the engine whistled and moved off. The road runs parallel to the train line, and we filmed it from the van until it entered the tunnel near the station.'

'Was there anyone around on the track who could have got on to the train?'

She checked with the others. 'No, we didn't see anyone.'

'How long did the whole scene take, from when the train reversed out of the station to when it arrived back?'

'I'd say no more than about twenty minutes.'

'And for how long did the train stop at Far Moss Hill?'

'Five minutes at the most. It was when we started to film that we noticed that the curtains were drawn. We were supposed to film a close-up of him looking out of the window, but we couldn't do it. We knew that something was wrong, but we didn't know how serious.'

'And you didn't notice anything else unusual?'

'No. We didn't see anyone or hear any shots. I can't imagine how on earth the killer was able to murder him and escape.'

The crew left Oldroyd and Craven together. Oldroyd sat in a chair with his hand over his mouth looking very thoughtful.

'See what I mean, Jim?' Craven said.

'Yes, it's a good one, isn't it?' said Oldroyd. 'It's certainly been meticulously planned by a clever person or persons from which we can conclude, I think, that the motive is something long estab-lished, not a spur-of-the-moment thing. It's very difficult to see how anyone could have got into that compartment after the train left the station, especially given that they couldn't get in from the other side as the lock was bust. The killer must have already been on the train or even in that compartment when it set off.'

'But where were they hidden, Jim? And where did they go? There are no hiding places in that compartment and no trapdoors from the ceiling or in the floor.'

'At the moment, Bob, I haven't a clue, but we're going to have to look much more closely at that carriage. Anyway,' he said, slapping his knees, something he had a habit of doing when he was ready for action, 'let's talk to the leading actors; they may have seen something earlier at the hotel and they may know more about who might have had a motive.'

The situation Steph faced on the station platform was difficult. Inspector Craven had instructed everyone who had been involved in the shooting of the scene to stay until they'd been spoken to by an officer. Extra chairs had been brought on to the platform and bottles of water were supplied by the café. There was a strange incongruity in the scene of people in Edwardian costume drinking from plastic bottles and tapping their mobile phones.

Two DCs were working hard and to save time were speaking to people in small groups and making notes. They were pleased when Steph appeared to help.

'OK, Sarge,' said one of the detectives. 'We're talking to all the people who were on the platform, could you deal with the ones who were in the carriage? They're sitting together over there.' He pointed to a group of people sitting on benches in shade provided by the station canopy.

'Sure,' said Steph. 'Has anything interesting come up?'

'No, everyone tells the same story. There was nothing out of the ordinary until the compartment door was opened except the curtain drawn across the door and side windows.'

'OK.' Steph went across to the train group and introduced herself. 'You were the extras on the train, yes?' They nodded. 'What was your role?'

'We were just playing ordinary members of the travelling public,' replied one who was dressed as a comfortably off gentleman with a waistcoat and gold watch chain. 'We sat in some of the compartments and got out at the station.'

'There aren't many of you.'

'That's deliberate. If there were too many of us, we would crowd the platform and make the shot difficult. It's only meant to be a quiet country station.'

'Were you directed to which compartments to sit in?'

'No. We just sat in the ones that were open and looked out of the window. It was a bit dull, particularly when Dan Hayward was late and kept us all waiting, which he did today.'

'Were any of you in the compartments next to Hayward's?'

'I was in the one to the right of his,' volunteered a middle-aged woman in an elaborate bonnet.

'And did you see or hear anything unusual?'

'I heard someone moving around, but I just thought it was Mr Hayward.'

'What about the compartment on the left?'

'That was locked. I expect because anyone coming out of that one at the station would be in the line of the shot and might obscure Mr Hayward's character.'

'OK. Did the rest of you hear or see anything?'

The group exchanged glances. One of them – a woman in a long velvet skirt and matching jacket with white frills at the wrist, who fanned herself with an oversized hat that was embroidered with flowers – replied, 'No, it was just a regular shoot, and it was going well until that moment.'

'What about the gun? Did any of you hear a gunshot?'

They shook their heads, which did not surprise Steph. The murderer would almost certainly have used a silencer.

'Did any of you know the victim?'

They shook their heads again. 'Only in the sense that he's quite well known,' replied one. 'But none of us have worked on a film with him before.'

'Well thanks anyway,' said Steph.

'Actually, there was just one thing, but I don't know whether you'd say it was unusual,' said the woman with the hat.

'What was that?'

'When the train got into the tunnel, it slowed down, didn't it?' She turned to the others.

'Yeah, I suppose it did, but so what?' said a man dressed in the moleskin trousers, faded jacket and stripy shirt of an Edwardian workman.

'Did any of you see anything or anybody in the tunnel?' asked Steph.

'No, there wasn't much light in there,' continued the woman sarcastically, and then she sighed. 'Look, can we go soon, I'm getting very hot in this costume? We've been hanging around for nearly the whole day.' The whole group looked completely jaded.

Steph smiled sympathetically. 'I understand, but you'll have to wait until one of my superiors – Inspector Craven or Chief Inspector Oldroyd – gives you the word. I don't think it will be long.'

She saw the disappointment on their faces and left feeling the same herself. It didn't seem as if anyone involved in the filming had seen much that could help the investigation. She disliked taking bad news to her boss.

Anna Whiteman sat behind the table facing Oldroyd and Craven. She was also suffering from the heat in her Edwardian costume. Her legs were stretched out under the table, and she had hitched her long heavy skirt up slightly. The buttons on the neck of her blouse had been unfastened. Oldroyd thought she seemed very calm and composed.

'Did you see anything unusual on the platform?' Oldroyd repeated the question that had now been asked of so many witnesses, none of whom had yielded any useful information.

'No. Dan got into the compartment, the train backed out, it came back about fifteen to twenty minutes later and he was in there dead. God! That was enough. I'm sure you find it as baffling as the rest of us.'

'Quite. What exactly did you see on the platform?'

'Gerry went over to see what was happening and I followed him. He was angry; he thought Dan was playing around. He pulled the door open, and there was Dan. I looked away and leaned against the next compartment when I saw the blood. I'm not good with that kind of thing and I knew something horrible had happened.'

'You are staying in the hotel with him and the others?'

'Yes.'

'Did anything happen while you were there?' asked Craven.

'Not much. Dan came down to breakfast very late this morning and had a row with Gerry. I think Gerry found him difficult; Dan could be so annoying.'

'Did Blake ever threaten him in any way?'

'No. He was very exasperated, but other than that very patient, actually. More than I think I would have been.'

Oldroyd looked at her. She was young but very confident and apparently not much affected by what had happened. 'Did you get on with Hayward?'

Whiteman shook her head. 'No, I think it's fair to say. I had little contact with him outside work, but I did work on another film in which he was involved. He's the kind of man who behaves as if it's still the nineteen-eighties, and he can touch women, leer at them and make suggestive comments all the time without anyone objecting. I hear he's been through a number of wives and relationships. I just kept away from him and didn't respond to his attentions.'

'Do you know of any other enemies he may have had?'

'No. I didn't know the man well enough. He was universally disliked amongst the younger actors because of his arrogance and self-centred disdain for what he was doing as if it was all beneath him. But I can't think that this was a motive for anyone to kill him.'

'How did the previous filming with him go?'

'Fine. I didn't play in any scenes with him as I did in this film. I just behaved professionally and avoided him socially.'

'Would you agree that you're not sorry to see the back of him?' asked Craven.

Whiteman looked at him. 'I had no feelings for the man, Inspector. What has happened is terrible. It's true that I would have preferred to work with someone else, but it would be indulging the actor ego to a chilling extent if I were to have him eliminated so that I could have a different actor in his part in the film. Don't you agree?'

Oldroyd smiled at this effective put-down. She was a cool customer, but he felt that perhaps her real feelings remained concealed.

The next person Oldroyd interviewed was Christopher North who, unlike Whiteman, seemed genuinely shocked and upset. He sat in the office still in costume: a heavy black Edwardian suit with a waistcoat and watch chain. He, too, was hot, and his face was red and sweaty. His voice was shaky and weak.

Craven gave the actor a glass of water.

'Thank you,' he said, wiping his brow. 'I've known Dan a long time; we worked on a lot of films and TV shows together and I always got on well with him. He could be difficult, I know, especially for directors. But he was what you'd call an interesting character and we've always had those in the acting profession; it's full of prima donnas and fragile egos but that's what makes us an interesting group of people.'

'Did he have any enemies apart from angry directors, rival actors and rejected women?' asked Oldroyd.

'That's quite a list, Chief Inspector,' replied North, managing a smile. 'Yes, he wasn't popular with a number of people, but I don't know of any individuals who would have actually wanted Dan dead.'

'I see,' said Oldroyd thoughtfully. 'You say you've known him a long time . . . What do you know about his early life and career?'

'Well, not a lot of detail. He was brought up round here, in Ilkley or Skipton I think.'

Oldroyd perked up, looking surprised. 'Was he? I didn't know that.'

'Yes. He went to RADA, and didn't come back to Yorkshire much except to visit. I'm not sure whether he's still got family here or not. He never spoke fondly about this part of the world.'

Again, Oldroyd was surprised: that was unusual for a Yorkshire person, although he knew that not every native of the county was as devoted to the place as he was. Had something happened that had made the actor feel negative towards the area where he'd been born?

'He got minor parts in London theatres,' continued North, 'and worked his way up. Then he got into television. I worked with him many times on the stage and the screen. We always worked well together, but I don't think he was a happy man.'

'Why do you say that?'

'His personal life was a mess. Candida was his third wife. He recently separated from her, and she has filed for divorce on the grounds of adultery. He had no children, which was probably a good job. Professionally he was a good actor, but he wanted to be a great one and more famous. He thought he was typecast in certain roles, and I guess that's why he could be difficult: he didn't really want a lot of the parts he was offered but he had to do them because he needed the money.'

'Did he have any financial problems? Money worries?' asked Craven.

'Dan was always a bit short of cash. It was his happy-go-lucky lifestyle; he got through cash quickly. He believed he was going to be badly treated in his divorce from Candida and would end up paying her a lot of money, but it was his own fault: he was the one who was constantly having affairs.'

'Might he have been capable of blackmail?'

'Dan? I don't think so. There was nothing malicious about him and he was so disorganised. I can't imagine him being crafty and planning anything like that. He loved being actorly and playing to his admiring public. There was nothing devious about him.'

'What did you see on the platform?'

North wiped his brow. 'Nothing much. I'm not very tall and my view was obscured. The train got to the platform, and nothing happened. Dan didn't get out. Gerry and Anna and a few others who were nearer than me went over to see what was going on and then all hell was let loose when they found his body.'

North paused and sighed. 'You know, the more I think about it, the more I think that this is the way he would have liked to go: a big dramatic gesture and a mystery which enthralled people. The old bugger's the centre of attention even after he's died.'

~

Oldroyd and Craven were discussing what they'd heard in their interviews so far.

'She didn't have much time for the victim, did she, Jim?' Craven said.

'Anna Whiteman?' Oldroyd replied. 'No. She was difficult to read, but there doesn't seem to be anything there which would constitute a motive for murder. Unless she's not telling us everything. North and Hayward appear to have got on well so nothing there either. None of the people we're talking to today had the opportunity to carry out the murder, so if they are involved it is as a partner in the crime.' He turned to Steph who had just entered the room, having returned from her interviews with the extras on the platform. As she sat down next to them, he asked, 'Anything to report?'

'Not much, sir. As far as I can see, everybody on the platform and everyone on the train seems to have seen the same thing: Hayward got on the train which backed out of the station. When it returned, the only odd thing was the drawn curtain; then Hayward was found dead inside. The only thing that was at all unusual was that, apparently, the train slowed down as it passed through the tunnel.'

'And?' asked Craven.

'Nothing, sir, but it's the only scrap of additional information I was given.'

'But actually, that is interesting,' said Oldroyd, who had suddenly become a little more animated. 'That may have given someone the opportunity to leave the train or to get on to it.'

'But how would they get on, Jim? The lock on one side of the compartment was jammed and Hayward was sitting by the other door. Are you implying he might have let his killer in? There was no sign of a struggle.'

'It's not impossible, but I've no idea why.'

'Did any of those actors see or hear anything or anybody in the tunnel?' Craven asked Steph.

'No sir, but they said that, obviously, it was dark.'

Craven shook his head. 'It would be such an enormous risk for anyone getting in or out of that compartment. Even if it was dark, the chances of being seen must have been high and what about the noise of the door? Those are heavy slam-doors, and they make a loud noise when you shut them. I just can't see it.'

'I tend to agree with you, Bob, but we'll have to follow it up and have a look in that tunnel. We'll also have to have a word with the driver.'

'The only other possibly significant thing was that there was no one in the compartment to Hayward's left, as the door was locked. The actor who reported this said that it might be because anyone coming out of there would interfere with the filming on the platform.'

Craven frowned. 'Well, that's odd, because it wasn't locked when we arrived. All the compartments were open. Maybe it was just jamming a little, and they thought it was locked?'

'Maybe,' said Oldroyd and thought for a moment. 'OK. Who's next?'

'Sheila Jenkins,' said Craven, consulting his notes. 'She's the fourth of the principal actors who were staying at the inn; playing the part of the housekeeper who goes with the other two to meet the new owner of the house – that was Hayward's character – at the station.'

'OK, bring her in.'

Like Anna Whiteman, Sheila Jenkins did not seem unduly upset by what had happened on the set that morning. She sat upright in the chair wearing her rather severe costume, which consisted of a long black dress, tight at the waist and buttoned up to the neck. She looked every inch the part of the housekeeper. Her account of what had happened earlier that morning tallied with what North and Anna Whiteman had said.

'How did you get along with Hayward?' asked Craven.

'Dan had a reputation. You learned to work with him professionally and keep away from him outside that. I made a point of warning the younger actresses about him, although it often made no difference. He could be very charming and seductive.'

Oldroyd narrowed his shrewd grey eyes. Was that comment a result of her experience with Hayward? Was there a history there? If so, she wasn't saying anything directly about it.

'Did he have any enemies who might wish him harm?' continued Craven.

She shrugged. 'I'm sure Christopher has given you a list of people who had no time for Dan. He knew him better than I did. You can't be in this profession for very long without making enemies. There's so much jealousy and backbiting. It might be all "Luvvies and Darlings" at the Oscars but there's no love lost between many actors, believe me.'

'You don't make it sound very glamorous,' remarked Oldroyd.

She shrugged again. 'I suppose I've been around too long. It didn't take me long to get disillusioned, but it pays the bills and it's a much more interesting job than the type of drudgery most people have to put up with.'

'OK. Well, we need you all to stay in Oldthwaite for a while,' said Oldroyd. 'What do you think will happen with the filming?'

'I'm sure Gerry won't want to abandon the film, especially not for the sake of Dan; they didn't get on well, though I presume Gerry thought Dan would be excellent in that part. I suppose we'll go back to London and shoot some scenes and then come back here after a decent interval. The show must go on, you know.' She smiled in a rather sardonic manner.

'She seemed very cynical about things, sir,' observed Steph when Sheila Jenkins had left.

'Yes, and like Anna Whiteman, she didn't seem particularly upset about Hayward's death. I think we need to find out much more about the past lives of those two, and anyone else in the cast who had any previous connection with Hayward.'

'From memory, there were one or two who'd worked with him before, sir, but I'll check the statements again. There was an actor who was sitting with Hayward in the bar when Blake came to get him for the filming. She said she hadn't met him before today, but it was flattering to be chatted up by a famous actor. I didn't get the impression she was going to let the flirtation lead anywhere, however. This Hayward sounds like a bit of an old rogue.'

'Yes,' said Oldroyd. 'But I think young women today are more sassy and less impressed by male egos than they were in the past. Anyway, the other thing is Hayward's past. We got a glimpse of his early life from North, but we need to find out much more. I'm giving that task to you, Steph, when we get back to HQ.'

'Right, sir, but I can start now. I can log in remotely on my laptop.'

'Oh yes, I keep forgetting,' replied Oldroyd sheepishly. 'Bob, let's go and talk to the engine driver and other people from the railway. We need to ask about the engine slowing down and whether anybody saw anything unusual.'

Oldroyd and Craven walked down to where there was a restroom for the railway officials, Oldroyd taking the opportunity to have another look at the train and the platform and to consider the puzzle. The door to the room was painted red with cream lettering like all the signs and notices in the station. It was opposite to where the engine was standing and still occasionally snorting out steam.

The detectives were admitted inside where they showed their warrants to the three or four people dressed in the railway uniform sitting in easy chairs around a table. There was a rudimentary kitchen area in one corner.

'OK,' announced Craven. 'I assume you were all on duty here when the incident occurred?' They all indicated that they were. 'We need to speak to those who were directly involved, so first of all the engine driver.'

'That's me, Philip Andrews,' said a grimy-faced man dressed in dirty corduroy trousers and a black shiny cap, who was drinking from a large mug of tea.

'And the guard who blew the whistle when the train backed out and was on the platform when it returned.'

'OK, me, Brian Evans.' Another man dressed in an immaculate uniform with a waistcoat, watch chain and shiny cap printed with the word 'Guard' above the peak put up his hand.

'Right. Mr Andrews first. We'll talk in here if the rest of you could give us a few minutes.' The others filed out leaving Andrews still drinking his tea. The detectives sat down.

'So,' began Oldroyd, 'it was your job to reverse the train back down the line and bring it back to the station?'

'Aye.'

'Were you alone in the cab?'

'Aye, we don't need a fireman on a short distance like this. I can stoke up a bit myself if I need to.'

'Did everything proceed as normal?'

'Aye, I did exactly what that chap, Mr Blake, said: I backed the train down to Far Moss Hill and then when I got the signal from those people filming by the track I drove back to the station.'

'Some people on board have reported that the train stopped in the tunnel. Is that true?'

'I don't think I actually stopped it, but I did slow down at one point because I thought there was something on the track. Turned out to be a fertiliser bag; plastic, you know. They get blown about a bit if the farmer doesn't dispose of them properly. You can't see anything clearly in the tunnel until you get close.'

'I see. Was there anything else unusual in the tunnel?'

'Nothing that I could see.'

'Right, I think that's all then,' said Craven.

Andrews finished his tea. 'Can I move the engine now? It needs to go back into the shed for the night. Mind you, I can't see us doing any more filming anytime soon so it'll probably be in there for a while.'

'I'm sure you're right,' said Craven. 'Yes, that will be fine, but you must leave the carriages at the platform; that's the murder scene. Nothing must be moved, and nobody must cross the incident tape and go inside.'

'Right you are, then.' Andrews got up and left.

Brian Evans came straight in.

'Sit down, Mr Evans,' said Craven. Evans sat upright on the same chair Andrews had occupied, the silver buttons on his uniform shining. 'It was your job to blow the whistle when the train left and then you were an extra standing on the platform when the train got back.'

'Yes, it's a regulation that a train has to be dispatched properly, even if it's only going a mile or so. Normally the guard would blow the whistle from the back of the train, but we didn't use a guard for this little manoeuvre.'

'We understand from the actors on the train that the compartment next to Hayward's was locked. They assumed that the director didn't want any of them to sit in there. Was that right?'

Evans shook his head. 'I don't know anything about that. I wasn't instructed to lock it.'

'But it wasn't locked when I arrived,' said Craven. 'Did you see anyone unlock it?'

'No, and that would be difficult. You need the right key, and it's only railway officials who have them.'

'OK. Was there anything unusual about the train when it left or when it returned?'

'Not when it left; when it got back a few of us noticed that the curtains were drawn in the compartment where Mr Hayward was supposed to come out.'

'And what happened then?'

'Mr Blake went over to see what was going on. Miss Whiteman followed him, and I was nearby on the platform. He opened the door, and Mr Hayward was dead inside. Then it was a bit chaotic, people screaming and shouting. I tried to take control a bit using my authority as an official. I cleared a space around the compartment and then called the emergency services. It was obvious that he was dead.'

41

'Well done. It was important that the murder scene was kept clear of people,' said Craven.

Oldroyd had been listening carefully and experiencing some frustration. Every account of what happened seemed to be the same; surely someone had seen something different, some small detail that could explain how and why Hayward had died. 'Is there anything you can remember that was at all unusual about the carriage or what was happening on the platform, however trivial it might seem?'

Evans shook his head. 'Not really. The problem is you're not expecting something like this to happen so you're not really on the alert.'

'No, I understand. If you do remember something let us know.'

'I will.'

When Evans had gone, Oldroyd sighed. 'Everyone's telling us the same story, Bob. This murder was extremely well planned, and the perpetrator doesn't seem to have left a trace. However, there's always a clue somewhere if you're on the ball. I'm wondering about this locked compartment. How come it was locked when the train left but open when you got here? And who unlocked it? Was it just jammed when the actors tried the door? We need to look into that. Anyway, let's go back and see if Steph's found anything.'

'OK, Jim.' Privately Craven was gladder than ever that he'd called Oldroyd in to assist him. This case was not going to be easy.

Janice Green was in her office facing out on to the station car park. She was fielding regular telephone calls about the dramatic events of the day. News had travelled quickly around the area. It was exhausting and dispiriting. The money from the production company was very welcome, but after this they would probably discontinue filming here and move to another venue. This meant that the railway would not feature in the film and that would lead to loss of revenue.

Suddenly there was a loud knock on the door that led out into the car park. Her desk was by the window and by leaning over she could see who was outside. When she saw who it was, she groaned and then murmured to herself, 'Oh my God, not now!' But the person probably knew she was in there. Granville Hardy, one of the volunteers, was nothing if not sharp and persistent.

Green summoned up her reserves of patience and called, 'Come in!'

A bald, bespectacled man of medium height wearing plain brown trousers, a checked shirt with tie and a tweed sports jacket entered the room and sat down without being invited.

'Granville, I hope this is a quick visit. I've got a lot on at the moment. The police are all over the place and people are calling in constantly to see what's going on. Anne's not in today so I'm doing everything by myself.'

The man sat still in the chair with an expression on his face that was half frown and half smirk. He appeared to be completely unimpressed by the stress Green was under. The light glinted on his rimless glasses.

'I said no good would come of this, didn't I?' he said in a whining voice. 'This railway is part of our heritage; it's not here for people to take it over and make silly films.'

Green closed her eyes and shook her head. 'Is there really any point going through all this again? This railway is struggling with its costs, Granville, it needs the money from ventures like this if it is to survive. Can you not see that?'

'What about the money lost from the paying public while the railway is shut?'

'I've explained that before: ticket revenue doesn't in any way match what we're paid by a production company for the privilege of shooting scenes here and also what we gain in publicity from people seeing the railway in films, whether you like those films or not.'

'It's not even authentic,' said Hardy, completely ignoring the points Green had just made to him and changing the subject. 'I hear the story's supposed to be set in Edwardian times, but they're using that Fowler 4MT tank engine and they weren't introduced until nineteen twenty-seven. I ask you: how ignorant can you get? It will make us look like fools.'

Green looked up to the ceiling. 'Do you really think most people know that much about railway engines? As long as it's a steam engine they'll be happy. If the film crew had the train pulled by a diesel engine, I grant you there might be some complaints.' Green was hoping that this comment might induce a smile from Hardy, but the man was not famous for his humour and his face retained a deadpan expression. 'And talking of the Edwardian period,' she continued. 'Look at the impact *The Railway Children* had at the Keighley and Worth Valley.'

Again, Hardy ignored her. 'So you're not going to stop it even after this has happened? A terrible crime tarnishing our reputation?'

Green wanted to say that there was no such thing as bad publicity and the murder might well bring the public flocking in, but she decided that might not go down well.

'I don't think I'll need to, Granville. I think after this they'll pull out and go somewhere else.'

'Good,' said Hardy. 'It will be good riddance from me.'

'Clearly,' replied Green. To her relief, Hardy got up and went to the door.

'I'll say good day then,' said Hardy.

'And to you.'

He opened the door but Green continued. 'And can you take that banner by the entrance to the car park down? You know, the one opposing the filming. I think that *is* something which will create a bad impression.'

Hardy glanced at her in an inscrutable way and left without another word.

~

Back at the incident room, Steph had so far drawn a blank with her research into Daniel Hayward's past. She explained this to Oldroyd when he and Craven arrived back.

'I've got lots of information about his acting career, sir, but not much to give us any leads except his love life. His reputation as a womaniser comes through with newspaper reports of his affairs and his divorces. He's always smiling in photographs. It made me wonder if he actually enjoyed the notoriety of being a bad boy. I suppose we'll need to track down his ex-wives at some point, particularly the last one.' She brought something up on the screen. 'Candida Nelson. It was an acrimonious and very public split, and it appears she's going to divorce him. I wouldn't be surprised if she still bears him a lot of ill will. Apparently, he conducted several affairs and spent large amounts of money, both of which he concealed from her.'

'At least that's something to go on.'

'One curious thing, sir, is that I can't find any record of his early life in this area. One or two biographical sketches mention that he came from Ilkley, but I can't find any details, and nothing about his family or his school. It made me wonder if Daniel Hayward was his real name or just a stage name.'

'Well done, Steph, that's brilliant!' said Craven.

'Yes,' said Oldroyd. 'And if he was using a stage name, he seems to have kept it a closely guarded secret. It's more evidence that, for some reason, he wanted to make a complete break with his life here. It was a long time ago, but we need to find out what it was. It may still be relevant to the case.' He looked at his watch and yawned. 'Well Bob, I'm not sure we can do much more today. I'll leave you to tidy up and secure the site and we'll be back tomorrow.'

'OK Jim.' He smiled at Oldroyd. 'At least we've established that something unusual was going on which is quite reassuring to me. I was afraid that I'd missed something obvious, and you would see it straight away.'

Oldroyd and Steph laughed. 'Don't worry, Bob, it's another puzzler all right,' said Oldroyd. 'And I haven't got much of a clue yet.'

'By the way,' said Craven, who had just remembered something. 'When you arrived, did you notice a banner hanging on the fence near the car park entrance?'

'Can't say I did. Did you, Steph?'

'No, sir.'

'Maybe you came in a different way. It says "Stop The Filming Now". It appears that someone was opposed to the film crew being here.'

'Really? Well, we'll have to find out who. Steph and I will be off now. We'll just call at that hotel on the way back; see if any of the staff noticed anything unusual.'

'Righto Jim, see you both tomorrow.'

It was still warm in the early evening as Steph and Oldroyd drove the short distance back to the Wharfedale Bridge Inn. Sheep and newborn lambs were grazing in the lush fields full of buttercups and daisies, and bordered by drystone walls. The police officers passed some magnificent horse chestnut trees with fresh green leaves and candelabras of pinkish-white flowers. The car trundled over an ancient stone bridge from which there was a fleeting glimpse of the river flowing swiftly over its rocky bed and overhung by trees on either bank. A chaffinch landed on the parapet of the bridge, and snatches of its song came into the car through the open window. Contemplating the scene, Oldroyd felt that he didn't want to go back to the town; he could stay forever gazing at this beautiful landscape at its sublime best at this time of year.

At the hotel they spoke to the manager, Christine Gray, in an office behind Reception. She looked shaken by the news that one of her famous guests had been murdered.

'We were delighted to have them here, Chief Inspector. What's happened is just terrible. I was passing the dining room this morning and they were all together having breakfast. I can't believe . . .' She shook her head.

'Yes,' said Oldroyd. 'It's been an awful shock for many people. Can I ask if you or any of your staff noticed anything unusual at any time during the period Daniel Hayward and the others were staying here?'

She thought for a moment. 'No, I don't think so, but I'll ask the staff. I noticed that Mr Hayward and Mr Blake were having an argument this morning. Mr Blake stayed in Leeds overnight, but he came back this morning. It sounded as if Mr Hayward was not ready to go down to the station and start filming.'

'Yes, you're right; we know all about that. Were there any other disagreements between Hayward and the others?'

'Not that I saw.'

'Did Hayward seem to be his normal self as far as you could see?'

'Yes.'

'And nothing odd has happened while he's been staying here?'

'No.'

'OK, well thank you for your time.' He turned to leave but then remembered something. 'On a different subject, could you give me a brochure for the hotel?'

'Of course.' She produced one from a filing cabinet and Oldroyd and Steph left.

'Are you thinking of coming to that inn to stay, then, sir?' asked Steph as she drove over Blubberhouses Moor and back to Harrogate whilst Oldroyd was glancing through the brochure.

'Yes. I think I might bring my partner Deborah. It looks very inviting in there, doesn't it?'

'It does, sir; beautiful dining room and gardens and I noticed they've got a spa with a swimming pool. I'll bet the rooms are really nice.'

'Yes, I think she'd like it. You don't always have to go a long way from home to have a nice break.' The more Oldroyd thought about it, the more he was inclined towards the idea of mixing business with pleasure by coming to stay with Deborah at the Wharfedale Bridge while he was working on the case. There was plenty for Deborah to do while he was otherwise engaged, and he wouldn't have to drive back home every night. It would be more relaxing for him at the end of the day. He would suggest it to her when he got back home that evening.

When the detectives left, Christine Gray went into her office. Her feelings at the moment were similar to those of Janice Green up at the railway. It was excellent for business to have famous actors as guests, but now one of them had been murdered and it looked as if the others would leave if the filming was postponed or cancelled altogether.

She felt guilty for looking at the situation like this when someone was dead but the demands of running a place like the Wharfedale were heavy, and there was always strong competition from other Dales pubs and hotels.

She decided that she would speak to all the staff about the situation and encourage them to continue as normal. She looked at the time. The two main receptionists Lauren and Amy were about to change over, and it would be a good time to have a word with them both. She went over to Reception, called them into the office and sat them down. They were both in their twenties and still relatively new to their jobs. She explained that the police had been asking if anyone had seen anything odd at the hotel since the actors had been staying.

'We all heard them arguing this morning, didn't we?' said Lauren. 'But I haven't seen anything else unusual. I don't know about you, Amy.' Amy shook her head and Lauren turned to Green. 'It's awful that Mr Hayward was killed, but he wasn't easy to deal with.'

'Why?'

'He was one of those men who leer at you and make suggestive remarks. He tried to look down my blouse more than once.'

'Me too,' said Amy. 'He told me several times how nice I looked but you could tell from his expression and his tone of voice what he was thinking. If that happens, I normally tell them to get lost, but obviously you can't do that in this job when the person is a guest.'

'Now, I understand why you might think that,' said Gray. 'But you know after that training session we had that you should always report things which make you feel uncomfortable.'

'Don't worry, we would have done if it had gone on, but anyway he's gone now,' said Lauren, and her expression made it clear that she was quite relieved.

Gray continued. 'So there's not been anything else at all suspicious? You two see the most, as you're on the reception desk.'

'Actually,' said Lauren. 'What about that funny little man who was in room six last night? He checked out very early this morning, didn't go for breakfast. He was glancing around all the time as if he didn't want anyone to see him.'

'OK,' said Gray rather sceptically. Once suspicious things were mentioned it was tempting to start seeing them everywhere. 'I'll mention that to the police when they're next here. So anything else?'

They both shook their heads.

'Well, stay on the alert. It will be good if we can help the police solve this crime. Then everything can quickly get back to normal. I can't see people wanting to come to stay in Oldthwaite while people are being shot. Also, I think there might be a chance that one of the detectives might stay here. In fact, it's possible it will be the chief inspector who's in charge of the investigation. He took a brochure and I wonder if he might stay here rather than go home each evening.'

'Chief Inspector Oldroyd? Ooh, that would be cool! He's famous round here for solving murders. He's always on the telly!' said Lauren.

Gray smiled. 'OK, then that's something to look forward to, so I repeat, be on the lookout for anything unusual.'

∼

Soon after dark, Oldthwaite station was almost deserted and the atmosphere rather ghostly. An owl called from the top of a large oak tree near the footbridge over which passengers crossed the line. The clear night provided some moonlight. It was still warm in the early summer air. The locomotive had departed to the engine shed, but the carriages remained where they'd stood ever since the train had arrived at the platform and Hayward had been found dead. Incident tape still cordoned off the compartment that was the murder scene, and a solitary police constable was on guard.

It was an extremely boring work assignment, and he kept himself awake by periodically walking up and down the platform. Suddenly he stopped, seeing movement out of the corner of his eye. There was a figure wearing a balaclava over their head climbing over the wall further down the platform. The figure looked stealthily from side to side and then walked slowly in the shadow of the wall towards the carriage.

The PC frowned. 'Stop!' he called. The figure reacted immediately by running back down the platform. The constable gave chase.

As soon as he was away from the carriage, another figure that had walked carefully and unnoticed down the track to behind the carriage opened the track-side door to the compartment next to the one in which Hayward had been shot and clambered in. Moments later two figures climbed out of the same door carrying some large objects, made their way down the track and into the darkness beyond the station.

The constable returned having failed to catch the intruder and completely unaware of what had happened while this diversion had been created.

Two

'The Signalman', written by Charles Dickens in 1866, is a chilling ghost story in which a signalman who operates a box near to a dark railway tunnel entrance has strange spectral experiences, each of which prefigures a tragedy. It was dramatised by the BBC in 1976 with Denholm Elliott playing the haunted man.

Twenty-four hours after the actors had met for breakfast in the Wharfedale Bridge on that fateful day, the survivors met in the dining room again but in very different circumstances. Outside it was another beautiful day and the sun was slanting through the trees and on to the inn lawn. The French windows on to the patio were open and birdsong drifted inside. It was difficult to believe that the horror of the previous day had taken place.

The room was so quiet, you could hear the chink of cups on saucers and knives on plates. None of the other guests seemed to be saying very much. The events of the previous day had cast a pall over everything.

Whiteman, North and Jenkins sat round a table drinking teas and coffees, but eating very little.

'I didn't sleep a wink last night,' said Jenkins, yawning.

'Me neither,' replied Whiteman, nibbling unenthusiastically at a piece of toast.

'Does anyone know what's going on today?' said North glumly.

'No idea,' replied Jenkins. 'We'll have to wait until Gerry appears. We're obviously not going to be filming any time soon.'

'It might put the whole film in jeopardy,' remarked Whiteman. 'I mean, the whole project's tainted, isn't it? Gerry might not want to carry on and then there's finance to consider. All the scenes with Dan's character will have to be shot again with a different actor in the role. And will we want to come back here? Will the railway want us? If not, there's the expense of paying another vintage railway somewhere, unless they change the storyline.'

'I suppose you're right,' said North. 'I hadn't really thought of it like that. Oh, here's Gerry now.'

Blake came into the dining room looking very tired and harassed. They all exchanged greetings. Blake sat down at the table and took a deep breath.

'I suppose you're all wondering what's going to happen?'

'Yes,' said Whiteman. 'Do you want coffee? There's some left in this pot.'

'Thanks.' Blake sat back in his chair and breathed out heavily. 'I've been on to Henrietta and the backers; they're not taking any decisions yet about the way forward, but clearly we can't proceed with any more filming here for the moment and I assume everyone will want to get away as soon as they can. I'm going down to tell everyone at the station. I'm going to check with the police, but I think we'll have to wait until they give the go-ahead before we can leave the area. Until then you can continue to stay here in the hotel and the company will pay.'

'OK, and thanks,' said Jenkins. 'I assume when we do leave here, you'll contact us about what's going to happen next.'

'Of course, but I'm half hoping it won't come to that and we can continue here. I know you'll be thinking that this may be the end of the film, but I don't feel that way and I'm going to fight to save it from this disaster.'

'Good,' said North. 'All power to your elbow.'

'Where's Frances?' asked Whiteman.

Blake immediately looked uneasy. 'She's . . . not feeling well. She'll be down later. Anyway.' He drank the remainder of his coffee. 'I must be off. None of you need to come down to the station unless you want to. I'm sure the police will contact you if they want to speak to you again. Bye.' With that, he strode out of the room.

'He seems like a man in a hurry,' observed Jenkins with a little frown. 'I wonder what's going on with Frances. Do you think they've had a row? She didn't come out of her room last night.'

'Maybe they have,' said Whiteman. 'Everything seemed OK yesterday, though.'

North sighed. 'So what are you going to do today? I think Gerry's right: we can't leave until the police give their permission. I'm going to stay here at the hotel and relax for a while. I'll find a nice chair on that patio.'

'Fancy a walk, Sheila?' asked Whiteman. 'We could go up to the Bolton Abbey estate. It's gorgeous up there. We can go into Bolton Woods, and I'll show you the Strid.'

'The what?'

'The Strid. It's where the River Wharfe passes through a narrow passage in the rocks. It's very dramatic.'

'Great idea. Let's get ready. I don't think anyone will need us for anything today. How about you, Chris? Are you going to stay here all day?'

'Oh, don't worry about me. I'll go for a drive around the area later on. I think I'll be ready to get away from this place for a bit.'

∼

Oldroyd's partner, Deborah, was a psychotherapist who ran her own practice in Harrogate, having moved from nearby Knaresborough to live with Oldroyd in his apartment overlooking the Stray. A big advantage of her being self-employed was that she could be flexible when it came to taking time off.

Over breakfast, Oldroyd showed Deborah the brochure from the Wharfedale Bridge Inn, and she went on to the website on her laptop.

'So I thought we could snatch a few days together there while I'm working on this case. Why not? We've got our incident room up the road at the railway station and I wouldn't have to drive back to Harrogate every night. While I'm at work you could use the spa and get some treatments or go walking.'

'Mmm . . . Well, I think you've sold it to me. Will you be back in the evenings or not?' she asked playfully. Deborah was used to their social life being disrupted by her partner's work, but she was always very understanding and patient, which was one of the things Oldroyd liked about her. She seemed to appreciate that detective work could be very demanding and did not always fit into a nine-to-five working day.

'I don't see why not. At least most of the time. Unless we hit an emergency situation, and I have to race across the moors pursuing a suspect.'

'Well heaven forbid! Five K is your limit, isn't it?' This was a teasing reference to Oldroyd's involvement in the Harrogate parkrun, which was one of the ways in which Deborah was trying to improve his fitness. 'I think I can rearrange my clients. It's a quiet week as a number have gone away on holiday. So, yes, you're on.' She smiled at him, and he couldn't help but think how he loved that crinkly smile below her brown eyes and dark hair. 'You know I can't resist spa treatments.'

'Well, I was pretty sure you'd say yes when you saw what was on offer. But we'll be able to fit in some walks too.'

'Yes! So I'll ring and make the reservation. I can book my treatments at the same time. And I'll be there in the afternoon; I've got some clients this morning.'

'Good. Well, I'll be off then.'

'What about packing a case, Jim?'

'Oh, I really don't have time. Just put a few things in for me, will you? Toiletries and walking gear, too.'

Deborah smiled. 'Anything else, your lordship?'

'No, that will be all,' he replied with a false haughtiness. 'Drop everything off at our room at the inn.'

Deborah laughed. 'Get off, you cheeky bugger, before I just book the place for myself and see if there are any intriguing single men around.'

'Well, there might be . . . but the only male among the principal actors staying there is quite a bit older than me, so I don't think you'd be interested.'

'I might if he's very wealthy and famous.'

'Well, it's Christopher North. You must have seen him in dramas on the telly.'

'Yes. How interesting! He's a strong possibility.'

'He's quite famous, but I don't know how wealthy. Actors tend to spend a lot as well as earn it, don't they?' Oldroyd laughed. 'I think you'll have to put up with me. Anyway, see you later.'

Oldroyd found the drive over Blubberhouses Moor from Harrogate to Wharfedale very enjoyable as he contemplated how nice it was going to be to relax after a day's work in such a beautiful setting, and spend some quality time with Deborah. The beauty of the moorland, blue sky and fleecy white clouds gave him energy and optimism as he faced the new day. He passed the golf ball radomes of the American base at Menwith Hill. They could look sinister on a misty day, but today they looked positively jolly in the bright sunshine.

∼

'Well, you're a lucky sod, that's all I can say,' said Andy Carter, his handsome face smiling at his partner Steph as they had breakfast in their apartment in Leeds near to the River Aire. They were sitting outside on their little balcony looking across the water to tastefully converted Victorian warehouses, and the river, bordered by shrubs and trees with fresh foliage, looked unexpectedly attractive for a waterway that had been derelict and heavily polluted not that long ago.

'That fraud case is as boring as hell,' continued Andy. 'And Inspector Harvey himself is just about as bad. So there you were in the office and the boss rang up wanting help with an interesting case.' He shook his head. 'I can't believe it.'

'Well, what could I do? Did you expect me to say that I was too busy, but that you would tell Inspector Harvey to bugger off, and join him shortly? Don't worry, you might get a chance to help later. If you're a good boy and work hard on your own case.' Steph's eyes sparkled at him mischievously as she finished her coffee.

'So what's your theory about what happened, then?' asked Andy. 'How was that bloke bumped off in a closed compartment with no one else inside? The boss will expect you to have an angle on it.'

'I know, but it's a puzzler. We know the train slowed down in the tunnel and I think someone could have got on at that point. They could have had a key to the compartment door. And no one on the train noticed because it's dark in a tunnel.'

'"Dark in a tunnel". What an amazing insight! I don't think the boss appreciates the calibre of the people he's got on his team!'

'Shut up, you sarcastic sod. You're only jealous,' replied Steph, laughing.

'And don't tell me,' continued Andy. 'They didn't see the killer get out of the compartment because they were blinded by the light when the train came out of the tunnel?'

'Get lost! Anyway, I'm off to Oldthwaite. Enjoy ploughing through those figures with Inspector Harvey and interviewing accountants, won't you?'

'I will, but I'm also waiting for the boss to call me in when he feels he needs a little extra brainpower. By the way, after this murderer got on the train in the tunnel and shot the victim without being seen, then how did they also get off the train without being noticed?'

Steph stuck out her tongue at him, and left.

Oldroyd was still in very good spirits as he arrived at Oldthwaite, and he was humming a tune from a Haydn string quartet as he swung into the car park. Classical music had always been important to him since he'd been taken to concerts as a boy by his father. This time he did notice the banner calling for the filming to end. Well, now it had, for the moment at least. But who had put that there? It could prove to be an interesting lead.

When he got to the incident room, he found Craven and Steph already there.

'Good morning everybody; bright and early I see.'

'Yes, sir,' replied Steph, sounding very upbeat. 'This weather and the beautiful countryside lift your spirits, don't they?'

'They do, and I'm going to take more advantage of this marvellous setting.' He explained about staying at the hotel with Deborah.

'Ooh, lucky you, sir! And why not?'

'That's what I thought.' He turned to Craven who looked a little more tense as he worked through a pile of statements. He clearly felt responsible for the case, even though he'd brought in Oldroyd, his superior, to oversee things. The crime had been committed on his patch and it was up to him to sort it even if he had help.

'Sorry . . . Morning, Jim,' he said. 'I was just checking through all these, but it certainly seems like no one saw anything. One interesting thing though; it includes a statement by Frances Cooper, Blake's wife. She was sitting on the platform watching the filming, but she saw nothing unusual. The reason I say it's interesting is that we haven't spoken to her yet and I've been wondering, you know Blake told us she was here for a bit of a break between jobs? What if there was more to it than that?'

'Go on,' said Oldroyd.

'Well, it's a bit of a long shot, but she's an actor and may have worked with Hayward. We know he was a womaniser, so what if there was something going on between them, and they arranged to meet here at the hotel behind Blake's back? They had the perfect opportunity when Blake stayed in Leeds the night before the murder.'

'Well done, Bob. That's certainly worth following up. Cooper's still at the hotel, isn't she?'

'Yes. I've instructed everyone to stay in the vicinity until we're happy to release them.'

'Why don't you go round and interview her, and Steph and I will go to see this railway chief exec? What did you say her name was?'

'Janice Green.'

'Right, well we need to find out who's behind that banner opposing the filming and whether there were any other issues in the railway which might be relevant, though I'm not sure what. We also need to check out that tunnel at some point and the press will be wanting some information.' He stood up and rubbed his hands

59

together. 'OK, it's a lovely day, and there's a lot to do. I love the challenge of a case like this, let's get cracking.'

Whiteman had driven herself and Jenkins to the riverside car park at the Cavendish Pavilion, a famous café and beauty spot on the River Wharfe near the entrance to the ancient Bolton Woods, and they were now sauntering down the wide path towards the Strid.

In the woods, the trees were covered in their new bright green foliage, while the ground was thick with wildflowers such as red campion, stitchwort, wild garlic and cranesbill. Mallards and colourful mandarin ducks swam in the river while wagtails fluttered from stone to stone. A chorus of birdsong was dominated by the falling, chattering song of the chaffinch and the loud, busy song of the tiny wren. Like Oldroyd and Steph, the two women felt the calming effects of the beauty around them and walked along for a while without speaking.

'Oh, it's so wonderful to be here, isn't it?' said Jenkins, at last. 'I needed to get away from that hotel for a while.'

'Me too,' replied Whiteman with a sigh. 'Do you think we'll be allowed to leave soon?'

'I should think so, I can't see that the police will need us.'

'What do you think about the film? Do you agree with what I said at breakfast about carrying on here?'

'Probably. It's difficult to see how it can continue. They've got to find a new actor, and they might hit financial problems because they'll still have to pay the railway even if they pull out of filming. Who knows what the producer and the backers will decide? I suppose a lot will depend on the insurers.'

'They'll have to pay us as well. I know it might seem to be bad taste to talk about it, but I want my contract honoured. I need the money,' said Whiteman.

'Me too. I've already emailed a copy of my contract to my agent, and told her the situation. So you're not alone. Maybe it will cost them more to cancel the film than to carry on. Wow, look at that!' Jenkins pointed to a large heron that was flapping slowly down the river, its long neck held in and its legs sticking out at the back. They watched as it glided to a halt and stood motionless at the side of the water. They walked on again.

'Do you have any idea who might have killed Dan?' asked Whiteman, abruptly.

Jenkins looked taken aback at the question. 'No. As I told the police, I know he wasn't popular, but to kill him is a different matter.'

'Do you think anyone else is at risk?'

'I don't think so; I've never really thought about it,' replied Jenkins.

'Well, what if Dan's murder has nothing to do with him personally? What if there's some maniac around who simply hates actors? Did you notice that banner up at the station about stopping the filming?'

'Yes . . . probably some crank who thinks filming defiles the railway or something. People like that are annoying but usually harmless.'

'Maybe.' Whiteman shuddered. 'I don't know whether I really want the film to go on. I think it's cursed after this murder. Perhaps more bad things will happen if we try to continue.'

'That's very melodramatic,' said Jenkins, laughing a little nervously. 'I know we actors are a superstitious bunch, but surely you don't think we're all at risk?'

Whiteman didn't reply. They were deep into the woods and had reached a strange place. The wide river narrowed dramatically as it plunged down a waterfall into a channel only six feet wide with hard rocks at either side. The whole of the river was compressed into this space, and it boiled and swirled as it passed through. They stood on the rocks above the water near to the waterfall.

'This is the Strid,' said Whiteman. 'It's very dangerous. It's said that no one has ever survived falling in because the powerful currents trap you underwater. The water has worn holes at either side under the rocks where we're now standing.' Jenkins instinctively stepped back a couple of paces. 'There is a place where people can jump across . . . but it's very risky.'

Jenkins shuddered. It was such a beautiful spot overlooked by beech and oak trees; it was hard to believe it was also potentially lethal until you went to the edge and saw the water roaring down the waterfall, and then boiling and surging through the narrow channel below you.

'Wow! I certainly wouldn't like to fall into that. So have people been killed here?'

'Yes,' replied Whiteman. 'Quite recently a couple were drowned, and their bodies found downstream. I think they were staying around here on their honeymoon. It's thought she fell in and he jumped in to try to save her.'

'How tragic!' declared Jenkins.

'Yes, it's a place full of ghostly legends about people who died here in the past.'

'Well I'm not sure I—'

Suddenly, Jenkins screamed, and Whiteman grabbed hold of her. She wasn't near the edge but had nearly stumbled into another hazard of the rocks near the Strid edge: huge potholes that had been ground out by the water over thousands of years. The one Jenkins had nearly fallen into was five feet deep.

Laughing, they ran away from the edge and sat on a bench under the trees.

'Oh my God! I was hoping for a calm day after yesterday,' said Jenkins. 'That's enough excitement. This is such a beautiful place and yet—' She shuddered. 'Let's go back to the café and get some lunch.'

Whiteman agreed and they walked back along the path in a lighter mood. But across the water the still and rather sinister heron watched them pass, and somehow the danger of the Strid and the fate of those who had fallen in remained with them, despite the sunlight and the trees.

When Oldroyd and Steph went to interview Janice Green, there were reporters outside the old railway station and even a TV crew awaiting their opportunity. Oldroyd was quickly recognised by the media, and they threw questions at him.

'Chief Inspector! Was Daniel Hayward really shot during filming or was it just for publicity?'

'Was it a stunt that went wrong? Did someone use a real gun instead of the fake?'

'Was he shot by a rejected lover? He got about a bit in his love life, didn't he?'

Oldroyd stopped and confronted them. 'I'm not making a statement now, but there will be a press conference this afternoon.' He and Steph pressed on to Green's office, despite being besieged by more questions.

They found Green behind her desk looking rather harassed. It was already turning into another hectic day, she told them, and she didn't have much time to talk to the police. She had to deal with the aftermath of the murder and with calls and emails from the media as well as from the concerned public. There were also cranks ringing in to claim they knew who'd done it. The best of these ideas was that Hayward had been killed by the ghost of a railway guard who had been hanged for murder in the 1920s and was said to still haunt the railway.

After the introductions, Oldroyd and Steph sat down and Oldroyd asked Green about the anti-filming poster.

'It was put there by one of our volunteers: Granville Hardy. He's a pain,' she replied, 'but he's contributed a lot to this railway in terms of time and money, so I try to tolerate him.'

'So, he's opposed to the filming because he thinks it trivialises the railway?' asked Oldroyd.

'Something like that. The railway and its engines are a very serious business to Granville. Far too serious to be used for frippery like films. It's a kind of desecration to someone like him. He also tries to argue that the railway loses revenue when it is closed to the public, ignoring the money we get from the film production company and the huge publicity from the film itself. I think he knows this is nonsense. It's just that he doesn't like the filming; it's too intrusive. Deep down he would probably even prefer it if the general public didn't ride the trains, either, and they were reserved for proper railway buffs like him who can properly appreciate them. But he knows we need money from visitors to survive.'

'Other than putting up the banner, what has he actually done to further his cause?'

Green shrugged. 'No doubt he's spoken to people and tried to recruit them. I don't think he's had much success. The others who are serious train fanatics like him can see the advantages of having the film crew here. Other than that, he's just made himself a nuisance to me by constantly coming in and complaining.'

'He's never threatened violence of any kind?'

Green laughed. 'Granville?! He's far too timid. It's all talk with him. Not that he's mentioned anything violent. He wouldn't be capable.'

'Not even if it was the only way of stopping the filming?'

'No, impossible. I just couldn't see him doing it.'

'OK.' Oldroyd looked around at the well-organised office. People thought of vintage railways as little amateur concerns where a few enthusiasts fired up some steam engines and took people for rides, but in fact they were serious businesses involving budgets, meetings, health and safety, catering, training and maintenance. Skilled professionals were involved, such as the capable woman before them now. He imagined that disagreements between the practical, business-oriented people like her and the romantic enthusiasts might be a common occurrence.

'Would you say the atmosphere amongst the staff and supporters at the railway is good at the moment?' he asked.

'Well, it was,' replied Green, 'before this happened. I haven't had time to talk to people yet, but I imagine it's hit morale pretty hard. I'm calling all the staff together at lunchtime and we'll see how everyone is.'

'Prior to yesterday though, were things going well?'

'Yes, it's just coming up to the main season and we've also had the boost of the filming. Contrary to what Granville thinks, most staff are really proud that their railway is being filmed and it enthuses them.'

'So you've had no conflicts or staff problems?'

'No – except for Mark Bingham.'

'Who's that?'

'He was employed in the café kitchen, but he was a bad time-keeper. Always late, and his skills as a chef weren't brilliant. I found out he'd lied about his qualifications, so we had to let him go.'

'When was this?'

'About a month ago.'

'OK. We'll need you to provide an address; we'll need to talk to him.'

'You surely don't think that he murdered Dan Hayward to stop the filming and get revenge on the railway?'

'It's unlikely, but we have to eliminate anyone with a possible motive. People can react very badly to getting the push. Not far from here a chef who was sacked at a pub returned one night and set the building on fire. Luckily no one was hurt, but the offender is now doing time for arson.'

'Charming. OK, no problem. I can text the details to you.'

'Thanks, I think that's all for now. But about the media?'

'What about them?'

'Are they causing you problems?'

'Yes. I'm getting calls all the time from reporters wanting information.'

'Right. Don't worry, I've informed them that I'm going to hold a news conference here this afternoon. I'm used to them. As part of that conference, I will say that the police do not want people contacting the railway about anything to do with the case. We are in charge of the investigation, so they should leave you alone and put all their questions through us.'

Green's eyes lit up. 'That's wonderful, Chief Inspector. I've got enough to do without having to talk to reporters. Thank you.'

'You're welcome. Some of them will still try to get to you, because they think you might tell them something I won't, but just refer them to me. It's better not to engage with them at all. They twist and exaggerate what you say. Before you know what's happened, Hayward will have had some crooked dealings with the railway or there'll be a ghost in that tunnel. Could you also ask your staff not to talk to anyone from the press or the general public about the case? That's often how the media get hold of stories, from people who unwittingly tell them things and then find what they said all over the papers.'

Green nodded. 'Yes, I'll tell them. And I'll definitely leave the media to you.'

When Craven arrived at the Wharfedale Bridge it was quiet in the mid-morning lull between breakfast and lunch. He showed his warrant card to the receptionist and asked to speak to Frances Cooper.

'I think she's out there, sir.' The receptionist pointed to the large French windows and the garden beyond. Craven walked through on to the wide patio flagged with Yorkshire stone. He'd seen Frances Cooper briefly the previous day, and recognised her now sitting in a wooden garden chair reading a book. There was a coffee pot, cup and milk jug on a round table next to her. She was wearing a bold red jumpsuit and designer trainers and stood out from the other guests in their practical walking clothes.

He introduced himself and apologised for disrupting her peace. She closed the book and sighed. 'Please sit down, Inspector,' she said in a rather languorous voice. 'I assume it's about that terrible business yesterday. I told that constable who took my statement all I know about it.'

'Yes, I'm sure you did. It's not particularly the events at the station yesterday that I want to ask you about; it's your relationship with Daniel Hayward.' Craven had developed a wiliness over his years as a detective. He knew that coming straight to the point could catch an interviewee unawares. Cooper looked up at him in surprise and he saw that her eyes were a little red as if she'd been crying.

'What do you mean?' she asked; her voice was a little unsteady.

'You were both actors. I wondered if you'd ever worked together.'

She paused before answering. 'Yes, we did, on a number of films. And we were once on stage in *Lady Windermere's Fan* in the West End.'

'So you knew him well?'

'Yes.'

She was clearly finding this difficult. It seemed a little brutal, but Craven pressed ahead with his advantage in order to get to the truth.

'Were you ever intimate with him?'

Her reaction to the question was unexpectedly abrupt. She looked away and said nothing. Then to his surprise she put her hands up to her face and started to weep. Craven waited patiently until she was able to speak.

She took a tissue from a small handbag and wiped her eyes. 'I was going to keep it all a secret, but why should I?' Craven's strategy had clearly worked. 'Dan and I had an on-off relationship over many years going back to before I met Gerry. I thought it was all over, but we met again last year on the set of *The Red Hand*. It was another period drama and we both had relatively small parts. Dan was bored with it, like he was with this one. I suppose I was a distraction, but I've always found him difficult to resist and we became lovers again.'

'How did your husband respond?'

'He didn't know. And I ended the affair after filming.' She sighed and took a drink of her coffee. 'Then recently I heard from him. He was going to be in a film directed by Gerry. He seemed to find this hilarious, and he said we could meet up here in Yorkshire if I came up with Gerry and wouldn't that be exciting.' She looked at Craven. 'I know what you're thinking: what a terrible way to behave towards your husband, but the truth is, Gerry and I haven't been getting on all that well recently. We've always had to spend a lot of time apart and it's taken its toll on our relationship.'

'I understand that it's hard in the world of theatre and acting to lead a regular life,' observed Craven as a way of trying to show empathy with her.

'Dan seduced me with the thrill of the idea. When we arrived here, we waited for an opportunity and it came when Gerry went to visit his friend in Leeds. While he was away, I spent the night with Dan.'

'I see.'

'But the whole thing was a disaster. Gerry found out. Apparently, he'd suspected that it wasn't over between me and Dan, so he'd paid an investigator to watch us. He was in the hotel, and he saw me leave Dan's room in the early morning. We had a furious row last night which was made more terrible by the fact that Dan had just been murdered. It . . . it's just all too much!' She shook, shedding a few more tears.

Craven waited again. 'So your husband must have been very angry with Hayward?' he said after a while.

'He was. He said he was glad the bastard was dead or something like that. It was dreadful.' The terrible memory made her shake again.

'When the filming took place, he knew that Hayward had spent the night with you?'

'Yes, Inspector, I know what you're getting at: he had a motive to kill Dan. I confronted him with it last night, but he denied it. I don't believe Gerry would ever do anything like that. But if he did' – Cooper gave Craven a baleful look – 'I've lost my husband and my lover and it's my own fault.'

'Wow, it's a bit spooky in here, sir!' Steph shivered in the cool dampness.

Oldroyd and Steph had just entered the railway tunnel outside the station. It was quite a shock to experience the sudden darkness and the drop in temperature.

'Yes,' replied Oldroyd. 'It makes me think of Dickens' story "The Signalman" where the poor signalman whose box is by a tunnel has strange experiences which turn out to be premonitions of death on the railway.'

'Oh, stop it, sir!' said Steph as they picked their way over the ballast, old pieces of sleepers and bits of coal.

'Or maybe you prefer *The Railway Children*. Have you seen that film?'

'When I was little, sir.'

'I've always loved it. Do you remember when the children have to go into the tunnel to find out what's happened to a boy who ran in but hasn't come out?'

'I think so, sir.'

Oldroyd was in fine dramatic storytelling mode. 'Well, he's fallen over the tracks and broken his leg. He pulls the leg off the track just as a train enters the tunnel and speeds past the children like a mighty dragon. And then they find him, and he's brought to their house to recover. Look here.' Oldroyd pointed to a refuge point in the wall of the tunnel. 'These were built so that railway workers could shelter away from the line when a train came through. I seem to remember the children hiding in one just like this.'

Steph was cold in the dank atmosphere and water dripped on to her head from the tunnel roof. It was dark and she could barely see anything. On this occasion she wasn't responding well to her boss's enthusiasm.

'What are we looking for, sir?'

They were now well into the tunnel and Steph found the echoing sound of her own voice unnerving. She kept imagining she could hear a train coming though she knew that was impossible.

'I'm not sure,' replied Oldroyd, who was fascinated by the old Victorian stone and brick work of the tunnel's construction. 'But one thing I haven't noticed is any plastic fertiliser bags. When Bob and I interviewed him, the driver said he slowed the train down because he saw something on the line which turned out to be a bag.'

Oldroyd had brought a torch which he switched on and shone around the track.

'That's odd,' he said, 'because there's nothing here; the bag must have blown away. I can't imagine anyone's been in here to move it. But there is another refuge, look.' He shone the torch into the dark recess in the wall. 'Someone could have skulked in there and got on to the train when it stopped. If they'd been dressed in black with their face covered, they could have avoided being seen by anyone on the train, but it would have been risky.' He stopped to consider the scenario.

'So they got on the train and murdered Hayward, sir, but what happened to them then? How did they get out of that compartment? Surely they would have been seen if they'd jumped off the train after it had left the tunnel? And wouldn't Hayward have tried to stop them getting on to the train in the first place?'

'Maybe he was expecting someone, and he let his murderer on board without realising it. But that would still leave us with the big problem of how they disappeared afterwards. Hmm.' He shone his torch on the roof of the tunnel where some small stalactites had formed. 'You know, being in here reminds me of that Jingling Pot case, I hope this one doesn't prove as difficult to crack.' He turned round. 'Right,' he said to Steph's relief. 'Let's go back. I've got that press conference soon.'

As he walked back towards the light at the tunnel mouth, Oldroyd switched off his torch and felt some disappointment. The search of the tunnel had revealed very little except to throw some doubt on the engine driver's story. He was beginning to see why Craven had called him in: this was turning into another real puzzler.

There was very little for Brian Evans, the railway guard, to do on the railway today. But as he'd retired from his job, and this was now his main occupation, he turned up at the station and passed time by sweeping the platform, even though it was already very clean. He watered the little flower beds and the hanging baskets, too. While he was doing this, he ruminated on something that was bothering him.

He was still stunned by the events of the previous day, and his personal involvement in them. He was quite proud of the way he'd acquitted himself in the situation, taking control and calling the emergency services. But something was bugging him. There was something he'd seen that was somehow not right and because of the shock of the moment, which had blurred his memory, he couldn't clarify to himself what it was.

The carriage was still stationed at the platform, so he went over to have a look. The compartment where Hayward had been found dead remained cordoned off with incident tape, but he was able to see inside. He looked carefully and then walked up and down peering into the other compartments. And then it came back to him. The day before, his brain had clocked something different in the 'murder' compartment and now he was able to pinpoint it. He looked into the next compartment to confirm his idea and found that he was right. But surely it didn't have any significance to the murder enquiry? Unless . . .

With a shock he realised that he may have discovered how the murderer was able to disappear from the compartment. He sat down on a platform bench and stared hard at the carriage. He would have to tell the police about what he'd discovered, but he didn't want to make a fool of himself. He would have to talk to some other people first to confirm his theory.

He pulled out his phone and called a number. The person on the other end of the line was intrigued by what Evans had noticed, and said they would come down to the station immediately to have a look for themselves.

Evans went back to the restroom for a drink of water; the excitement of his discovery had made his mouth dry. He sat and thought for a while and then returned to the carriage and double-checked what he'd seen. He was definitely right. Should he go straight to the police now? He might have done if he hadn't been afraid of looking ridiculous if he was wrong, and so continued to wait for the person he'd called to arrive. He was standing facing down the platform and waiting when a rifle shot rang out. A circle of red appeared on Evans' forehead, and he fell on to the platform.

Back at the Wharfedale Bridge, Gerard Blake was sulking in the bar, sitting at a table and drinking one whisky after another to 'drown his sorrows' as the saying went. Not only had his wife been unfaithful with a man he heartily disliked, but after that man's death, the film was now in real jeopardy. After telling the actors that they would not be required for the day, he tried to answer their anxious questions about what was going to happen now in terms of the future of the project. As he didn't know himself, it was impossible to give them any firm assurances and the meeting became tetchy and unpleasant.

He'd then returned to the inn and, avoiding his wife, had spent the rest of the morning on his phone to the producer, the production company and various other people concerned with the film without being able to establish a clear way forward. He was now exhausted, had a headache and his brain was becoming befuddled with the whisky.

He took a deep breath and rubbed his eyes. The whole thing was a bloody mess, and he didn't know what to do about any of it. He was about to order another drink when his wife, Frances Cooper, came into the bar and sat at the table with him. Blake tapped at his phone and didn't look at her.

'The police came to interview me,' said Cooper.

'Why was that?'

'They were interested in my relationship with Dan.'

Blake looked up sharply and put his phone down. 'How did they know about that?'

'They didn't really. I think that detective had a hunch. But then I told them what had happened.'

Blake laughed sarcastically. 'Why? Oh, I know! You still think I could have murdered him as an act of jealous revenge. We had all that out last night, didn't we? That philandering bastard is not worth my attention.' He was raising his voice.

'Don't shout in the bar,' pleaded Cooper. 'The truth is I don't know what to think. When Dan is murdered the very next day after I've . . . been with him, it's an awful coincidence.'

'You've done your duty, then, and reported it all to the police. I'll have them on my back now . . . as if I didn't have enough problems at the moment!'

'Well, if you're innocent you've got nothing to worry about, Gerry.' She reached across for his hand, but he pulled it away. 'I'm really sorry about what happened. It's just that, we've spent so little time together recently and I felt we were growing apart. I didn't know whether you cared for me any more.'

'So was that your way of finding out?'

'No, it's just, Dan always made me feel special and I felt lonely and . . . I never thought you would have me spied on like that.'

'When you agreed to come up here and he was going to be around I got suspicious. I had an idea that there was still something going on between you and I wanted to find out for sure.' He gave her a filthy look. 'That was a nasty trick, waiting until I went to Leeds for the night and then getting into his bed.'

'I know; I've already told you I'm really sorry.'

Blake got up. 'Look, I don't want to talk about this now. All we do is go round in circles on it. I have a crisis on with this film and I have to sort it out.' He marched out of the bar without another word. Cooper remained there sitting still and silent. After a few moments, a waiter came to the table.

'Can I get you anything to drink, madam?'

She didn't respond for a few moments. 'Yes,' she said finally, and gave him a wan smile. 'I'll have a gin and tonic please. Double gin.'

Steph stood next to Oldroyd on Oldthwaite station platform, which had received its second murder victim in two successive days. They had left the tunnel and were walking back to the station at the side of the track when they heard the crack of what sounded like a rifle shot. They ran back the rest of the way when they heard someone scream. The line was on a slight curve and their view of the platform was concealed by the 'murder' carriage. When they reached the station, they saw Janice Green and Craven, who had heard the gunshots and come running out, talking to a man in the uniform of the railway. The victim was lying on the floor; blood was trickling from his head on to the huge, smooth slabs of Yorkshire stone.

Another railway man was leaning over the figure feeling for a pulse. He looked up, white-faced, as Steph and Oldroyd arrived.

'What's happened?' demanded Oldroyd.

'It's Brian, Brian Evans. He's been shot! I think he's dead.'

Oldroyd knelt down and checked over the body. The man was definitely dead. 'Did anyone see who fired the shot?'

'I don't think there was anybody about except me. I was on the platform and heard the bang. It came from over there.' He pointed to the footbridge over the line.

Craven came over. 'I've already rung the ambulance and Tim Groves,' he said.

'Good. I'm going over there to have a quick look at that footbridge. It seems like the obvious place for a sniper.'

'OK Jim. I'll ask these two a few more questions.'

Oldroyd beckoned to Steph to follow him, and they walked briskly over to the footbridge and up the wooden steps. The crossing section was enclosed by a wooden boarding and a roof with a gap between the two. The boards were at just the right height for a person to rest a rifle on the top while remaining concealed if they crouched behind their weapon. Oldroyd looked over and saw a perfect view of the platform.

'We'll have to get Forensics to examine around here, but I'm pretty sure this is where they fired from.'

Steph looked over. 'They must have been a pretty good shot, sir.'

'Yes. To hit a target which might have been moving, it would have to be. Although I suppose the victim would have been walking directly towards the killer.'

'It was also risky. They could easily have been seen,' continued Steph. 'They must have urgently wanted rid of Evans.'

'Yes. It's possible that he knew who the killer was and was blackmailing them; or he gave away the fact that he knew something, and the killer couldn't afford that to be made public.'

'This killer is pretty ruthless and efficient, sir; they're going to take some catching.'

'Yes, extremely clever and able to react quickly when things don't go according to plan. I'll wager this murder was not planned in advance.' Suddenly he put his hand to his forehead. 'Oh, bloody hell! The press! I'm supposed to be speaking to them.' He frowned. 'I haven't got time for that now. Go over and tell them that there have been some developments in the case and that I'll speak to them tomorrow morning here at ten o'clock.'

'Right sir.'

'Though what I'm going to tell them, I'm not sure.'

'Don't worry, sir, you're always a match for them.'

'Your loyalty is touching,' he replied.

It was well into the afternoon when Deborah checked in at the Wharfedale Bridge. She'd driven past the inn many times on her way over to Skipton, but had never been inside. She was immediately impressed by the shabby-chic country-house style and looked forward to sinking into one of the lovely chintzy sofas and leafing through a glossy magazine of the kind she thought too expensive to buy.

Lauren was on duty at Reception, and greeted Deborah with a warm smile – especially when she found out who Deborah was – and showed her to the room. The atmosphere in the inn was very relaxed, but Deborah wondered to what extent the staff must be affected by the violent death of one of their guests. It was an interesting psychological question, but she wasn't going to let any professional concerns affect her while she was staying here. It was enough that her partner would of necessity be distracted by work. She smiled. There was no point in that happening to both of them. She'd got used to Oldroyd's problems with shutting off from work, and she knew how to handle him. She had encouraged him to write poetry and to take regular breaks from work, like his recent birding walk. Her influence had paid off. He was much less work obsessed, and less prone to bouts of depression than when she'd first met him.

She made herself a cup of tea, kicked off her shoes and settled into a comfy armchair, nibbling a locally made ginger parkin biscuit as she looked through the spa brochure. The treatments were very tempting: she fancied the Indian head massage and the luxury pedicure – a bit pricey but why not? Through her bedroom window she could see a helicopter parked on a flat grassy area. Wow! she thought, I'm staying here with some seriously rich people. The biscuit was delicious, and she was contemplating taking another when her phone beeped. She read the text from Oldroyd and shook her head. Another murder had taken place; how awful! It also meant that he would almost certainly be late for dinner.

She lay down on the bed, closed her eyes and relaxed. Never mind. That meant there would be time for a swim in the pool in the spa complex and maybe a treatment too. She smiled again. Nothing was going to stop her enjoying this break.

'Well, this killer doesn't hang around, do they? I was here only yesterday.'

Tim Groves was his usual jocular self as he examined the body of Brian Evans on the platform of Oldthwaite station. Oldroyd looked on, smiling at Groves' grim humour.

'It appears not.'

'I'll know more after the post-mortem, but it looks like a rifle bullet, and pretty good marksmanship: right between the eyes.' Groves looked up towards the footbridge with its carefully maintained lattice ironwork. 'I think you're right. The shot would have come from that direction.' He looked around at the pretty buildings restored to their Edwardian splendour. 'It's more like the station during wartime here, isn't it? People arriving dead in train carriages or shot down on the platform. Are you sure there are no spies involved?'

Oldroyd laughed. 'At the moment, I wouldn't mind handing this one over to MI5, Tim, but I think we'll find the answer in the normal motives rather than in espionage.'

'Good luck with it then. I'll clear up and be off. I don't want to spend more time than necessary on the most dangerous station platform in Britain.'

After breakfast, Christopher North drove to nearby Ilkley and spent the day in the beautiful little town where the famous moor climbed up steeply behind the pleasant streets. He walked up a section of the moor to White Wells House which housed the only remaining plunge pool from when Ilkley was a thriving spa town in the eighteenth and nineteenth centuries. Famous visitors included Charles Darwin and Madame Tussaud. He enjoyed the panoramic views across Wharfedale, back towards Bolton Abbey, and up to Simon's Seat and Great Whernside. He returned to the town via the picturesque Ilkley Tarn.

By the time he was taking refreshment in the Ilkley branch of the famous Bettys Café he was feeling better after the stressful experiences of the previous day. He sat alone at a table drinking coffee, eating one of the iconic Fat Rascals, a large, rich, fruity scone, and reflecting on a number of things.

The truth was he had not been completely honest with the police about his relationship with Dan Hayward. Like many people he had always been drawn to Hayward's colourful character, but he had also learned about his other side: lazy, exploitative and often disloyal. North knew Blake looked up to him and listened to his advice, and he'd considered advising the director not to cast Hayward in the film. In the end he'd decided not to interfere, but he now wished he had.

When he'd worked with Hayward on a film shoot in London, he'd gone to a bar in Soho to meet some of the cast. As he arrived, the group were sitting at a table near to the entrance behind a screen and Hayward had his back to the door. North had heard him say: 'Old Chris . . . he's a bit of a has-been, isn't he? Well past his sell-by date if you ask me,' to some laughter from the others. North had cringed and paused before joining the group, which mostly consisted of young actors who found Hayward entertaining. There was a moment of slight embarrassment, although nobody suspected that North had heard anything. He was sullen and angry for the rest of the evening, finding Hayward's bonhomie hypocritical and repugnant.

But worse than this two-faced behaviour was the fact that Hayward hadn't honoured his debts. Like many entertaining mavericks, his private life, including his finances, was chaotic. He was constantly short of money and survived by charming loans out of his friends, loans that were rarely repaid. North himself had succumbed a while ago, loaning Hayward a substantial sum of money, none of which he had got back. North needed that money back now. Most actors never formally retired, it was just that they received fewer offers of parts once they got past a certain age and were less energetic. He needed to invest that money so that he could enhance his pension. He had been divorced several years before and lived alone.

He smiled grimly to himself as he ate the last morsel of the Fat Rascal and thought again about the day before. Poor Dan. It was a very unpleasant fate.

But every cloud had a silver lining. North stood a better chance of getting his money back now that Hayward was out of the way than he had when the old rogue was alive. He could make a claim on the estate.

He paid his bill and left the café feeling much more positive about his situation.

'First of all,' said Oldroyd, 'I think we're safe in assuming that these two murders are linked unless we discover that Evans had some vicious enemies. My guess is that he was silenced because he knew something. He was there when the train arrived in the station, and I think he saw something and worked out how the murder was done. That may also have given him an idea about who the killer was.'

'Could he have been trying to blackmail them?' asked Craven.

'I don't know. He might have just naively and unwittingly given away the fact that he knew something and the killer moved quickly.'

The detectives had convened in the incident room to review the evidence and the suspects so far with a sense of urgency. This second killing coming so quickly after the first had given them a jolt and they had alert and serious expressions as they sat around a table.

'So,' said Craven. 'We've got a bit of a lead, because the killer is clearly familiar with firearms. So far, they've used a handgun and a rifle, neither of which are easy to acquire. And they clearly know how to use them. I've got people at the Skipton station looking into whether there have been any thefts from gun clubs recently, especially in this area. I think it's the most likely way to get hold of firearms, especially a rifle.'

'Fine. So, do we have any clear suspects yet?' asked Oldroyd.

Craven reported on his interview with Frances Cooper. 'I think that makes Blake the top suspect so far in terms of motive. But he must have had an accomplice, because he was on the station platform the whole time Hayward was in the carriage being murdered.'

'Well, the motive is clear enough. But if he is the person behind this, he must have planned the murder before his private detective brought him confirmation of his wife's affair. And he's employed a skilled and ruthless hitman or woman who had an ingenious way of disappearing.' Oldroyd shook his head. 'I don't know. It seems a bit of a stretch to me, unless he teamed up with someone else.'

'There's Granville Hardy, sir, the rail buff opposed to the filming,' said Steph. 'But he doesn't sound like the kind of person who would commit a brutal murder.'

'No, but nevertheless it's time we tracked him down and spoke to him,' added Craven. 'And apart from those people, Jim, we've nothing on anyone else, although I suspect, given Hayward's past life, there will be plenty of women with a grievance against him and men too whose partners Hayward may have seduced. But even if we find people with a motive, it's linking any of them with the murder that's the problem.' It was a challenging situation, but Craven's expression conveyed nothing except his resilient doggedness.

'I think this makes the further research into Hayward's past more urgent,' said Oldroyd. 'Steph, I think you need to go back to HQ and help Andy. Bob and I will manage here. We'll have to investigate Evans too, but I suspect we won't find anything. I think the poor man just knew too much.'

'Right, sir,' replied Steph, who hid her disappointment. There was nothing she liked better than working out in the field with her boss.

'Bob, I think we'll do exactly what Steph suggested and pay the railway fan a visit. Janice Green will be able to give us his address.'

After lunch at the Cavendish Pavilion café, Sheila Jenkins and Anna Whiteman walked down by the Wharfe in the other direction from the Strid in order to explore Bolton Abbey. The abbey stood picturesquely by a bend in the river across which there was a famous set of stepping stones plus a bridge for the faint-hearted.

The two actors wandered around the ruined sections of the medieval monastery closed by Henry VIII in 1539 and then into Bolton Priory, the parish church for the area. After this they sat on the grass by the river, a popular picnicking spot, surrounded by people.

'We used to come here quite a lot when I was little,' said Whiteman, as she watched young children paddling in the shallow water at the edge of a pebbly beach and trying to catch small fish with their nets.

Jenkins looked at her. 'I knew you came from Yorkshire,' she said. 'But did you live near here, then?'

'Not far away,' replied Whiteman, with a dreamy expression, as if she were thinking about the past. 'We had some happy times here with my parents. They're both dead now.'

'Oh, it must be quite sad for you to come here.'

'Yes, it is.'

'Did you have brothers or sisters with you when you came here?'

'Yes. My brother. He's a few years older than me. We used to do exactly what those kids are doing now.' She looked again at the children playing. 'He's down in London too so we see each other quite a lot. If I ever have any children myself, I'll bring them here on a visit. It's a great spot, isn't it?'

'It's beautiful,' replied Jenkins, and she stood up. 'Shall we walk back now? It's getting on, I fancy a cocktail in that lovely bar.'

'Me too.' Whiteman laughed as she got up. As they started the walk back to the Pavilion, she cast a final glance back to the stepping stones as some kids splashed into the river.

As her partner continued to deal with a case that had just become more complex, Deborah was relaxing in the spa pool at the Wharfedale Bridge. It was fairly empty on this midweek afternoon, and she swam a number of lengths unimpeded by other swimmers. Then she got out and lay on a lounger by the side of the pool. The floor-to-ceiling glass windows of the pool area afforded wonderful views of the Wharfedale fells. She spent some time contemplating the patterns made by the drystone walls climbing up the fells and the stone barns in the fields.

The large glass doors that led outside were open, and one or two people were sunbathing on the patio area. It was a hot afternoon and Deborah decided to stay where she was in the shade and read for a while. She settled down, resting her head on a towel, and opened her book.

Someone walked past her, and she glanced up to see that a woman of about her age was about to dive into the pool. The woman cut a striking figure in her high-leg, halter-neck swimsuit and Deborah noted the contrast between this and her own rather practical Speedo.

I'm a feminist but . . . she laughed inwardly.

She was vaguely aware that the woman swam a few lengths before getting out and occupying another lounger nearby. Deborah continued to read but gradually, to her surprise, became aware of quiet sobs coming from the other woman. After a while she put her book down and looked across. The woman was facing away from her and shaking slightly with the sobs. Deborah considered whether she should say something. She waited a while and when the crying didn't stop, she got up and went to where the woman was lying and leaned over.

'Are you OK?' she asked.

The woman turned round abruptly, and Deborah saw that her eyes were full of tears which she had been dabbing with a now-soaked tissue. 'Oh! No, not really,' she said, surprised that someone had spoken to her. 'But it's my own fault. My husband and I are having a few . . . difficulties and . . .' She waved her hand weakly. 'You don't want to know the details.'

'Of course not, if you don't want to talk about it,' said Deborah. 'But how about a drink in the bar? That might make you feel better. It's no good just lying here if you feel like this.'

At first the woman shook her head, but then seemed to change her mind. 'It's very kind of you; that would be nice.'

'Good. I'm ready for a G and T. I'll meet you in the bar in twenty minutes. How about that?'

The other woman nodded. Deborah and Frances Cooper left the pool and headed for the changing rooms.

The bar was quiet in the late afternoon and the two women sat at a table in the corner that afforded them privacy.

In circumstances like this, Deborah never revealed that she was a therapist; this knowledge made some people react negatively, such was the continuing suspicion in society concerning mental illness and 'shrinks' amongst certain groups in society. Nevertheless she used her skills to enable people to feel safe and to talk if they needed to. It was often much easier to confide in a sympathetic stranger about a personal problem than to someone closer who might be involved.

Frances sipped her drink and seemed more composed. There was something about Deborah that seemed to invite confidences. 'As I said, it's all my own fault. I've been unfaithful to my husband, and he's found out. We had a terrible row.'

'Well in my experience, things are very rarely all one person's fault. I presume you weren't getting on too well before this happened.'

Frances frowned. 'He's in the film industry, and he's here for this film they're making on the railway. I came with him because we spend so much time apart. I feel that I come second to his work.'

'That's a classic of marital difficulties; all couples need to be together for substantial periods of time or the relationship will falter. Did you talk about it with him?'

'I tried to when we were together, but he's always so distracted by work. It's hard to get him to stay in one place for very long.'

'And I suspect the other man made you feel wanted.'

'Exactly.'

'And you've had a confrontation about it?'

'Yes. He was very upset. He even used a private detective to spy on me. And it's so awkward now. A number of the cast are staying here, and I find it embarrassing because I'm sure they know what's going on, and I don't feel like talking to them.'

'OK. I don't know your husband. Employing a private detective sounds a bit extreme but it might just mean that he wanted to know the truth and not that he's acquiring evidence so that he can ditch you. Deception is never a good thing in relationships.' She paused to take a sip of her G and T. 'Well, I think the way forward for you is this . . .'

And she made her suggestions, being careful not to be patronising or prescriptive.

~

Janice Green gave Oldroyd Granville Hardy's address, but it was hardly necessary to know the number of the house once you were in the right street – a row of nineteenth-century houses quite near the station that looked as if they'd been built for railway workers – as the exterior of the house and the small garden were full of railway memorabilia. Old signs from level crossings mingled with red plates bearing station names. Flowers had been planted in a metal funnel taken from a steam engine. A huge set of old hand-operated railway signals were leaning against the wall of the house.

'I think this might be the right house,' said Craven with a wry smile as looked around. It was now six o'clock and the weather had turned a little heavy and overcast. At the end of the cobbled street was the entrance to some allotments. He could see some rickety greenhouses and bamboo canes sticking out of the ground. Runner beans or sweet peas, he thought. Craven had an allotment himself in Skipton.

'I would think so,' replied Oldroyd. 'I can't think that there would be two railway nerds in the same street.'

He knocked on the door, which was opened by a small, nervous woman wearing an apron.

'Yes?' she asked in a quiet voice.

'Mrs Hardy?'

'Yes.'

Oldroyd explained who they were, and they showed their warrants.

'Oh, you'd better come in,' Mrs Hardy said. 'It's a terrible business, isn't it? A man being killed at the railway.' They walked down a short entrance hall and into a sitting room. There was an unusual whirring noise coming from somewhere in the house.

'I'm afraid it's two men now,' said Oldroyd as he and Craven sat down in old, cracked leather armchairs. He explained about the murder of Brian Evans.

'Oh!' exclaimed Mrs Hardy. The colour drained from her face and she half collapsed on to another chair. 'Brian? We've known him and his wife for years. He was a lovely man. Who would want to hurt him? Oh goodness, poor Gladys!' Tears formed in her eyes.

'I'm sorry to have to bring this news to you,' said Oldroyd. 'If you do know of anyone who was an enemy of Mr Evans, please tell us.'

She dabbed at her eyes with a small lacy handkerchief and struggled for a moment to answer. 'No, I don't know anyone, but Granville knew him better than me. I expect you've come to see him anyway.'

'That's right. Is he in?'

'He's in the loft.'

'The loft?'

'Playing with his train set. He stays up there for hours sometimes. I call myself The Train Set Widow.'

'Has he been in there all day?'

'I don't know; I've been out shopping in Ilkley and I didn't get back until four. It'll be better if you just go up. He doesn't hear anything because of the noise. There's no point me calling him down.'

The detectives mounted the staircase up to the first floor and then a narrower and steeper one up to the loft. Here the whirring and grinding noise was much louder. It was coming from behind a door upon which Oldroyd knocked. There was no response, so he knocked again more firmly and shouted: 'Mr Hardy. It's the police. We want to speak to you.' Suddenly the noises stopped, the door opened and Granville Hardy, wearing the uniform of the Wharfedale Railway, peered around the door.

'Who is it?' he said, sounding rather irritated and clearly not welcoming this interruption.

Oldroyd once again made the introductions. Hardy's brow furrowed. 'Well, I don't see how I can help you. Of course I felt sorry for that poor actor, but as I said to Janice Green yesterday, nothing good was ever going to come out of trashing the railway and making a silly spectacle out of it.'

Oldroyd was tempted to present some of the arguments in favour of the filming that had been used by Janice Green but decided against it. Instead, he intensified the seriousness and urgency. 'It's not just Daniel Hayward now,' he said. 'Brian Evans, who I think you knew well, was killed this afternoon.' Hardy seemed genuinely shocked.

'What? Brian? What happened?'

'He was shot on the station platform by a sniper.'

'Good God!' Hardy was now taking the thing more seriously. 'Come in, find a seat if you can.'

This was more easily said than done. Oldroyd and Craven entered the loft room with its sloping ceiling to find an enormous model electric train set on a raised platform that wound around the whole room. Several tracks containing passenger and goods trains passed through model stations, through tunnels and over countryside that was reproduced in extraordinary detail including cows and sheep grazing in the fields. Tiny figures sat in miniature signal boxes or handled minute suitcases on platforms. Hardy ducked underneath the platform and appeared in a place between the tracks that was clearly the control centre. Here he sat in his railway uniform beside a panel containing a number of electric switches from which he could operate trains and signalling on the tracks. Oldroyd half expected him to say that he couldn't speak to them just at the moment because the six o'clock express was due, and everything had to run according to the timetable.

However, the shock of the news he had just received seemed sufficiently powerful to render Hardy temporarily oblivious to the trains. He sat on a stool surrounded by his pride and joy but looking forlorn and rather ridiculous in his uniform. Oldroyd and Craven managed to cram themselves on to a couple of chairs in one of the few spaces on the floor.

'I've known Brian for over forty years. We were at school together in Skipton. What on earth's going on, Chief Inspector?'

'We're hoping that you can help us.'

'How?'

'Well as you were, by your own admission, hostile to the whole business of the filming, we have to regard you as a possible suspect,' said Oldroyd with brutal frankness. Hardy sat upright on his stool. 'Where were you yesterday morning between ten and twelve? And also this morning between roughly the same times?'

Hardy looked completely bewildered. 'This is ridiculous, Chief Inspector. Why would I kill someone on the railway I love and then shoot one of my oldest friends?'

'Just answer the question, please.'

Hardy took a deep breath. 'At both times I was in my allotment just down the street. Since I retired, I tend to work there in the mornings and then come up here in the afternoons.'

So, no trains run on his railway in the mornings, thought Craven with a smile.

'Can anyone corroborate that?'

'I'm afraid not. Most of the other allotment owners have jobs so they only tend to be there in the evenings or at weekends. I'm usually by myself on weekdays.'

'OK. I assume you'd never met Daniel Hayward?'

'Correct.'

'But if you targeted him as an interloper on your beloved railway, maybe Brian Evans discovered something and you had to get rid of him.'

Hardy laughed. 'That's absurd.'

But Oldroyd continued. 'Do you possess any firearms?'

'No.'

'Have you had any training in the use of firearms?'

'No, Chief Inspector. This really is ludicrous; you can't seriously suspect me of any of this.'

Oldroyd remained stony-faced. 'I can assure you that I and my colleague here have seen some very unlikely people turn out to be violent. Anyway, if it wasn't you who killed Evans, were you aware that he had any enemies? Anyone who would wish him harm?'

Hardy shook his head. 'No. Brian got on with everybody.'

Oldroyd stared at Hardy for a while and then got up. 'OK, we'll leave it there for the moment, but don't leave the area. We will most likely wish to speak to you again.'

'I've no intention of going anywhere, Chief Inspector. I've got all I want here.'

I wonder if your wife feels the same way, thought Craven as he and Oldroyd descended the steep stairs. Before they left the house, they heard the sound of the little electric trains moving along the tracks again. Everything was behind schedule, but the controller would bring things back into order.

∾

'The poor woman was in quite a state; she was crying by the pool, so I did my best to help her.'

Oldroyd and Deborah were eating dinner in the rather opulent dining room of the Wharfedale Bridge as she told him about her encounter in the afternoon. Deborah was eating a mushroom risotto with truffle and purple sprouting broccoli. Earlier, Oldroyd had told her about the second murder and how the case was developing. He was now enjoying some belly pork with caramelised apple sauce and pork crackling. There was a nice bottle of red to accompany the meal.

'That was very good of you. You say her name was Frances?'

'Yes.'

'Then you'll have to be careful. It was almost certainly Frances Cooper, the wife of Gerard Blake, the film director. He's a suspect in the murders. His wife, who you met, had an affair with the first victim, Daniel Hayward.'

Deborah put her knife and fork down. 'Oh goodness, I'd no idea. She said her husband was here for the filming, but I'd no idea he was a suspect.'

'Of course you didn't. Don't worry, she didn't know who you were, either. I presume you didn't tell her.'

'No, I said we could meet up again some time tomorrow, but I don't want to interfere with the case. Should I avoid her?'

Oldroyd took a sip of wine. 'No, that would be very unkind if she's in distress. Just avoid any discussion of the murders. Also, I have to tell you that she is a suspect, too.'

'What?'

'Not a serious one. But she has a history of involvement with Hayward so there's always the possibility of jealousy and revenge as the motive. Inspector Craven interviewed her here this morning, so that makes it very unlikely that she could have committed the second murder. We'll have to look carefully at the timings.'

'I see. It's not often you go into the details of your work. It's very precise and logical, isn't it? And you have to keep an open mind about everything.'

Oldroyd finished chewing a piece of the belly pork before replying. 'Yes, we do. Some of the most charming and cooperative people turn out to be killers. But by all means meet up again. You might find out something interesting.' He took another sip of wine and his grey eyes twinkled at Deborah.

'Hey, I'm not being recruited as an unpaid extra detective! We have strict confidentiality rules in my profession.'

Oldroyd laughed. 'I'm only joking. Anyway, let's change the subject. I need to relax; it's been a stressful day. Did I tell you Louise is applying for a job?' Oldroyd's daughter Louise had been studying in London on a master's conversion course in social work.

'No, you didn't.'

'Yes, it's in Tower Hamlets in a unit helping women who've been abused by their partners. Just an entry-level job, but she needs the experience.'

'Well that time she spent volunteering at the refuge will be useful. It'll probably get her the job. She'll make rapid progress in the profession once she gets established. She's very capable.'

'I'm just glad she's found something she really wants to do. Also she's met someone at last.'

'Oh, that's good. It must have been so difficult after what she went through in Whitby.'

'I know. Anyway, how's Chloe?'

Deborah's daughter, also a psychotherapist, had recently moved to Liverpool with her partner Ivan who was a veterinary surgeon.

'OK. There's a lot to do on the house, but they've got the money to do it. Ivan earns a packet. He's partner in that practice.'

Moving on from their offspring, they talked about a holiday in France they were planning for later in the summer.

Oldroyd sighed with contentment; this was exactly what he needed in order to switch off from work: relaxed conversation and good food. He finished his belly pork and then, when he thought Deborah wasn't looking, he picked up the dessert menu. But she spotted him with it.

'Jim! I don't think so. We're not on holiday and it's not a special occasion.'

'Oh, all right – spoilsport! Just coffee then.'

Deborah started to think about the next day. 'Can you spare any time for a walk tomorrow? The forecast is very good again. It would be lovely to get into the woods; they're so beautiful at this time of the year.'

'I can't promise anything as we're still waiting for a break-through, but I'll see what I can do after lunch.'

'Well, I'll go for a short walk and then I'll probably go into the pool again.' She looked at him as she lifted the wine glass to her lips and smiled. 'At least we can be together in the evenings like this.'

'Absolutely,' replied Oldroyd, and he raised his glass.

The long evening twilight of June was starting to fade as Mrs Hardy climbed slowly up the narrow staircase to the loft room, from which the noise of the electric model trains could still be heard. She pushed the door open and entered to see her husband sitting motionless on his stool and apparently deep in thought. He seemed unaware of the trains that looped round him as they moved continuously along their circuits.

'Granville! Turn it off!' Hardy looked up and then flicked some switches. The whirring ceased. 'Don't you think it's time you stopped? You've been up here for hours.'

'Have I? I didn't realise.'

She came closer to him and leaned over the railway track. 'What's going on, Granville? You've been very strange since the police came; you've barely said a word to me.' She stopped and took a deep breath. 'Do you know anything about all this terrible stuff going on at the railway?'

He looked at her sharply. 'No.'

'Because I'm really worried. First that actor and now poor Brian Evans. It's dreadful. Why did the police come here? Do they suspect you?'

He sighed. 'That Janice Green's been talking to them. Because I've been so opposed to the filming, they seem to think I might have sabotaged it by killing an actor.'

'But that's ridiculous.'

'Of course it is. And why on earth would I kill Brian? He's one of my oldest friends.'

'So what's wrong?'

Hardy put his head in his hands. 'I don't know; I just think the railway's never going to be the same again. It's all tarnished with these murders, and we've lost one of our best people. Who's going to come here after all this?'

'You'd be surprised. People are ghoulish; they like to see where awful things have happened.'

'Maybe some do, but it's hardly a family outing, is it, to the "Murder Railway"? If we lose money, some of them on the committee will want to start selling some of our best locomotives like our A3 King George IV. It's a wonderful engine. Then the whole thing goes into a downward spiral. Some of us have worked for years on that railway. I just knew nothing good would come out of that blasted filming.'

'I think you're being too pessimistic. The main thing is you had nothing to do with any of it.'

'I didn't.'

She looked at him hard; did she believe him or not?

'Well come down now. I think you're getting completely obsessed with railways, this one and the real one. It's time you got some other hobbies.'

'I don't want any other hobbies.'

She shook her head and went back down the stairs. Hardy didn't follow her, but neither did he switch anything back on. The tiny trains remained frozen between the destinations they had passed hundreds of times already that day as he sat on the stool in silence and gazed at the toy station.

Three

The Ladykillers is a classic Ealing comedy from 1955. Five crooks including characters played by Alec Guinness and Peter Sellers plan a robbery while meeting at a house owned by an innocent old lady who knows nothing of their intentions. The rickety house is situated above a busy railway line and, when the plot goes wrong, the comedy darkens as the smoke rises from the steam trains passing below.

Early the next morning in Leeds, Andy had already left for Harrogate and Steph was about to drive over to Skipton when her phone rang. It was her mother. It was strange that she should call at this time and Steph immediately wondered if something was wrong.

'Mum?'

'Oh, I'm glad I got you, love, before you're off to work. I nearly rang you last night but it was too late, and I didn't want to disturb you. I won't keep you long.'

'What's happened?'

There was a pause. 'Your dad called me.'

'What?'

'Last night at half past ten. He wasn't drunk, but he said it'd taken him a long time to summon up the courage to do it.'

For a moment Steph was speechless. Her father, Kevin, had left the family when Steph and her sister Lisa were still young and little had been heard of him since, although he did usually send something for them at Christmas and birthdays. Sometimes Steph threw her present away. She remembered the bruises on her mother's face and arms. His departure back to London came after a long period of drunken behaviour and physical abuse. One terrifying night would always remain vivid in Steph's memory: she heard shouting and came downstairs to find her father brandishing a knife and her mother with a cut lip pleading with him not to use it. Not long after that incident he'd left, as if he knew that he'd crossed a line.

'What did he want?'

'Oh, he was saying he was sorry about everything; he'd ruined his life and all that stuff.'

'Do you believe him?'

'I don't know what to think. He didn't sound particularly happy; I don't think he's in a good place. He sounded different, not so full of himself, more sober. He wasn't full of self-pity or anything.'

'Mum, don't have anything to do with him. You know how he treated you for all those years.'

'No, it's not that. He never mentioned seeing me. It's you and Lisa that he wants to contact.'

'Oh.'

'Yes, he said he wanted to get in touch with you again and see how you've grown up. He asked me to give him your number.'

'What did you say?'

'I said I'd have to ask you first. I was firm about it. I told him I didn't think either of you would be keen to see him after what happened and then all these years having passed.'

'Well, you're right.'

'But he didn't get angry like he would have done in the past if he didn't get his own way; he seemed to accept it, said he understood how you must feel. So maybe he has changed, at least a bit. I don't know. Anyway, it's up to you. He's your father and—'

'Mum, you know he's never been a father to me.'

'No, not in that sense. But he is still your biological father, Steph, and you can't change that. If you and Lisa want to see him, I don't mind.'

'Mum, that's so generous of you, but . . . I don't know. I don't think he deserves it.'

'Well can you tell Lisa about it? I'd rather you did instead of me explaining it all again. Then let me know what you think.'

'OK Mum, I will and if he rings again trying to rush you, tell him where to go. We're in a different world now, Mum, we don't have to kowtow to men all the time.'

Steph's mum laughed. 'All right, love. Anyway, you have a good day.'

When her mum had rung off, Steph sat down and shook her head to clear it. This was totally unexpected, and had brought back some very unpleasant memories. She got up and made for the door. It wasn't something she could process at the moment, and she had to get to work. She would also need to call her sister, and that might not be easy. She had no idea how Lisa would react to this news.

Inspector Craven's day began with some good news. An officer at Skipton station had located an old report of a break-in and theft at the Airedale Rifle and Pistol Club near Keighley. The theft was still under investigation, but it could be a promising lead in their hunt for the railway shooter. He decided to follow it up immediately.

Craven rang the club and then drove from Skipton along Airedale to the outskirts of the old mill town of Keighley. He found the gun club at a small retail park down a lane by the river. Even here in an area that was semi-industrial, the flat fields by the river were beautiful in their late-spring freshness. Oystercatchers flew, kleeping overhead, and Craven spotted a heron by the river. The door was opened by a burly man of about forty wearing a flat cap in the old Yorkshire style. His accent was strong.

'Don Bates, pleased to meet tha,' he said, extending a friendly hand to Craven. 'Come in.' Craven followed him into a rather scruffy office and through another door into a long narrow room. Here the walls were lined with cabinets containing rifles and pistols. Craven could hear the distant sound of gunshots that were presumably coming from the target area. 'So tha want to ask me about t' break-in?'

'That's right.'

'It's a few months ago now, back at th' end of February and we've had everything repaired. Ah told t' coppers who came at t' time all about it. Haven't tha got all t' details in a report or something?'

'Probably, but I'm investigating the shootings at the Wharfedale Railway and there's a strong possibility that the murders were committed with the firearms that were stolen from here.'

Bates' face lost its cheery smile. 'Right. Bloody hell!'

'So, to confirm: a rifle and a pistol were stolen, and they haven't been recovered?'

'That's right.'

'And how did the thief get in? I assume you've got good security here or at least you should have with all these guns around.'

'Yes Inspector, everything's in order here ah can assure tha. This was the first and only time we've been burgled. It was a professional job. They disabled th' alarm and crowbarred t' door.' He turned to the cabinets. 'These are strong metal, not easily broken into. They brought an oxyacetylene torch in and burnt t' locks off.'

'But they only stole one rifle and one handgun?'

'Yes, plus a silencer for the handgun and ammunition for both.'

'Did that strike you as odd?' asked Craven.

Bates shrugged. 'Why?'

'After going to all that trouble, wouldn't you have expected them to take more than that?'

'Aye, ah suppose so if they were going to make any serious money selling 'em.'

'Exactly, which suggests they were stealing them for another purpose: to be used.'

'Ah see what tha mean.'

'I understand there was CCTV of the intruder?'

'Yes, but they were well covered up.'

'You didn't recognise them?'

'No.'

'Do you know of anyone who might want to break in? Maybe someone who had a grudge against the club or something?'

'T' other police asked me that, but ah can't think o' nob'dy. If there were anyone like that, wouldn't they be more likely to cause damage or steal more stuff as tha said, you know, make it worse for us?'

'I think so.' Craven examined the cabinets again. 'Does anyone in this club come from Oldthwaite or the Skipton area?'

'Ah don't think so, but ah'll check for tha. T' members 'ere are all from Keighley and t' little villages around here. Skipton has its own gun club which is nearer to Oldthwaite.'

'OK thank you, that was very helpful,' said Craven.

As he drove back to Skipton, he felt pretty sure that the weapons used to kill Daniel Hayward and Brian Evans had been stolen from that club. The robbery was a significant distance away from

Oldthwaite and it had taken place several months ago, so that it would not appear to be connected to the murders. But Craven was not fooled. It was further evidence of the planning that had gone into the murder of Daniel Hayward. Did they steal the rifle as a backup if anything went wrong with their first attempt to kill Hayward? It made sense, as something unexpected had happened, and whatever the reason at the time for taking it, the rifle had come in handy.

When he got back to Skipton station, Craven had a look at the grainy black and white CCTV footage of the break-in that, as Bates had said, showed a muffled figure entering the club during the dead of night. This ghostly person took on a sinister and tantalising fascination as they were most likely the killer. Craven played the sequence many times and magnified the images, straining to see any distinguishing features but without success.

However, two things remained clear: there was at least one dangerous person on the loose. And they were pretty handy with firearms.

'I think I'll just have some toast. I'm still a bit full from that meal last night,' said Oldroyd.

He and Deborah were at breakfast at the Wharfedale Bridge.

'That hasn't always discouraged you in the past,' she remarked with a smile as she ate her bowl of muesli.

'True,' he replied as he smiled back. 'Then, unfortunately, I'll have to get to work.' He looked with a combination of enjoyment and regret out of the window on to the gardens on another fine day. 'I'd much rather be walking with you in Bolton Woods on a day like this and doing a bit of birdwatching, but duty calls. We've got to catch whoever's behind this before they kill again.'

'Is that likely, do you think?'

'As we haven't established a motive for the murder of Hayward, it's difficult to say. We think the second person was killed because he knew something, but we can't be sure and therefore we can't rule anything out, I'm afraid.'

'I see. Well, be careful. I get nervous when you're on a case where there are guns involved.'

He put his hand across the table on to hers. 'I know. But we'll get there soon, and I've got Steph, Andy and Bob Craven working with me. We look out for each other.'

'OK. Well, I'm going for a solitary walk up on to the moors. It's great being by yourself in that peace and quiet. I'll tell you if I see any interesting birds. I might speak to Frances Cooper again later.' She sat back in her chair, drank from her cup of coffee as Oldroyd munched his toast, and then noticed something on the wall opposite. 'Look at that painting; it's exceptionally well done, isn't it? I don't normally go for realistic art, but that is outstanding.'

Oldroyd turned round to see a large oil painting of Bolton Abbey with the river and the stepping stones.

'It looks as if you could just walk into the scene.'

Oldroyd looked at Deborah and then back at the picture. 'Yes,' he said with a thoughtful expression on his face, and then paused. Something had given him an idea. 'Anyway, I'd better get off; I've got to speak to the press. They'll be off their heads with excitement over this one: a film actor murdered on set and a railway volunteer shot on the platform.'

'Rather you than me.'

Oldroyd laughed as he got up from his chair and prepared to leave. 'Oh, they don't bother me; I know how to play them. It's mainly a matter of keeping things rooted in the facts and preventing them from going off into colourful fancies which would make dramatic headlines. We're there for totally different reasons: I want

103

to solve the case and bring the perpetrator to justice. They want to create sensation and interest in order to sell newspapers or gain an audience for their television programme. They can help by broadcasting our appeals for help and I accept that they have a legitimate right to question the police. They know I'll tell them less in future if they misquote me or distort what I'm saying so they usually behave themselves and there's a kind of symbiosis between us.'

Deborah chuckled. 'Well now you're making it sound more interesting. I could come along and observe the psychological processes, but it would be too much like work. I think I'll stick to my walk!'

'OK, everyone, please listen carefully. I have some good news.'

After a brief call to Craven, Janice Green had called all the staff at Oldthwaite station together for an emergency meeting on the platform. She stood by the door to her office while ticket clerks, porters, guards, chefs and drivers, mostly volunteers, gathered around her in their various uniforms. Although the railway was closed, the staff still kept turning up and were keeping everything clean, functional and ready to resume operations. It was a sign of their devotion.

'I've been talking to the police, and we can open to the public again on Sunday if all goes according to plan.'

There was a quiet murmuring as people responded to this.

'There are conditions. We have to limit the numbers and a large area of platform one, including the place where Brian was shot, will remain cordoned off. This means that we'll have to use platform two, although one side of that will also be taped off.' There were some nods. 'The police have also given the go-ahead for us to move the carriage in which the actor was shot away from the platform, but it must remain closed. I suggest we take it to the shed straight away.' More nods.

Green paused and looked at her audience before continuing. 'The difficult question is: should we open the railway yet even if we can? Is it disrespectful towards the people who died, especially Brian Evans, who I want to pay tribute to at this point as one of our most stalwart volunteers?'

There were mutters and the shaking of heads and then someone spoke up. 'I think Brian would have wanted us to open. He wouldn't have wanted anything to stop this railway running.'

'Hear hear!' replied a number of voices.

'What about his widow? It's Gladys, isn't it? Has anyone spoken to her? She volunteers with us now and again, doesn't she?'

'Yes, and I've been round to see her,' said a woman from the ticket office. 'She's devastated obviously, but I'm sure she'll want the railway to open; it was so important to Brian. I presume we'll be doing some kind of tribute to him later?'

'Of course. When all this has blown over,' said Green. 'I will speak to her to make sure she's happy with us reopening, and I'll get messages on our website and Facebook page that we're open for business again. I think we may well get a rush of enquiries, so be prepared.

'On a different issue, it's important that everyone resists the temptation to speak to anybody from the press or any member of the public about these crimes and what you saw or what you think might have happened. If you do, things will find their way into the press, and it will cause problems for the investigation. If you have any information you should speak to the police.'

People nodded.

As they started to disperse Green remembered something. 'Oh, has anyone seen anything of Granville Hardy?'

'He's not been here,' said Andrews, the engine driver. 'He'll be in the house playing with his train set. He drives his wife mad with it.'

'Aye,' replied another man as he laughed. 'He's always been a funny bugger 'as that one. He'll be back though; he can't stay away from railways for very long.'

Green nodded, but she was not so sure. Hardy must feel vindicated in his campaign against the filming. But why wasn't he around saying, I told you so? Instead, he seemed to be hiding away. It was very strange.

While Green was speaking to her staff, Oldroyd with Steph alongside him was addressing a large group of journalists in the station car park. TV cameras were there, such was the interest in the developing story. Steph enjoyed these events as her boss always outmanoeuvred the hordes of media people with his witty put-downs and skilful control of the focus. Oldroyd stood at the top of a short flight of steps leading up to the door on to the platform. As he expected, the interest was intense with several voices calling out at once and cameras flashing. He noticed that the TV cameras were rolling.

'Chief Inspector! Is it true that two people have now been murdered?'

'Where will it stop, Chief Inspector? Has the railway got anything to do with it?'

'Is it true that the first victim had a number of jealous lovers?'

'Was the murder part of the film? Was it an on-set accident?'

Oldroyd seized on the last comment in order to take the initiative. 'OK, quiet please!' He looked at the reporter concerned. '"Part of the film". What on earth do you think they were doing here? Making a snuff movie?!'

There was some laughter and the reporter looked sheepish. 'No, I meant was there a murder in the plot of the film or something which went wrong, and someone was actually killed? There have been accidents with firearms on film sets before.'

'I see. The answer is no, the victim was meant to step out on to the platform and be welcomed by members of his Edwardian family, no shooting involved, and no mock guns or anything. Anyway, can I just clarify a few things before we go any further?'

Oldroyd then gave a concise account of the two murders and explained why he had postponed the press conference. He was unable to report much progress so far in solving the case but there were a number of lines of enquiry. 'As ever, you can play a part by communicating our requests to the public,' he continued. 'Anyone who we haven't already spoken to, but who was in the vicinity of this station on Wednesday or Thursday and who might have seen something unusual, should come forward and speak to us. However trivial a thing may seem to be, it might prove important.'

'Have you any idea about motive, Chief Inspector? It is true, isn't it, that Daniel Hayward had a shady past and must have made a lot of enemies?'

'I suppose it depends on what you mean by "shady",' replied Oldroyd. 'Obviously we are looking into his past in the search for people who had a reason to dislike him. I would ask you to show restraint in this area and not to go digging up lurid stories and speculating about who might be involved. That can be very upsetting for people who turn out to have no connection with the case.' He knew that this request would almost certainly be ignored. Where a reasonably well-known actor was involved there was always wonderful mileage for the media to uncover juicy material from the victim's past. There would be some new revelation about Hayward's past, probably with photographs, every day until the culprit was caught.

'We understand that the other victim was a railway volunteer by the name of Brian Evans?'

'Correct.'

'Are you sure the two murders are connected? There doesn't seem to be much to link them.'

'At the moment we're working on the theory that Mr Evans was killed because he knew something about the first murder, but we have no proof.'

'Was it blackmail?'

'We're not sure, but it would be very unlikely that there would be two unconnected murders in two days at the station of a remote vintage railway.'

'Is it true that you're also not sure how the killer was able to get into the compartment, kill Hayward and get out again undetected?'

'It's true that there are elements of mystery surrounding the circumstances of the first murder. Hayward was shot by a handgun in his compartment. We're not sure how the killer escaped, but we are developing some theories. Mr Evans was shot by someone on the footbridge with a rifle.' These details prompted some exclamations.

'That's a lot of firearms, Chief Inspector. It sounds as if there's a dangerous person around.'

'I was coming to that and you're right. This killer is ruthless but not, we believe, a deranged person who might kill at random. However, everyone should remain on their guard and report anything suspicious.'

'Is it true that you're allowing the railway to open again?'

Oldroyd was surprised. How did they find things out so quickly? He swore that sometimes they seemed to know what was going to happen even before the police had decided what they were going to do! 'Yes, we are allowing a limited reopening of the railway from Sunday, although certain sections of the station and platform will be cordoned off. We realise that the railway needs the revenue, and we don't want to cause unnecessary difficulties for them.'

'Do you think that allowing a reopening of the station will be safe, Chief Inspector?'

'Yes, I do. I don't think the killer has a grudge against railways, or the people who use them. We all want to see this railway, which is such a great asset to this area, functioning normally again. In the meantime, we are going to find these killers. We are pretty sure that more than one person is involved.'

After the press conference, the detectives convened in their incident room at the station. They sat around a small table as Craven reported on his visit to the gun club.

'It's pretty much as you thought, Jim. I'm sure Forensics will confirm that the bullets are from the batch stolen from that club, and they'll match the weapons that were also taken.'

'Good work,' replied Oldroyd. 'The only problem is, it doesn't take us much further in finding out who it is, does it? The only things we really know about them are that they have some experience with firearms, and they can plan a clever murder.'

'None of the people with some kind of motive would appear to fit into that category,' observed Craven. 'And they mostly have alibis. I think the killer was hired by someone else. Whoever it was, they're definitely dangerous, and we need to take extra care in apprehending them.'

'Yes. And I agree that this isn't an individual effort; there may have been a number of people involved. The killer would definitely have needed help with the first murder.' He paused to consider the tasks ahead. 'OK, we'll need to interview Evans' poor wife when she's able to speak to us. What's the situation there?'

'I've got officers assisting her, and her daughter's come over from Bradford to stay with her for a while. She's profoundly shocked obviously, but I think we can call later and see how she is.'

'Right. We'll do that, but I'm not sure she'll be able to tell us much.'

'Sir, I've got something here in relation to a possible motive,' said Steph, who had been quiet so far, part of her mind still thinking about the phone call from her mother. 'Andy found this yesterday afternoon when we were researching Hayward's past.' She got a picture up on the screen of her laptop. 'It's from several years ago and it was in some kind of cinema magazine.'

Oldroyd looked at the photograph, which showed a bunch of smiling people sitting in a bar. The caption read: 'Our photographer found the cast of *Natasha* directed by Gerard Blake relaxing at Mancini's'.

'You can see Hayward there,' said Steph, pointing at the murder victim looking rather younger. 'But look who he's sitting next to. And he's got his arm round her.'

'Well done, now that is interesting,' said Oldroyd, looking carefully at the image. The woman was Sheila Jenkins. 'It certainly looks as if they were an item at some point. If so, she kept quiet about it when we spoke to her, always a mistake.'

'The other thing about that photograph, sir, is that it says that Gerard Blake was the director of the film. So he and Hayward had a history of working together. Maybe they fell out years ago over something and Blake planned his murder, so maybe it wasn't just about Hayward's recent affair with Blake's wife.'

'Yes, that would explain why he got Hayward cast in that role in the film despite claiming to dislike him.' Oldroyd leaned back on his chair. 'So, what else have we got?'

'Not much, Jim. I followed up on that chef who was sacked at the railway, but he's been out of the country for months in Australia,' replied Craven.

'OK then. Steph, can you get over to the hotel and speak to Sheila Jenkins? Show her this evidence.' He pointed to the photograph.

'Sir.'

Oldroyd looked at her questioningly. She was usually very keen and engaged, but today she seemed a little detached.

'Is everything OK?' he asked, genuinely concerned.

'Fine, sir,' she replied. It was not the right moment to say anything about her mother's call. 'Just a bit tired today. I didn't sleep well last night.'

Oldroyd smiled at her and then turned to Craven. 'Bob, we need to have another look at that railway carriage. I've had some ideas about how the murderer managed to disappear.'

North, Whiteman and Jenkins had finished a late breakfast together at the Wharfedale Bridge for the third morning running and the process was becoming rather tedious. They sat at the table sipping the last of their coffee. They were fast losing energy and were tired of hanging around with nothing to do. They wanted to get back home.

Whiteman sighed. She looked tired and stressed. 'How long is this going on, do you think? I just want to get back to London.'

'It's been complicated by the second murder yesterday,' replied North. 'Somehow I don't imagine the police were expecting that. They may want to talk to us all again about whether we knew the man who was killed or anything about him.'

'Bloody hell!' Jenkins swore as she slammed her cup down. The crash of china and the rattling of the spoon in the saucer caused a waiter to look over at their table. Luckily nothing was broken. 'Why the hell would any of us know anything about some local bloke who dresses up in an old uniform and pretends to be a porter or something?'

North smiled. 'Don't be unfair to people who volunteer at these tourist attractions. They get a lot of pleasure out of it.'

Jenkins shook her head and frowned.

'How do they even know that the murders are connected?' said Whiteman. 'Maybe that guard or porter whoever he was, was knocking off someone's wife and they got their revenge.'

'Or maybe he knew something and had to be silenced.'

'Oh my God, it's beginning to sound like the plot of a complicated murder mystery!' said Jenkins.

'Well, I suppose it is,' said North, 'and they won't let us go until they're satisfied that we aren't involved.'

'Anyway, that detective, Oldroyd, is staying here, isn't he? I've seen him with his wife or partner, whatever. They were having dinner last night,' said Jenkins.

'Yes, I saw them too,' replied Whiteman. 'By the way, has anyone seen Frances recently?'

'Not to speak to,' replied North, 'but when I got back yesterday afternoon, I saw her in the bar in conversation with the inspector's partner.'

'Really? Do they know each other? I wonder what's going on there?'

'Well, it could be that Frances has confided in a stranger,' he remarked perceptively. 'If she's having a difficult time with Gerry . . . sometimes it's better to talk about such things with someone who's not involved at all. That's probably why she's avoiding us because we know Gerry and so on. She's too embarrassed to talk to us.'

'Very impressive,' said Jenkins. 'You could be a counsellor yourself.'

North laughed. 'So what are we all going to do today?' he asked.

Whiteman shook her head. 'I've no idea.'

'Why not have a trip over to Ilkley or Harrogate, they're beautiful towns. I was in Ilkley yesterday and I—'

North was interrupted by one of the receptionists. 'Sorry to intrude, sir, but Detective Sergeant Johnson from the murder investigation team is at the desk and she wishes to speak to Sheila Jenkins. She said it's urgent.'

The carriage in which Daniel Hayward had been shot had already been moved from the platform to a nearby engine shed when Oldroyd and Craven left the incident room. They crossed the footbridge and picked their way over some sidings to reach the old Victorian stone building, its roof still scarred black at the entrance by generations of steam locomotives.

'Did you do any trainspotting when you were a lad, Bob?' asked Oldroyd, with a wistful look in his eye.

'Not particularly. I'm a bit younger than you, Jim. Steam engines on the main lines were a bit before my time.'

'Well, I don't remember much. I was only five or six when steam trains stopped, but I remember being taken to York station and a fabulous Gresley A4 Pacific pulling up with an Edinburgh train. I can still recall the name: "Bittern". It was so powerful and exotic. Wonderful!' He shook his head at the memory.

'You want to watch it, Jim. You're turning into a nostalgist for the good old days.'

'Not me, they didn't exist as far as I'm concerned. Anyway, here we are.'

They left the railway lines and went down a path at the side of the building and then through a door into the shed. They were immediately faced by the huge driving wheels, over six feet high, of a steam locomotive. It was a lovingly restored Jubilee-class engine from 1934. Oldroyd was tempted to climb up the metal steps and into the cab, but reluctantly decided that it would be a frivolous waste of time in the circumstances. The shed was dark, but as their eyes adjusted to the gloom, they could see other giant locomotives still and silent like sleeping dragons. There was also a line of vintage carriages. It was quiet, apart from the sound of someone whistling in the distance and the occasional hammering. The detectives made their way over to the source of the noises to find a workshop area where two men in oil-stained overalls were repairing a locomotive that had had its funnel and various sections of pipework removed. Oldroyd presented his warrant card to one of them, a large, strong-looking man of about thirty-five, and explained that they needed to examine the carriage.

The mechanic looked surprised. 'They've only just brought it back in here, Inspector – we assumed you'd finished looking at it.'

'And you are?' asked Oldroyd.

'Terry Hopkins. And this is Jack Smith.' He indicated the other man who was a little younger, slimmer and smaller but still power-ful-looking. He had a full beard and wild hair, smeared with black engine oil. Smith was walking towards them, wiping his hands on a dirty rag.

'I work for an engineering company and volunteer here in my spare time,' continued Hopkins. 'The boss is a railway man himself and he's always letting me off early to come and do some work down here. Isn't that right, Jack?'

'Oh, aye. He's very good about it.'

'And what do you do?' Craven asked Smith.

'Motor mechanic in Barnoldswick,' replied Smith. 'I've got the day off today. I'm working tomorrow.'

'So do you two do all the maintenance work here?' asked Oldroyd.

'More people volunteer now and again, usually at weekends. We supervise what gets done,' said Hopkins.

'OK, so were either of you around here on Wednesday or Thursday when the murders took place?'

The two workmen shook their heads.

'Not until today, Chief Inspector, I've been busy at work all week,' replied Smith. 'And I take it you have too?'

'Yep,' said Hopkins.

'Have you seen anything unusual recently?' asked Oldroyd.

'Such as what?' said Smith.

'Anybody hanging around; any strangers seen near the station or the shed; anything at all suspicious?'

The mechanics looked at each other and shook their heads again.

'If you remember anything let us know. In the meantime, we need to have another look at that carriage.'

'Yes,' replied Hopkins. 'Over there just outside the shed. I'll come over and open it up for you.'

They walked across the lines again to where the vintage carriage stood in a siding. Oldroyd asked Hopkins to unlock all the compartment doors and then the engineer returned to the shed.

'Right, Jim, do you know what we're looking for?' asked Craven as they climbed into the 'murder' compartment.

'I'm not entirely sure, Bob.' Oldroyd sat down and looked around carefully. 'Have you ever played that game called Spot the Difference?'

Craven sat down next to him. 'Yes, of course.'

'Well, I think what we need to do is to compare this compartment with the others and see what's different about this one.' He sat looking across at the painting of the steam train in the countryside on the panel above the seating opposite. 'But to save time, I have a clue about where to start. Deborah was looking at a picture in the hotel this morning and she talked about it being so realistic that she felt she could walk into the scene. This set me wondering in a vague way about how the killer could have escaped from this compartment.'

'You don't mean they vanished into that scene with the train,' said Craven, pointing at the picture. 'I know you don't believe in magic, Jim.'

'No. But let's have a look at it.' He got up and examined the picture panel. 'This is fastened with bolts; look, you can see the square end. So let's have a look next door.'

The detectives moved to the compartment to the left. On the wall shared with Hayward's compartment there was another railway scene, this time depicting a train steaming along by the sea, with happy beachgoers waving to the passengers. This panel was secured with cap nuts.

Oldroyd got excited when he saw this. 'OK, now let's have a look at the other compartments.'

He moved rapidly up and down the carriage opening doors and popping in until he'd seen them all. He had a smile on his face. 'I've spotted the differences, and I'm going to borrow some tools. Just wait here, Bob.'

He almost ran back to the shed. Craven sat in the compartment, again smiling at Oldroyd's infectious enthusiasm about solving these seemingly impossible mysteries.

Soon Oldroyd returned with some spanners. 'Bob, go next door and take off those cap nuts.'

Craven obliged, and when he was done, Oldroyd was able to pull the bolts out from the other side. Oldroyd then pulled off the picture panel to reveal that a section of the wall had been cut out.

'Pull the panel off at your side, Bob.'

Craven did so, and the detectives found themselves facing each other through the compartment wall.

'Good Lord!' exclaimed Craven. 'So this is how the killer got out?'

'Exactly.' Oldroyd climbed through the hole. 'The difference that I spotted was that in all the other compartments these picture panels are each fastened separately with screws flush to the wooden wall, but here there are bolts which go right through the wall and fasten the two picture panels back to back.

'I think this is what happened. You remember that this compartment was to the left of Hayward's and had been locked so none of the actors playing passengers could get in. The killer climbed through from here before the murder, replacing the panel on Hayward's side but leaving the cap nuts and the panel on this side off. Everything looked normal on Hayward's side and, even though it wasn't properly fastened, it would have stayed in position long enough for the killer's purposes. After shooting Hayward, they climbed back through the hole and probably used some kind of suction pad to get the panel on Hayward's side in place with the bolts through the holes. The second panel on this side was put on to the bolts and then the cap nuts were screwed on. Hey presto, the hole between these two compartments was concealed again!'

'So, in a sense, they did go into the picture,' said Craven, shaking his head.

'Yes. In fact, they went through one picture on Hayward's side and came out of another one on this side.'

'Well Jim, I take my hat off to you again. That hole must have been the way the killer got in and out of Hayward's carriage. I seem to remember that the curtains were drawn in this compartment as well as the one where the body was found. That would have concealed anything going on in here, but the door on the platform side was definitely unlocked. We had a quick search in here but found nothing. If what you're saying is true, then the murderer would have needed this compartment locked so that nobody could get in before Hayward was shot. But how come it was unlocked after the murder? And who unlocked it?'

'I'm not sure. Unless someone used the chaos and confusion to quietly unlock it. Nobody would have noticed. If it had remained locked that would have been suspicious.'

'True. But the more important problem is: where did the murderer hide in Hayward's compartment? If they weren't hidden, Hayward would have seen them as soon as he got in and raised the alarm.'

Oldroyd frowned. 'I can't answer that yet, Bob. We need to get another search done on these compartments. There must be somewhere to hide. And we need to get a full list of every person who has access to these sheds because it's clear that someone has been doing some work in secret. Also, there is the interesting question of how the killer knew which compartment Hayward was going to use, so that they could create the secret exit beforehand.'

'Nothing is left to chance with filming, is it? I suspect that the carriage and compartment were selected well before filming began.'

'So, we need to find out who knew, and when.'

'Yes. But another problem, Jim,' said Carter, still sceptical about Oldroyd's theory, 'is that we're assuming the killer escaped from this compartment after they'd climbed through from the other one.'

'Most likely.'

'Then they either had a key and opened the door on the platform side, which would explain why that door was unlocked when we tried it back at the station, or they went out the other side. But either way, the same problem arises as when we were considering whether they could have escaped from Hayward's compartment: it's extremely risky. The chances of being seen are high, whichever side or compartment you exit from, even if it happened in the tunnel when the train slowed down. Remember those doors make a noise when they're shut and there were no doors left open in that carriage when the train arrived at the station. Someone would definitely have remembered a door banging. Then, even if you weren't seen by anyone else on the train, you could be observed walking out of the tunnel. Someone put a great deal of effort into planning this murder, so why would they be content with such a weak link, risking the whole enterprise?'

Oldroyd sighed. 'I agree. In fact, all the evidence suggests that nobody joined or left the train between when it left the station and when it returned. So how did they get out? Or where were they hiding? They seem to have vanished into a puff of smoke, so to speak.' He sat back on the bench seat of the vintage carriage and looked around the compartment again. The happy waving holidaymakers in the picture seemed to be taunting him. The truth was that, despite his ingenuity, he had only uncovered part of the solution to this mystery.

Steph took Sheila Jenkins into a small room behind Reception that had been vacated by the staff. They sat down on either side of a small table. Jenkins had regained her composure.

'I've an idea what this is about, Sergeant.'

'Go ahead,' replied Steph.

'You've found out that Dan and I were once together, so you think that I may have had a motive for killing him.'

Steph raised her eyebrows. 'That's pretty much it. But there is also the question of why you didn't disclose this to us when we questioned you earlier.'

'How did you find out?'

'We unearthed a photograph of you together and it was pretty obvious you were in a relationship. It was in a bar at the time you were filming *Natasha*.'

'Oh God, I remember: Mancini's. It was all lovey-dovey in those days. I thought I'd met the man of my dreams. But that was a while ago, Sergeant, and it ended badly. I don't like to think about it. Dan and I were able to work with each other OK when we had to. But other than that we kept out of each other's way.'

'So what happened?'

Jenkins looked away and out of the window. Cars were passing in the road outside, and a gentle wind moved the leaves on the bough of a tree. She was thinking about the past. 'He was very charming, and a lot of women fell at his feet, me included. He usually went for women a bit younger, who were less experienced and easier to impress. I came from a sheltered background. I was in London and not long out of drama school. He promised he could use his contacts to get me parts, then he wined and dined me, and I fell in love with him. It was as simple as that.'

'And then he started to cheat on you?'

'Yes, he did. And it all went sour. I found out he'd been doing it for some time.' Jenkins faltered. She looked down and seemed to be struggling to continue.

'I realise that this is very personal, but you clearly blame him for a lot of pain that you suffered at that time.'

'Yes, I do. But as I said, it's a long time ago now and I'm over it. I was very young, and he exploited my relative innocence. It happens to a lot of young women in the acting world. But I didn't wish him any harm, if that's what you're thinking. He wasn't worth my attention.'

Steph looked at her doubtfully. 'I'm seeing a lot of anger in you. It sounds as if what happened affected you very deeply and that's not surprising. You must have felt a desire to take revenge on him.'

Jenkins shrugged. 'True. I imagined doing all sorts of things to him at the time, but I never acted any of them out. I've got a new life now and a partner, why would I risk all that for the sake of getting revenge on that bastard? Anyway, I was on the platform at that station when the train came in with his dead body inside so how could I have shot him?'

'We're working on the assumption that more than one person is involved in these murders,' replied Steph. 'Where were you yesterday in the early afternoon?'

'Anna and I were walking around the woods and by Bolton Abbey and we came back here for a drink in the bar. I was with her for most of the day, which she can verify.'

'Was it just the two of you?'

'Yes.'

Steph paused and thought before continuing. 'OK, so why didn't you tell us about you and Hayward right from the beginning?'

Jenkins shook her head. 'Yes, I know it was wrong, you people always find things out in the end, but it was so long ago, and I didn't think it was relevant. Basically, I just didn't want to go there.' She looked at Steph. 'Sergeant, I heartily disliked, even hated the man, but I didn't kill him.'

Steph was inclined to believe her.

Oldroyd and Craven returned to the engine shed to find Jack Smith working on an enormous crankshaft that lay on a long work bench.

'Did you find what you were looking for?' he asked.

'I think so,' replied Oldroyd without divulging any details. 'Can you tell me when it was decided that that particular compartment where the body was found was to be used in the film?'

'OK,' replied Smith, wiping his hands again and stroking his grubby beard. 'It was a while ago. I remember Janice Green coming round to the shed with some people, I think they're called locations experts or something?'

'Something like that.'

'They looked at all the vintage carriages and the locomotives and decided what they wanted for their Edwardian setting. We had to work on that carriage and tart it up a bit, you know, as it was going to be filmed. They selected a particular compartment where the main character was going to sit, and we paid special attention to that as the interior was going to be filmed.'

'Who is "we"?' asked Oldroyd. 'In other words, who knew which compartment was going to be used?'

'Lots of people, Chief Inspector. There was a whole team of us: the carriage was painted, and that compartment was redecorated in the Edwardian style. We cleaned and polished the engine until it gleamed. We wanted the railway to look at its best.'

'Naturally.'

'We were all very excited about the railway being filmed except that weirdo Granville Hardy.'

'Was he part of the team that renovated the carriage?'

'Yes, he does a lot of work for us, I'll give him that, but he's such a crank; said filming was not right for the railway; the film crews would take over and all sorts of paranoid crap.'

'So,' said Craven. 'We need a list of the people who help here. Would that include everyone who worked on the carriage?'

'I would think so. I'll check with Terry to see if any other people were drafted in, and we'll add them to the list.'

'Where was that carriage when it was being prepared for the film?' asked Oldroyd.

'Just about where it is now, on the sidings outside the shed.'

'So it was accessible to anyone day or night?'

'Yes, I suppose so. We can't lock up any of the engines or other rolling stock. Even if they're in the shed, there are no doors and there never were. The doors on the carriage would be locked.'

Oldroyd looked round. 'Is this land fenced off? Would it be difficult for an intruder to get in?'

Smith shook his head. 'We've got some fencing up around here near this shed and the station, but to be honest all anybody would have to do to get in would be to walk down the railway line. It's just not possible to make this area into some kind of secure compound.'

'I see. Have there been any incidents of people breaking in, vandalising stuff or pinching things?'

'Not much, occasionally we have to chase some kids off. It's fairly remote out here, so there aren't many people knocking about at night. We lock all the buildings that are lockable, so the money and valuables are kept safe. I don't think anyone's going to make off with a hundred-ton engine.'

The detectives laughed, thanked Smith and left.

'I think when we get that list, the killer must be on it, Jim,' said Craven as they returned to their office at the railway station. 'It has to be someone who had access to a key to open the compartments and that person must also have had the technical know-how to create that secret way into the next compartment. It must be someone who works on the railway, but they also needed accomplices.' They sat down. Oldroyd was thinking hard.

'You're right, Bob. There's enough evidence, I think, to suggest that more than one person was involved in these murders, but at least one of them had an intimate knowledge of the railway and practical experience. We're making progress; they didn't expect us to find out about those picture panels concealing the hole through the wall. They hoped that killing Brian Evans would keep things secret. We'll have to see what they do when they learn that we're on to it. The problem is that we have no motives for any railway people to kill Hayward except Hardy and his eccentric opposition to the filming. Somehow, I don't find that convincing. Do you?'

'No, Jim. We must be looking at some kind of alliance. But the people we know who might have had a motive don't even come from round here and don't know anybody who works on the railway.'

'Or so we think. There must be a connection somewhere. We'll have to dig deeper into the pasts of all these people to find it.'

'I suppose the two men we've just spoken to, Smith and Hopkins, must be major suspects given that I imagine they had the most detailed knowledge of everything.'

'Yes. But we don't know who else had the capability. It seems as if access was not difficult. Everyone on that list will have to be interviewed and maybe some kind of motive will turn up.'

Craven nodded. On this issue it would most likely be the old-fashioned police slog through many suspects that would get them there in the end.

At this point Steph arrived back from the hotel after her interview with Sheila Jenkins.

Craven went to make coffee while Steph reported back to Oldroyd.

'I'm not sure about Sheila Jenkins, sir. She acknowledged that she and Hayward were once together, but she could hardly deny that, given the evidence. She vehemently denied any involvement in his murder, but there was still a lot of bitterness in her about the way he'd treated her. She claimed that she'd moved on and felt no animosity towards Hayward, but she had no really convincing explanation as to why she didn't tell us about their relationship at the outset. It's amazing, isn't it, how so many people think the police won't find things out if they don't tell them.'

'It is,' replied Oldroyd. 'They seem to think that if they admit to something this will incriminate them, not realising that it looks worse if they try to conceal it.'

'Yes, well anyway, I don't think we can eliminate her. She has a clear motive, though it does seem to have taken her a long time before taking vengeance, if she did.'

'Maybe this was an opportunity which presented itself. We're pretty sure now that more than one person was involved in these murders.' He told her what he and Craven had discovered at the train shed.

'Then the working theory is that one of the people who we know had a motive, teamed up with someone else who could fix things on the railway and carry out the murder?' asked Steph.

'Something like that. Although there may have been a third person who committed the actual killing.'

Craven came back into the room with the coffees. 'Thanks, Bob.' Oldroyd looked round to see if there were any biscuits. Then he saw Steph's frowning expression. They both knew what the other was thinking. She and Deborah had a pact to keep their partners away from food that could cause them to put on weight – which they both had a tendency to do. Top of the list was biscuits in the office.

Oldroyd gave Steph a half smile and drank his coffee, thinking while he did so. 'I sense that there's much more to find out about this case yet,' he said. 'But let's summarise what we know. There is someone involved who has the technical know-how to adapt that carriage. But the possible identity of that someone includes quite a list of suspects who are connected to the railway, and the film crew. We have identified three people with a motive: Sheila Jenkins, Gerard Blake and possibly Granville Hardy. Of these only Hardy could have been involved in the actual murder as the other two were on the platform.'

Craven's phone pinged and he looked at the incoming message. 'Ah, now that's interesting,' he said.

Oldroyd and Steph looked up.

'I've had some people at Skipton looking into Hayward's finances and, not unexpectedly, they were pretty ropey. The key thing is that he was lent a sum of money a couple of years ago by one Christopher North and there is no sign that he paid any of it back.'

'Good,' replied Oldroyd. 'Now that is a promising lead. I wondered if the sordid issues of money and debt might crop up. Hayward's just the kind of character who would live beyond his means and cadge funds from other people. Why don't you catch up with North, Bob? He should be at the hotel.'

'OK.'

'Meanwhile Steph and I are going to speak to Andrews, who drove the train the day of the murder. I want to ask him again about whether he noticed anything unusual happening that day, especially in that tunnel.'

Jenkins came back to the dining room after her interview with Steph, but the table was empty.

Then Whiteman appeared behind her. 'What was all that about?' she asked. She could see that Jenkins, who gave her a wan smile in greeting, was shaken.

They both sat down at the table again. 'Christopher's gone back to his room.'

'Look, let's get out of here,' said Jenkins, looking around her to see if anyone was listening. 'We'll take Christopher's advice and go into Ilkley. I'll tell you all about it on the way.'

'OK, let's go in my car. I'll just go up and get a few things.'

'Me too.'

They left the dining room deserted and there was still no sign of Frances Cooper.

'I have something to confess,' said Jenkins as soon as the car pulled out of the car park and they began to drive down the beautiful road towards Addingham.

'OK,' said Whiteman.

'You remember when I told you to be wary of Dan?'

'Yes.'

'Well, I was speaking from experience. He and I were a couple for a while in the early noughties.'

Whiteman, though driving, was compelled to glance at her companion. 'Really?!'

'Yes, and it ended badly. The police found out, and that's why they came to question me. I should have told them earlier.'

'Bloody hell! Why didn't you? It looks suspicious.'

'I know, I know, but I didn't want it all dragged up again. I didn't think they'd take something from so long ago so seriously.'

'What happened between you and Dan? If you don't mind me asking.'

Jenkins looked out of the window as they entered the village of Addingham with its picturesque long main street and old pubs. 'It's OK. I told the sergeant. I was young and wanted to get established in the acting world. I met him on the set of a film. I had a very minor part. He's a great charmer, at least he seemed to be to me at that time. I can see through him now. He's just another in a long list of predatory men who exploit young women. We weren't as aware of it in those days as we are now.'

'So you were happy for a while?'

'Oh yes, he moved into my flat in Notting Hill. I was lucky; my parents are very well off and they helped me pay the rent. They didn't like Dan. They were suspicious because he was quite a bit older than me, and they were proved right. But for a while it was very exciting. He said he would get me parts in plays and films, but not much happened. He exaggerated the amount of influence he had in the acting world.'

'So he had a young girlfriend, and a nice flat to live in at her expense?'

'Exactly, and I didn't realise what was happening. He was always short of money, and I got tired of subsidising him. I felt I was being used. But then – and this is between you and me – the relationship suddenly went rapidly downhill. I got pregnant, and he couldn't get rid of me fast enough.'

'No! The bastard!'

'Yes. Naively, I'd thought this might strengthen the bond between us. We could have had a family together, but he wanted me to have an abortion straight away. He didn't want any responsibility. And then I found out that, yes, he'd been cheating for a while. I think it's a strategy for men like him: always have another woman primed to replace your current official partner. He made me feel a fool: he'd been up to all sorts, and I didn't know.' Her tone became more bitter as she relived the experiences.

'And then what happened?'

'He persuaded me to have an abortion.' Jenkins looked at Whiteman and her eyes blazed with anger. 'And I'll never forgive him for it.'

'Did you tell the police any of this?'

'Everything except the abortion. I don't like talking about that.'

The car was approaching Ilkley and they could see the Cow and Calf rocks up on the edge of the famous Ilkley Moor.

'I see. I can understand how you must feel, but if the police find out you've kept things from them again, they'll be doubly suspicious of you.'

'I don't care. There are some things which go deep, and you don't want to talk to official people about them. What happened is just between me and him.'

Whiteman glanced at her again. Jenkins was staring straight ahead, a faraway look in her eyes.

Gerard Blake, like the rest of the cast and production team of *Take Courage*, continued to be deeply frustrated. He didn't know what to do with himself. It was all a bloody mess! The breakdown in his relationship with his wife had made a bad situation even worse. The cast and crew were still not allowed to leave the area, and he was besieged by complaining actors and technicians wanting to know what was happening about the film, when would they be paid and when they could leave. It was all out of his hands, which did not make it feel any better.

He'd taken to spending most of the day crouched in a corner of the bar at the Wharfedale, drinking whisky and messaging people on his phone. He refused to share the room with Frances and had moved into a single bed on the other side of the hotel. He now sported a three-day growth of beard and a permanently sullen look that unsettled the hotel staff.

As he was sitting alone in the bar again looking at his watch and waiting for it to open, although it was still early in the morning, he tried to gather his thoughts, specifically those concerning Frances. He was still too angry to think about her rationally. He was not sorry that he'd sent someone to spy on her, even though the strategy had confirmed his worst fears. The problem was that, although he was devoted to Frances, he'd never quite trusted her. She was high maintenance and expected him to pay her a lot of attention even though he had a demanding and time-consuming job. It wasn't fair that—

His train of thought was interrupted by his phone ringing. It was the film's producer, Henrietta Fawkes. He was expecting the call and hopefully some answers as to where they went from here with the filming.

'Henrietta? I'm OK, yes.' Blake listened for a while. At first he seemed relieved, but then a frown developed on his face. 'Are you serious? I've no idea when, or if, we'll be able to film here again. To demand we wrap it up here in two weeks is ridiculous, I mean I've got to find another actor for God's sake! Maybe he might be good, yes – I'll give him a call. He could be doing something else.' Here there was another silence as Blake listened to more unpalatable news. 'Very well, I'll try, I've got no real choice, have I? No. Well, we're all just waiting for the police to allow us to leave – they're all completely pissed off, just like I am – yes, I will, that should quieten them down a bit. Fine, OK for now. Bye.'

The call ended, he sighed deeply and sat back in his chair. Fawkes had said the company was still committed to the film and they would honour the pay and contracts of all the actors and support crew. That was the good news; the bad was that they would have to complete the outdoor shots within two weeks, otherwise the expense would become too great and then the whole film would be at risk. His reputation as someone who delivered films was at stake. There were a hundred and one things to think about, but he had no choice other than to give it a try. The best approach was to try to see the situation as a challenge.

He got up and walked briskly out of the hotel towards his car and was soon driving down to the station.

His private life would have to go on hold until he'd sorted all this out. It was all very daunting and at this point he was inclined to wish that Hayward had survived, whatever his feelings about the man.

While her husband dashed off in a rush of determined activity, Frances Cooper was still in bed. She had been finding it difficult to sleep, especially now that Gerry had moved to a room of his own and was virtually refusing to talk to her.

She sat up, rubbed her eyes and looked at her phone. She'd missed breakfast, but didn't feel like eating. Like her husband, but for different reasons, she didn't know what to do with herself. It had been soothing and useful the day before, when she had talked to that nice woman who was the partner of the detective in charge of the murder investigation. Deborah had helped her to plan a way forward. But when she was alone again it was difficult not to succumb to anxiety about her situation and to feel that she had made a shocking mess of everything. Now there had been two murders and Gerry was trying to deal with the crisis concerning the film. He had no time to talk about their relationship.

She finally managed to get out of bed and into the shower. At least she was able to enjoy the reviving sprinkle of water as she thought about what to do for another day of waiting. She was not a lover of the countryside, and did not go on long walks up hills and by rivers. But here she was, like so many of the others, marooned in a country hotel, miles from home. She'd done enough sunbathing in the inn garden and couldn't concentrate on reading books.

She thought about driving to Leeds and doing a bit of shopping, but she had no one to go with. Unless . . . unless she could persuade Deborah to go with her. They could pass a pleasant day together, even if the shops did not approach the ones in London. There must be somewhere nice they could have lunch.

She was a little more animated as she dried and got dressed. It was a pity she hadn't taken Deborah's number, but she was confident of finding her around the hotel somewhere. Maybe she would ask the staff if they knew where she was.

As Craven left the station to seek out Christopher North, he saw a sleek grey Porsche sports car turn into the station car park. A woman wearing an expensively tailored trouser suit and sunglasses stepped out and walked towards the station entrance. Intrigued though he was, Craven got into his car and drove off to the Wharfedale Bridge.

The woman spoke to the first person she saw wearing the railway uniform, who pointed towards Janice Green's office. Inside the office, Green heard a knock and called, 'Come in.' She was surprised by the rather glamorous figure who appeared. She'd never seen her before. The newcomer held out her hand.

'You must be Janice Green. Hello, I'm Candida Hayward, Dan Hayward's wife. Can you tell me where the police are?'

'Are you sure you're OK? You don't seem yourself.' Oldroyd and Steph were about to leave to interview Andrews, but Oldroyd decided to ask his normally lively and engaged detective sergeant again about how she was feeling. Maybe she would tell him something now that Craven had left the office. He was right. She looked at him and sighed.

'Well, sir, something personal has cropped up.' She told him about her father wanting to make contact.

'I see,' said Oldroyd. 'And how do you feel about it?'

'Very ambiguous. He treated my mother badly. But on the other hand he is my father. Maybe I should give him a chance if he has reformed himself. I need to talk to my sister first.'

'I can appreciate that it's difficult,' Oldroyd said. 'I suppose I always try to believe that people can change for the better. A lot of people in our profession get cynical and think certain people are evil and can never change. If you did agree to see him, you're not committed to anything. If you don't feel he's any different then you don't have to see him again. But if you don't give him the chance then you might always wonder whether you might have been able to reconnect. What does your mother think?'

'She's leaving it up to us.'

'That's very gracious of her. Maybe—'

Oldroyd was interrupted by a knock on the door. Candida Hayward entered, introduced herself and sat down. She lounged back in her chair and crossed her legs. She was someone who was on the list to be interviewed but had saved them the trouble of tracking her down.

'Of course, Dan and I were separated,' she said languidly, her long painted nails wafting in the air. 'We were about to get divorced. I was up at Granada Studios. I'm filming a series there about a woman who has an affair during the war while her husband is away in the army. I play the rich aunt who lives in the countryside. It's absolute tosh, but it's a tough world for actors, Chief Inspector. We have to take whatever parts we can get. Dan was the same. He did some terrible stuff.'

You don't do too badly out of it, judging by your car and your clothes, thought Steph.

'Anyway,' Candida continued. 'I heard about what happened and I thought, well it's not far over to Yorkshire, I'll just pop over and see if I can be of any help. And here I am.'

Oldroyd looked at her with his penetrating grey eyes and frowned. She seemed to regard the death of her husband – albeit her estranged husband – with remarkable equanimity. Why had she turned up at this point? Was it just a desire to help? He decided that a certain bluntness was appropriate.

'I can't help noticing that you don't appear to be at all emotionally upset by the death of your husband. It's almost as if you're glad to see the back of him.'

She sniffed. 'Well, I wouldn't go so far as to say that, Chief Inspector. But our relationship was, as the legal phrase goes, "irretrievably broken". There's only so much philandering you can take from a partner before it destroys all feeling.'

'Did you wish him harm because of how he treated you?'

Her eyes widened. 'Good God! You're surely not thinking about me as a suspect! I couldn't hurt a fly; far too delicate. Anyway, I was over in Manchester, the people there will vouch for me.'

'You say you and Hayward were about to be divorced. Was he making things difficult? Maybe he was worth more to you dead because you would inherit more than you might get in a divorce settlement.'

She laughed derisively. 'That's very melodramatic. Maybe I got my lover to help me. If I had one, which I don't at the moment. It all sounds more like crime fiction than fact if you'll excuse me for saying so. It's true, I was about to divorce him, but I was very confident that I would get a good settlement.'

'Very well. Then did you know anyone who might wish your husband harm?'

'I'm sure you're already aware of Dan's womanising. There must have been many people out there who bore him a grudge. Actors too, there's a lot of rivalry and we can be very nasty to each other.'

'So we understand. But was there anyone in particular who you would say was an enemy of your husband?'

'Not that I was aware of.'

'Do you know anyone who works on this railway?'

She laughed. 'Certainly not. I've never been to this part of the world before, though Dan came from round here. He was never keen to come back.'

'No,' said Oldroyd distractedly. 'OK, well thank you for turning up. Sergeant Johnson will take a few more details from you before you leave. Your husband's body is still being examined by the forensic people, but you'll be informed when it can be moved.'

Steph escorted Candida out while Oldroyd sat thoughtfully at the desk. Hayward's wife was the second person to remark on Hayward's apparent alienation from the area in which he'd been brought up, and in which he'd died. Oldroyd felt that this had to be related to the case. But how?

Deborah appeared at Reception in the inn. She was well equipped with a rucksack containing food, map and warm, waterproof clothes. She was wearing sturdy walking boots. Amy the young receptionist was very eager to please.

'It's such a lovely day,' said Deborah, smiling back. 'I'm off up the fells. Can I leave details of my route with you? I'm just going up on to Barden Moor and back down to the river.'

'Of course, madam.' Amy got a notepad and wrote down what Deborah had said.

'Oh, good morning, Deborah,' said a voice behind her. It was Frances Cooper.

'Good morning, Frances. Isn't it a gorgeous day?'

Frances looked at Deborah in her walking gear. 'Yes it is . . . and I can see that you're ready to go walking. I was going to suggest a trip into Leeds.'

'That's a good idea, but I can't today. I'm all set up for the walk. Maybe tomorrow?'

'Yes of course. Off you go and have a good time.'

'I will.'

After more apologies, Deborah left and almost immediately another person appeared at Reception. Candida Hayward had decided to stay for a couple of nights in the area to see how things panned out. She stopped when she saw Cooper speaking to Amy.

'Oh my God, not you!' she said with contempt.

Cooper's face fell. 'Candida? What are you doing here?'

'I could ask you the same.'

'I came up here with Gerry; he's directing the film.'

'Oh, of course. And I suppose it was just a coincidence that Dan was here too. Did you manage it one final time then?' Her voice was getting louder. Amy was embarrassed and looked away.

'Don't make a scene, Candida. What is it to you anyway? You were about to divorce him.'

'Indeed I was. And why? Because women like you were always jumping into bed with him.'

Cooper walked away in disgust, and Hayward turned to the cowed Amy and proceeded to reserve a room.

The fine day was starting to become a little hot and sultry with a thin veil of cloud overhead as Deborah strode out on a section of footpath by the river. The forecast was suggesting the possibility of rain later, but she was determined to complete a circular walk up on to Barden Moor and back down to the riverside fields before the weather turned.

She didn't mind walking alone. In fact, solitude without feeling the need to sustain conversation tended to intensify the sense of peace she experienced when in a landscape like this. She stopped at intervals to look over the water, which was full of grey wagtails, dippers and the recently arrived sand martins beginning to make their nesting holes in the sand banks ready for this year's nests. She exchanged greetings with one or two walkers coming in the opposite direction and negotiated a number of stiles before heading away from the river, across a road and on to a path that would take her up on to the moors. She crossed a meadow full of grazing cows from which she steered well clear, although the animals looked at her with nothing more than passive curiosity.

She felt lucky to be walking over fields like this on such a beautiful morning. She hoped that Jim would make some progress today in this difficult case. It was good that her flexible working life allowed her to be with her partner occasionally when he was spending time away from Harrogate. She knew her presence helped to defuse the stress he experienced. And then she thought about Frances again. Her personal instincts inclined her to offer help to anyone in Frances's situation, but she recognised that she needed to be very careful. The last thing she wanted was to make things more difficult for Jim.

The path climbed slowly, and the terrain became rougher. She paused when the path reached a dense copse of trees and took out her map. Now she had reached the wilder countryside the birdlife changed: she could hear curlews and lapwings. Sheep were grazing on the fellsides. She looked back down towards the river and saw the inn in the distance and the ruins of Bolton Abbey closer by. She took a deep breath of bracing Yorkshire air and consulted the map to make sure she was heading on to the right path. It was a sublime moment which made what suddenly happened all the more shocking.

A hand was planted firmly over her mouth and a knife was placed against her neck by a person who came quietly from behind her.

'Now just take it easy and everything will be fine,' said a deep and menacing male voice. She struggled a little but felt herself held by a powerful grip. 'Don't do that or I'll cut right through your throat.' His tone became more threatening so she went still. 'There's no one here to help you. Now just walk where I direct you, stay calm and quiet and give me your phone.'

She handed him her phone and he pushed her towards the woods. Her legs were weak, and she was in shock, but she managed to keep walking. They wound their way through the trees until they came to a clearing. There was an entry to the wood from the road and a car was parked just inside. He stopped, took the knife away and gagged her mouth with a thick cloth. She tried to break free, and he hit her hard on the head with the handle of the knife.

She groaned and fell to her knees. He produced another cloth and blindfolded her. He pushed her forward again roughly and she felt herself falling over some kind of barrier and then she was forced to climb inside a small space.

Her rucksack was pulled off and rope was bound round her legs and then her wrists. A door slammed. She was in the boot of a car! A few seconds later they drove off.

The movements of the car told her that they went for some way along winding roads, but not very far, until they stopped. By this time, she felt car sick.

Her assailant opened the boot, untied the rope around her legs and helped her out. She tried to cry out, but the sound was muffled, and he slapped her over the head again.

She was pushed forward into a building. Something in the acoustics told her it had a high ceiling. A chain was placed around her waist, and it felt as if this was being tied to something. She collapsed, and found herself lying on a gritty stone floor. Then, as suddenly as he had appeared, her kidnapper left. She was alone, wherever she was.

She tried to move but she was definitely tied to something, and she was still gagged and blindfolded. Her mind raced and she could feel her heart beating fast. It was all a massive shock and she started to cry.

Time passed painfully slowly and all she could do was lie there on the cold floor. Her head ached and she felt blood running down her face. What would happen now? She was being held captive somewhere quiet and empty, but she could hear sheep bleating and birds calling in the distance. After several hours there was a pattering on the roof. The forecast rain had arrived. She had no idea what time it was or how long she'd been there and eventually she was so exhausted that she fell asleep.

Four

Shanghai Express, 1932, directed by Josef von Sternberg and starring Marlene Dietrich, was one of the first film dramas to be set on a train. It concerns a number of English and American travellers en route from Peking to Shanghai during the Chinese Civil War. The passengers are held hostage on the train by a Chinese warlord.

Philip Andrews, the engine driver at the Wharfedale Railway, lived in a cottage on the fellside off the road from Oldthwaite to Skipton. It took a bit of finding, but eventually Oldroyd drove his old Saab up a narrow lane with freshly flowering cow parsley at either side. The cottage itself was very tumbledown, with paint peeling off the door and window frames. A few hens wandered about a yard and a cat sitting on the window ledge meowed at the detectives as they passed. At the back of the house there were some dilapidated sheds and, further beyond, a field containing a barn. It was the sort of country property that with some investment had the potential to be renovated and, given a lick of Farrow & Ball paint, look very smart indeed. Not that Oldroyd approved of this. In his opinion there were more than enough second homes and holiday properties in the Dales.

'My grandad lived in a place like this above Birstwith somewhere,' said Steph as they got out of the car, and she looked around.

'Me and my sister loved going and we stayed there sometimes in the summer holidays. We used to see all sorts of animals like foxes and weasels. There was a pond with frogspawn and later on frogs. It was great, but I couldn't have lived there; it was too far out. It was very dark and quiet at night – a bit spooky.'

'Fascinating place though, isn't it?' replied Oldroyd. 'Look at that date over the door: "1757 TW". Those will be the initials of the builder. Anyway, we'd better get on.'

He knocked on the door and after a few moments Andrews appeared dressed in dirty corduroy trousers and a checked shirt with braces. He was rather pale, and he screwed up his eyes at the light from outside.

Oldroyd and Steph presented their warrant cards. Andrews didn't look as if he had the energy to bother with them, but he beckoned them in.

Inside the main door, there was a large kitchen with a stone floor, a table and a Rayburn stove. There was a pile of wood in a basket at the side. The stove was lit, and very warm. They sat in old spindle-back chairs around the dining table. Andrews rested his elbows on the table.

'I've told you all I know about that film star being murdered and I know nothing about Brian Evans. I wasn't even at the station when that poor bugger was shot.' He hung his head. 'I've known Brian a long time. There's a few of us – Granville Hardy's another, though he can be a funny bugger – we were there not long after the railway trust was set up and it bought the line from the government. We've worked on it ever since. I was an engine driver for a long time on the railways. I worked on engines out of Skipton shed. I was only fifteen years old, just out of school, and there were some older blokes who'd worked on steam engines in the nineteen-sixties, and they used to talk about it a lot. When this railway reopened with steam engines, some of them were the first drivers and I was keen to learn from them. I've been the main driver for the Wharfedale for a while now and I've taught a lot of the younger ones how to do it.' He seemed to have forgotten that Oldroyd and Steph were there, as he lost himself in nostalgia about the past.

'I want to ask you again about exactly what happened on the day of the murder of Daniel Hayward,' said Oldroyd, returning to the reason for their visit.

Andrews, brought back to reality, sat back wearily in his chair. 'I've told you everything.'

'Did you notice anything unusual about that carriage before you left the station?'

'No, we picked it up from outside the shed and took it down to the platform.'

'Was there anyone else around the shed area?'

'Only Terry Hopkins; he helped me to couple up.' Steph made a note of this. 'I think there were some more people knocking about in the shed, but I couldn't see who.'

'OK. So, for the filming, you reversed the train out of the station and down the line to Far Moss Hill?'

'Aye, and that was unusual. We normally pull the carriages down to the end of the line at Westby. There's a double track there so we can decouple the engine, take it to the other end of the train and pull it back to here.'

'But to save time with the filming, you just reversed to Far Moss.'

'Aye, that's right.'

'Without stopping?'

'Aye, but we went slow because we're not used to going backwards like that.'

'Did you see anyone or anything in the tunnel when you backed through?'

'No.'

'When you reached Far Moss you got the signal to start, and set off back towards the station. Did you notice anything at this point?'

'No. I could see the filming crew alongside us on the road and then we got to the tunnel.'

'Yes, so think carefully here. Was there anyone or anything unusual in the tunnel when you passed through for the second time?'

Andrews thought for a moment. 'No, only that thing on the line. I slowed right down, but it was only a plastic bag as I told you. You can't see stuff that clearly in there, there's smoke and steam from the engine.'

'We've been into the tunnel and there was no sign of a plastic bag.'

Andrews shrugged. 'Maybe it blew away or someone moved it.'

'Did you slow down enough so that someone could have got off the train?'

'Maybe, but they would have had to jump. Wouldn't someone have noticed?'

Oldroyd tended to agree. 'Did you hear any doors banging?' he asked.

'No.'

'And was there anything unusual on the last section back to the station?'

'Nope, we got back and then all hell broke loose when they found the body.'

'What did you do?'

'When I heard all the hullabaloo, I got out of the cab. I could see everyone milling about that carriage, but I'd no idea what was going on. A few of us went into the restroom and waited. Then the police came.'

'Did you go to look at that carriage at any point?'

'No. It was cordoned off by the police.'

'But you eventually moved it back to the shed?'

'Yes, but I never went inside. It was locked up.'

Oldroyd had got to the end of his questions. He stood up and thanked Andrews, who seemed relieved that they were leaving and showed them out.

'Nothing much new there, sir,' observed Steph as they drove back down the lane in the Saab.

'No, I think it's clear that no one got off that train at any point until the end. But what I find curious is Andrews himself.'

'How, sir?'

'He looked exhausted and stressed.'

'It's been a bad time for them all on the railway and he's lost one of his friends.'

'I know, but to me he looked like a man tormented by something.'

'Perhaps there are other things going on in his life.'

They reached the main road. Oldroyd didn't answer and remained quiet and distracted on the drive back to Oldthwaite. Too distracted to notice a car passing by driven by a figure wearing a hood. As they arrived back in the village, dark clouds were coming in slowly from the west and soon they blotted out the sun. Oldroyd shivered as he got out of the car, although it was still warm. He felt a sense of foreboding.

The Wharfedale Bridge is acting as a useful holding pen for suspects, thought Craven with a wry smile as he returned once again to the inn. He found Christopher North sitting at a table in the garden wearing shorts and sandals in the warm weather. He had his glasses on and was reading *The Times*. He looked up as Craven arrived and frowned.

'Oh dear. I've been half expecting you, Inspector. Please take a seat. I've just had a coffee. Would you like one?' Craven sat down, but declined the coffee. 'I expect you've found out about the money,' continued North.

'Correct,' replied Craven, noting that North appeared unconcerned about their discovery, unless his blasé attitude was an act.

North put his newspaper down. 'I know I should have spoken sooner, but it's all been so traumatic. I never thought about Dan owing me money and that you might think this was a motive for me to want to get rid of him. Then yesterday I remembered and realised I could be in trouble.'

'Well, was it?' said Craven in his blunt Yorkshire way.

North laughed and then sat back in his chair. 'No, Inspector. Look, I'll tell you all about it. Dan could be very charming, but he spent money like water. He was always short of a bob or two as the saying goes. I've known him a long time and he came to me about eighteen months ago asking if I could lend him some cash, a fairly substantial amount. He said he had some debts he needed to deal with rather urgently, but he would pay me back very soon, and we were old friends, and I was such a good fellow and so on.

'I lent him the money; I must have been mad, but he was very persuasive. He was the kind of entertaining friend that it was always nice to have around, and you did things for him or gave him things even though you knew he was completely unreliable. Needless to say, he never paid me a penny back despite my reminders.'

'How did you feel about that?'

North shrugged. 'Not delighted obviously, especially as I suspected he was just spending it on his lifestyle: wine, women and song as they say, at least not fast cars.'

'Why was that?'

'Dan didn't drive much, if at all – once said he didn't like driving. I expect he was over the limit most of the time anyway, but you can get around in London fine without a car.'

'It's about the only British city where you can,' observed Craven.

'True. But anyway, the point is that although I was cross with Dan, I would never have done him any harm, you understand. You sort of factored in with Dan that he would let you down, but he remained your friend.'

'Would you describe yourself as a rich man?'

'Not particularly, as far as people in my profession go.'

'Then you must have needed him to pay you back before too long a period had elapsed?' Craven's pursuit was relentless. 'You must have felt angry and resentful and maybe you thought that if he was dead, you might, as a creditor, have a better chance of getting your money back?'

This was uncomfortably near to what North had been thinking in Ilkley. He looked flustered, something that didn't escape Craven's attention, but continued to insist on his innocence. 'No Inspector, I must protest. I wouldn't do any harm to Dan and anyway I was there when that train reached the platform, so how could I have done anything?'

'We're pretty sure these murders are the work of more than one person,' said Craven. 'But we'll leave it there. You'll need to come down to the railway station and give the details of Hayward's debts to one of my detective constables. Otherwise remain here at the hotel for now, although I think we'll be able to allow you all to leave before long.'

'That's a relief,' said North as Craven ended the interview, leaving the actor feeling not a little uncomfortable.

When Craven was gone, North picked up his newspaper and tried to resume reading, but he couldn't concentrate. He had to hand it to the detectives: they were very sharp and extremely thorough. He hadn't thought that they would be on to Dan's debt so quickly, if at all. Neither had he been completely open even now; he'd played down his need for the money to be paid back and how angry he really was with his old friend. He drummed his fingers on the table, wondering if there was anything he could do to put them off his scent. Complying quickly with Craven's request would help. He went to get his laptop so that he could examine his bank details and give a precise report on what Dan owed and when the money had been lent.

When Deborah woke, she had a throbbing headache, and was still blindfolded and cold. There was dried blood on her face and her arms, legs and back were stiff. The gag was hurting her mouth, but it was too tight for her to move, and she was frightened of pushing it further into her mouth and suffocating herself. The blindfold had loosened a little, so she was able to nudge it up on to her forehead with her bound hands.

She peered around to try and make sense of her surroundings. It was very gloomy but when her eyes adjusted, she could make out that she was in a typical Dales barn. Up above her were rafters and a birds' nest on the ledge at the top of the stone wall. As she watched, a house martin swooped in from outside and landed on another nest built in the angle where a roof joist met a stone roof tile. Below, there were wooden stalls where the cows were housed in winter and some small piles of hay, the remains of the winter feed. The stone floor was smeared with straw and cow manure. She was lying against the wall by the door and was tied by a chain which went through a large metal ring that looked as if it would normally be used to restrain animals. There was a sturdy lock fastening the chain around her waist. A cursory pull demonstrated that she had no chance of freeing herself as it refused to move.

She lay back against the rough stone and tried to think calmly about her position. Her kidnapper had said nothing to her apart from rapping out orders. If he had wanted to rape or murder her, then surely he would have done so by now? Robbery was not the motive. She had her purse in the rucksack that was lying beside her, but he'd shown no interest in that either. The only thing he'd taken was her phone. There was only one explanation: she was a hostage. Which meant her captor had to be connected to the case Jim was working on.

Jim must have been getting close to solving the mystery, and now the murderer was trying to stop him from investigating any further by threatening her.

She got a sick feeling in her stomach as she realised that this meant her life could be in danger if Jim refused – or wasn't allowed to – cooperate. Her captor had already killed two people. She knew Jim would be distraught when he realised what had happened, but how would he play it? Neither Jim nor the police force generally would willingly put her at risk, but he couldn't call off the police from investigating a double murder. Would he withdraw himself from the case and hope that was enough?

These tormenting thoughts were interrupted by the sound of footsteps approaching from outside the barn. Deborah hastily pushed the blindfold back over her eyes. She tried to remain still, but she couldn't help shaking a little. There was the sound of the door being pushed open on creaky hinges and then the blindfold and the gag were roughly pulled off. A man stood before her, his face still obscured by a mask. He was carrying a metal bucket and a large bag, both of which he put down. From the bucket he took a small plastic bag containing some slices of bread, a hunk of cheese and a bottle of water.

'OK,' he said. 'This is what's going to happen.' She noted that the accent was local, but the voice was deep, and it was difficult to estimate his age. 'That boyfriend detective of yours is going to get a message, telling him that you're OK. For now. That will change if he doesn't get off the case he's working on, and he can take those other two with him.'

'What difference will that make? Other officers will replace them.'

He produced the knife again, grabbed her hair, pulled her head back and held the blade to her throat. 'I didn't say you could speak!' he whispered fiercely. 'Keep your mouth shut!' Her whole body trembled but she managed to nod her head. He unbound her hands. 'Now eat something and drink the water.'

All she really wanted to do was drink, but she was frightened of what might happen if she disobeyed him, so she forced some food down and drank all the water. Her mouth was sore where the gag had been pressed against her gums and her wrists hurt. He opened the bag and produced a grimy-looking duvet. He gathered some handfuls of straw and laid them on the floor near to her. Then he gagged her again, but left the blindfold off.

'OK, I'll be back in the morning. Don't try anything silly. You can't get that lock off.' He pointed to the bucket. 'That's your toilet, don't do anything on the floor, there's enough shit on it already.' Before he left, he took a photograph of her with her phone.

When he got back to the incident room at the station, Oldroyd looked at his phone and saw, to his surprise, that there were no messages from Deborah. She usually sent frequent texts at times like this when she embarked on some activity without him.

However, he was too absorbed in thinking about the encounter with Philip Andrews to pay this any more attention. He sent her a message: 'How's it going?' and then put the kettle on.

'Going back to Andrews,' he said as he and Steph were sitting at the table drinking tea. 'I've got this feeling that there's something going on with him.' Oldroyd was a great believer in the synergy of rationality and instinct in detective work: ruthlessly follow the evidence, but also pay attention to what your antennae are telling you.

'How do you mean, sir?'

'Well, he was clearly distressed, and the cause seemed to be the murder of his friend Brian Evans.'

'Isn't that natural, sir?'

'Yes, but what if that anguish had been intensified in some way? I'm thinking something like this: what if, for some reason, he did play a part in the murder of Dan Hayward? He didn't seem at all upset the first time we spoke to him at the station. The difference today is that now his friend has been murdered, mostly likely because of what he knew. It's a fair bet that the killers weren't expecting to have to kill Brian Evans. Maybe Andrews wasn't told about that and was angry about it. He didn't expect to be part of an enterprise which involved murdering one of his oldest friends.' Oldroyd shrugged. 'It's just a theory, but I felt he was more than just very sorry that his friend had been killed, and that there might be deeper feelings involved, possibly guilt and betrayal.'

Steph nodded. 'It would make sense, sir, if you're right about him being involved.' Steph always took her boss's hunches seriously; she'd seen him turn out to be right so many times in the past. 'It would explain why he slowed the train down in the tunnel: to help the killer in some way. I agree that his explanation about seeing a plastic bag in the tunnel doesn't quite ring true.' She grimaced. 'It's just that, well, it's all a bit flimsy, isn't it? I mean he could just be upset because his friend has been killed. That doesn't mean to say he's involved with the people who did it. And haven't we virtually ruled out anyone getting out of that compartment undetected?'

Oldroyd sighed. 'You're right of course, but as usual in these hard cases we end up clutching at straws a bit until we finally solve it.'

Steph smiled. Her boss never doubted that they would eventually crack a case, however difficult, and she'd always admired this belief and confidence. He was also very generous in using the word 'we' in relation to finding the solution; he was the one who invariably came up with the answer to the most intractable mysteries.

The door opened and Craven returned. Oldroyd poured him some tea while he reported back from his interview with North.

'He played it down, Jim, but that money Hayward owed him must have been a significant issue. It's a clear motive in my view. I think he would rate his chances of getting his money back, at least part of it, higher when Hayward was dead, and he was registered as a creditor. I think it's worth investigating his own financial situation; let's see if he's a bit short himself and needs that money.

'On the other hand, I have to say, he seems a very unlikely person to be involved in violent crime. He comes across as a kind of gentleman actor of the old school.'

'Which could be an act,' said Oldroyd. 'One of the problems with this case is that there are too many actors involved. You can't tell if you're getting the real person or not.' He drummed his fingers impatiently on the table and then looked at his phone again to see if there was any message from Deborah. There was nothing. 'Damn!' he exclaimed. 'Today has been so frustrating somehow: leads which don't really get us anywhere. And I'm concerned about Deborah. She went walking alone up to Barden Moor this morning and I've heard nothing from her since about ten o'clock.'

'I wouldn't worry, Jim,' said Craven. 'There are some notorious bad spots for reception up on the fells. You get behind some big hill and everything goes dead. She'll have been trying to contact you.'

'I'm sure you're right. Anyway, I've got a blasted headache, so I'm calling it a day. I'm off back to the hotel so I'll see you both tomorrow.'

'Well, take it easy, Jim, and have a rest,' said Craven who felt fairly worn out himself after the hectic last few days.

'OK, sir.' Steph looked at her boss with concern. It was most unlike him to plead ill health as a reason to finish work early. He was obviously quite worried about Deborah. She thought she might take the liberty of calling him later in the evening, just to see that everything was all right.

As Oldroyd drove the short distance to the Wharfedale Bridge, the rain began to fall quite heavily which did nothing to improve his mood. He parked, walked hurriedly into the inn avoiding the downpour, and headed to the room half hoping she would be there. Maybe her phone had conked or run out of battery. These hopes were immediately dashed when he opened the door to reveal the room empty and quiet with everything where they had left it that morning. She had clearly not been back to the hotel since setting off for her walk. It was dark and cool in the room, and he could hear the sound of cars splashing through the rain as they went past the inn. A lonely, desolate feeling struck him, and his anxiety increased.

He went back down to Reception. Lauren, the other young receptionist, thrilled to be talking to the famous detective, smiled at him, and confirmed that Deborah had left the inn that morning to go walking.

'Amy was on duty, she said Ms Fingleton was dressed in walking gear, very stylish, and she told Amy she was going up on to Barden Moor, sir. Amy wrote it down.' She produced the record

Amy had made of the route and handed it to Oldroyd who she could see was concerned. 'Has she not come back yet?'

'No.'

'I haven't seen her since I came on duty at four o'clock but I might have missed her. Never mind, she was planning to go quite a long way, wasn't she, up on to the fells? The weather was very good when she left, she'll have been prepared for bad weather and taken waterproof stuff with her, won't she?'

'Yes, yes, she will have done,' said Oldroyd, a little comforted, and he smiled at her. 'Thank you, you've been very helpful.'

'You're welcome, sir,' replied Lauren, smiling back.

It was very typical of Deborah's thoroughness to be well prepared and leave information about her route. He went to the bar and to the other public rooms, but there was no sign of her.

He returned to the bedroom and looked at the note Amy had made. Deborah had been planning to walk past Upper Barden reservoir up to the top of Cracoe Fell and back down to the Barden Tower area. It was quite a challenging walk and the weather had turned wet. He pulled out his phone and tried to ring her again. He felt quite desperate now but there was no reply. He sent yet another text, then lay on the bed with the phone on the bedside table. He didn't know what to think. And his head ached. He closed his eyes and tried not to catastrophise about what might be happening to her. After a few minutes he was so tired that he fell asleep.

Suddenly the phone beeped, bringing him back to consciousness. He'd got a message. How long had he been asleep? He snatched the phone with a feeling of relief that she was finally getting in touch, only to have this immediately dashed. The message was indeed from Deborah's phone, but when he opened it, he saw a horrific photograph of her bound and gagged, crouched by some kind of stone wall. The message sent a terrible chill through him. His hand shook as he read.

Your partner is well – for now. She stays here until you leave the investigation. Enough people have died, don't let her be the next. No more messages from this phone – I know you can trace it. You'll be watched.

Oldroyd sat up on the bed and tried to control his feeling of panic. His heart was pounding. Why had he not considered that Deborah could be vulnerable when there were dangerous people around? Why had he brought her to the scene of these terrible crimes? Members of his family had been in jeopardy before in connection with cases he was investigating but they had never been targeted directly because of him personally. For a moment he loathed his job and wished he'd never become a detective.

Then with a supreme effort he got up off the bed and sprang into action. It would not help Deborah if he gave in to despair; she would be relying on him to do whatever he could to rescue her. He had to get help. Quickly.

He called Craven who had not long arrived back at the Skipton station.

'Hello, Jim. Are you feeling any better?'

'Bob, Deborah's been kidnapped.' His voice faltered. He could barely believe what he was saying.

'What?'

'I've had a message from the kidnapper with a photograph of her tied up. I'll . . . send it to you. They must have got her while she was . . . walking.' His voice trailed off. Craven had never heard Oldroyd sound so upset.

'Steady on, Jim. Sit down and take it steady.'

'It's OK. I'm in the hotel room. There's a message with the image.'

'Good God!' exclaimed Craven, looking at his phone as the image came through.

'They're trying to get me off the case, Bob. What am I going to do? I can't think straight. She's tied up there; she must be terrified . . . I . . .'

'We're obviously getting close to them, Jim, and they've decided to try and stop you.'

'But they must know that the investigation won't stop if I'm taken out,' said Oldroyd, unknowingly repeating what Deborah had said to her captor. 'I don't . . . I don't understand.'

'Maybe they do know that. But they also know that you are a famous detective, with a great record of solving cases and bringing people to justice. It's possible they think they've got more chance of evading capture if you're not involved. Look, Jim, stay there. I'll be over as quick as I can. I'm going to report this first.'

'OK. I'm going to contact Steph. I need to talk to people. It's a nightmare being by myself here.'

'OK.'

The call ended and there was silence again. Oldroyd could see out of the window. There was still a dark, rainy sky and the garden, so recently a sunny and welcoming place for the hotel guests, was wet and empty. He looked away. Where was she? Was she cold and wet? She must be alone and frightened. He couldn't bear to think about it. He needed to talk to someone he could trust and who would also understand. He called Steph.

Steph had reached the outskirts of Leeds and was driving through the rain when she got the call on her car phone. She wasn't expecting a call from her boss.

'Sir? How are you? I was going to call you later to see how you were and to see if you'd heard from Deborah.'

'Steph, something terrible has happened.'

She could tell straight away that something was badly wrong, and pulled into a lay-by so she could give him her full attention.

'What's wrong, sir?'

Oldroyd explained about the message he had received from Deborah's phone.

'Oh my God, sir, that's terrible. I'm coming straight back now.'

'You don't need to. Bob's on his way from Skipton.'

'I want to, sir. It's no trouble.'

'OK,' Oldroyd said, gratefully.

Steph rang Andy to give him the news. He had just arrived at their flat overlooking the River Aire in Leeds.

'Bloody hell! Held as a hostage?'

'Yes. Until the boss comes off the case. Can you believe it?'

'Hardly. It's a desperate action by desperate people, isn't it? How is he?'

'He sounded awful on the phone. I know he's very fond of her. You know how much happier he's seemed recently compared to those years when he was hoping to get back with his wife.'

'I know.'

'Anyway, I'll give you a call later. Bye.'

'Bye.'

Steph drove back down the Otley Road towards Bramhope as the rain continued to pour down. Her face was grim. They'd faced many difficult and dangerous things together over the years but never a hostage situation like this. They were entering uncharted territory.

The hours passed slowly. Deborah lay on the floor listening to the rain that continued to beat on the roof of the barn. The gag was sopping wet, and her mouth was sore, as were her wrists which were chafed from the nylon cord that had bound them together. The barn was cold, and water had begun to trickle in through cracks in the roof, dripping on to the floor and forming a puddle near her feet. She had wrapped herself in the duvet and was still reasonably warm, but the general discomfort and the suspense of not knowing what was going to happen next were difficult to deal with. She was grateful that her training and work as a psychotherapist was of some help. She distracted herself from the pain and occupied her mind with meditation, deep breathing and by setting herself mental tasks. She also replayed memories of good times in the past and hummed pieces of music to herself.

Jim would know what had happened by now. He would know what to do. He was a brilliant detective and she had faith in him. She used such thoughts to soothe and encourage herself, but it was extremely hard being alone all the time and she had some periods of tearfulness. Once she thought she heard some voices outside and tried to make a noise, but no one came. Then she heard an owl cry and wished she could see it. Maybe a barn owl would fly in and perch on the ledge. That would be company.

How would they find her? They would search all over the area, every possible hiding place. She knew she hadn't travelled a great distance in the boot of the car, so she was not far away from the hotel. Not far away from Jim. The thought was both reassuring and frustrating: if only he knew she was close by.

She was thinking about this as the light began to fade and she became drowsy; she was calling to him and he could hear her. He called back to her to be brave and to stay strong. She would get out of this, and everything would be OK.

She felt calmer and despite everything, she fell asleep on the dirty straw.

∽

Craven was the first to arrive back at the Wharfedale Bridge. He met Oldroyd in the bar and bought him a whisky. Oldroyd seemed a little more composed as they sat at a table. Luckily the bar was fairly quiet. Oldroyd shared with him all the details he knew about where Deborah had been heading on the walk.

'I've got all our resources ready for a search first thing tomorrow, Jim. I'm confident we'll find her. My team at Skipton know this area like the back of their hands: every house, farm, outhouse, shed, barn, and cave; anywhere a person could hide or be hidden. We'll start combing it all tomorrow as carefully as we can.'

Oldroyd looked at the red, weather-beaten face of his old friend and colleague. They'd worked together on many cases over the years, and if there was one person he could trust to carry out an operation like this, it was Bob Craven.

'Thanks, Bob.'

Craven put his hand on Oldroyd's shoulder. 'That's OK, Jim. Now, looking at that photograph. Deborah is lying on the ground near a wall. It all seems too rough to be inside a house, but they won't be leaving her outside with no shelter. So I deduce that she's in some kind of farm building with a roof like a shed or a barn.' He brought up the picture on his phone and pointed at it. Oldroyd winced as he looked. 'You see she's tied to something; you can just see the edge of it. I think it's a metal ring of the kind that you might secure a bull to and that suggests to me that she's in a barn.'

'Brilliant, Bob! Why didn't I notice that?'

'You'd have worked it out, Jim, if you weren't in a state of shock. So early tomorrow we'll be exploring every field barn in this area. I know we don't have a guarantee that she hasn't been taken further, but I don't think they would. It's not only a risk, but they would want to take her to somewhere they know, and we believe that this person is local.'

'You're absolutely right.' Oldroyd knocked back some whisky.

Craven looked at him and frowned. 'The question is, what are you going to do?' he asked.

Oldroyd shook his head. 'I've got to withdraw, Bob; I can't risk anything happening to her. I've thought about calling Superintendent Walker to explain what's happened and see what he thinks, but he's on holiday and I don't want to disturb him. I'm not sure what he could do anyway. The plan is this: you call a press conference and explain what's happened and that I am standing down from the case. Then ask for people to be alert and report anything unusual and so on. It will cause a sensation; the media love the suspense of a kidnap followed by a demand. You might get some leads from it.'

'You don't think it will put Deborah in more danger?'

This was a hard question, and one Oldroyd had agonised about since he received the message. 'It's a risk, but we have to take it if it leads to her being found. It wasn't one of their ransom demands to keep this away from the press, and they must know we'll be looking for her, anyway.'

'OK, Jim. I'll handle the press, don't worry.'

At this point Steph arrived and joined them at the table. She gave Oldroyd a searching look. 'How are you, sir?'

Oldroyd gave her a grim smile. 'Shattered, obviously, but I've got over the initial shock a bit.' He explained what he and Craven had decided to do. 'I want you and Andy to come over and join Bob's team and help with the search. Skipton station early tomorrow morning, OK?'

'Yes, sir.' She looked at her boss. 'Are you really going to come off the case, sir?'

Oldroyd shrugged. 'I don't think I've got much choice. We know these are ruthless people. I can't risk anything happening to her.'

'No, of course. It's an act of desperation, sir, they must think you're closing in on them.'

'Yes, which, ironically, is a good sign. I wasn't aware that we were getting that near and I need to go through what we've found so far and see what we might've missed. Don't worry, I'm working on ways I can stay involved. For the moment I'm going to go back to Harrogate and Bob will run things.'

'Are you going back now, sir? Are you OK to drive?'

'Well, if you could give me a lift back that would be great. I know it's out of your way . . .'

'Not at all, sir. You're welcome.'

'Thanks. I'll have to leave the cars here for the moment. Hers and mine.' This brought the memory of what had happened crashing back into his mind and his voice faltered. 'I'll have to make up some excuse to the hotel staff about why we're both leaving. Anyway.' He stood, making a big effort to compose himself. 'So I'm going up to pack a few things. Bob, call that press conference early tomorrow. You'll have to explain what's happened and ask for anyone who knows anything to come forward and so on. Make sure you say I'm off the case and I've gone back to Harrogate, you know.' Under stress he was repeating himself.

'I will, Jim, don't you worry.'

Oldroyd left the bar.

'Bloody hell, sir,' said Steph, watching him leave.

'I know,' replied Craven. 'I've never seen him like that. This is getting really serious.'

'Yes,' replied Steph, 'but if anyone can find a way through it all, he can.'

It was Friday night and in a pub in nearby Skipton, Terry Hopkins and Jack Smith, the volunteer engineers, were drinking at the bar with a few other friends who also helped on the Wharfedale Railway doing track maintenance and repairs. They were all local people who had been brought up to consider the Wharfedale, as they called it, an important part of their heritage. They were discussing recent events and the atmosphere was more subdued than normal. It was a warm evening, and the doors and windows of the pub were open.

'I can't imagine how the hell anyone managed to shoot that bloke in the carriage. No windows broken, no one got on or off. It's bloody freaky if you ask me,' said Hopkins after swigging from his pint.

'Wish I'd been there to see it, if you know what I mean,' replied Smith.

'Yeah, we do,' laughed another man. 'You like watching people get shot.'

'Get lost!' laughed Smith. 'It's like a mystery, isn't it? I've always liked a good mystery.'

'Be careful what you wish for,' said a fourth. 'Look at poor old Brian Evans. I reckon he saw something he wasn't meant to, so they got rid of him. That could have been one of us.' This sobering comment quelled any further laughter. 'Where are we living? Is it downtown Chicago in the nineteen-twenties?'

There was some shaking of heads at this, and silence as they tried to comprehend the shocking reality of the situation. Another round of drinks was bought and there was some chat about other things. But the subject of the recent murders was so compelling that it was difficult to move on to anything else.

'Two murders in two days. Where's it going to end?' asked Smith.

'I think that chief inspector will crack it. He seemed as sharp as a razor to me,' said the fourth man.

'Yeah. Apparently that actor was a bit of a womaniser, so I reckon it was some abandoned ex-lover getting her own back,' suggested Smith.

'But how do you think it was done? There was nobody in that compartment besides that actor.'

'I don't bloody know. It's like something on one of them magic shows; you know, an illusion or whatever they call 'em, with smoke and mirrors.'

'Well there was plenty o' smoke with that tanker pulling the train but I don't know about mirrors.' Hopkins took a drink of his beer and wiped his face with the back of his hand. 'I'm sorry folk have been killed, especially Brian, but what's worrying me now is what's going to happen to the railway? It's losing money all the time.'

'Janice will sort it out, don't worry. She's brilliant,' said Smith.

'Ooh! Fancy her then do you?'

'Cheeky sod, she's a bit older than me.'

'Beggars can't be choosers.'

Smith went playfully for the teaser, who ducked behind a wooden pillar. The banter and horseplay distracted them and released some of the tension the men were feeling.

'Jack's right though. I think Janice will negotiate something and we'll be able to open again soon.'

'Well I'll drink to that,' said Smith. 'Cheers.'

They all held up their glasses.

When Steph finally got home to Leeds, she briefed Andy on what had happened. He was watching a football match on television, so she went into their bedroom, taking the opportunity to call her sister, Lisa. She was still not ready to talk to Andy about her father and with all that was going on in the case she wished the issue had not come up now. However, she had to do something, and talking to her sister was the first step.

Lisa was a nurse and lived in Sheffield. She was a few years younger than Steph, and married with two small children. Her husband Gary was a painter and decorator. Steph wasn't sure how she would react to the news of their father's interest in seeing them.

Lisa answered the call almost immediately before Steph had a chance to change her mind.

'Hi, it's me,' said Steph. 'Sorry it's a bit late, but I've only just got home from work and something important's come up.'

'Oh, that's OK. Are you working on this murder on that old railway? I've seen it on the telly. Two people killed. It's awful. Be careful.'

'Don't worry. We always look after ourselves and each other. I'm in a great team. There's more to come on that story. I can't tell you anything, but watch the news again tomorrow. Anyway, listen, I've got something to tell you.' She explained what her mother had told her earlier. Lisa was quiet for a few moments.

'Bloody hell,' she said finally. 'I don't really know what to say. I never expected to see him again. I don't know whether I want to. I don't remember him as well as you do, but I do remember what he did to Mum and how we were frightened of him. I was always so glad you were there.'

'I know.'

'What does Mum think?'

'She's leaving it to us. I know a big part of her will not want us to have anything to do with him, but she won't say that because I think that she believes that we ought to at least think about it because he's our father.'

'Father! Him?'

'That's what I said.'

'I suppose it's good of her not to tell us what to do,' said Lisa. 'If I was in her position, I'd probably say, "If you have anything to do with him, I'll never speak to you again" or that sort of thing.'

Steph laughed. 'Yes. Look, I can't say any more about it now. I thought we could meet up soon, when this case is over, and talk about it. It doesn't feel right over the phone.'

'That's a good idea.'

They pencilled in a possible time before ending the call. Steph felt better having spoken to her sister, but it was a tricky decision they were going to have to make.

The next morning at eight o'clock found Steph and Andy driving from Leeds to Skipton. As it was Saturday, they had planned to have the day off together and go for a visit to Temple Newsam Park where the rhododendrons and azaleas were flowering, but they didn't begrudge coming on duty and taking part in the search for Deborah. They were both devoted to Oldroyd, their boss and mentor, from whom they'd learned so much, and this was the least they could do in the circumstances.

The rain had cleared, and it was another beautiful early June day. They went round the Addingham bypass and up the hill to Chelker Reservoir. Steph was driving and Andy glanced out to see that moorhens had laid their eggs in nests near the edge of the water. A little further on he could see the fellsides between Oldthwaite and Skipton: a classic piece of broad Yorkshire landscape. His enjoyment of all this, still something of a novelty to a Londoner from Croydon, was rather tarnished by the thought that, somewhere in the scene before him, it was very likely that Deborah was being held gagged and tied up. He looked up at the gorgeous blue sky and fleecy clouds as they passed over the green fields full of grazing sheep. He could see the fresh green of Bolton Woods in the distance. It didn't seem possible that all the horrendous things that had taken place in Oldthwaite could have happened in such a beautiful place as Wharfedale in early summer.

'Where did the boss say he was going to then?' asked Andy.

'He's going to go into work in Harrogate and communicate with us from there. Knowing him and especially in these circumstances, I can't see him being able to stay away from the action, although he obviously doesn't want to risk anything. I think he's got something up his sleeve.'

'I'll bet he has,' replied Andy, smiling.

When they arrived at Skipton station, they joined a briefing session led by Craven, who began by outlining what had occurred the previous day. He then turned to a large wall map of Skipton and the surrounding area and indicated the locations that were to be the target of the search.

'We know the victim's planned route for her walk from what she told DI Oldroyd, and the fact that she left details at the hotel reception.' Craven pointed this route out on the map. 'The assailant or someone else must have tracked her, probably from the point she left the hotel, unless they somehow had knowledge of the route she was taking. Now it seems to me unlikely that she would be attacked in the open fields or moors as there would be a greater chance of being seen and, looking at the map, I think that a likely place would be here.' He pointed to a spot that, although he didn't know it, was almost exactly where Deborah had been abducted.

'There is some cover from woodland alongside the path and there is a road nearby. I suspect they pounced on her after hiding in these woods. Then one of two things happened: she was either taken to a place of captivity nearby or transported, probably in the boot of a car, to somewhere more distant, but not very far away because we believe the killers are local and would take her to a place they know. The car could have been parked on this road or in the woods. There is a track at this point.' He pointed again.

'If the first option is correct, then we would expect to find her in a barn or similar building around that spot.' He explained why they had concluded that Deborah had been held in a barn. 'So all the structures near this point will be examined first. It wouldn't have been possible for the kidnapper to have taken her far in the open country.

'If it's the second option, and she was taken away by car, then that obviously widens the search considerably, but it also eliminates the barns which are isolated in the fields well away from the roads and inaccessible by car. We would be looking for something near to a road or well-surfaced track. I favour this second explanation mainly because these people appear to be excellent planners, and would have carefully chosen somewhere to place the victim rather than grab her and stuff her in the nearest barn.

'We don't know in precisely what conditions the victim is being kept. She may be cold, hungry, and so on. We need to locate her urgently before her health is affected. Also remember that the kidnappers are dangerous people, so be on the alert. Anybody want to ask anything?'

Craven answered a number of questions and then brought the briefing to an end. Steph and Andy were impressed with Craven's command of the situation, and it gave them hope that their boss's partner could be found.

'Craven's a good bloke, isn't he?' said Andy as he and Steph drove out of Skipton in a convoy of police vehicles which then split up to cover different areas.

'Yes, you can see the boss's influence, can't you? There's the same careful examination of the evidence as well as some trust in your hunches. I'll bet the kidnap happened almost exactly as he described it.'

'Yeah, it makes sense. So we'd better start looking carefully.'

Oldroyd woke up in his flat in Harrogate to a strange silence. He had become used to the sound of Deborah moving around, and the noise of the radio in the kitchen. She was always up before him and sometimes even went for a run round the Stray while he was still in bed. The quiet made him remember the years that he'd lived alone in this flat after his separation from his wife, and how much happier he was with Deborah as his partner: the interests they shared, and their similar sense of humour.

He got out of bed and opened the bedroom curtains to see that it was another beautiful day, but he felt wretched. He had not been able to sleep until sheer exhaustion overtook him in the early hours. He was tormented by the agony of not knowing where Deborah was, or what physical and mental state she was in. If he thought about it too much, his mind began to catastrophise about what might be happening to her and he started to panic. His heart would race, and he would become extremely agitated.

To try to remain calm he drank some tea, forced down a slice of toast, and tried to focus on any details that might give a clue as to what had happened. He went through everything that Deborah had done since arriving at Oldthwaite and what she'd said to him, and then he remembered Frances Cooper. She was a suspect in the case and had sort of befriended Deborah, who had helped her to cope with her damaged relationship with her husband, who was also a suspect. He now saw this behaviour in a more sinister light: was it a strategy? Was she really so upset as she seemed? And did she find out where Deborah was going on her walk and then pass the information on? To whom?

He grabbed his phone and called Craven.

'Bob.'

'Good morning, Jim, how are you feeling today?'

'Not that good . . . but listen. I wasn't thinking clearly last night. I've just remembered Frances Cooper, and the way she's been behaving.' He explained his suspicions to Craven. 'I think it's worth pursuing. If Deborah was taken in a car, which we think the most likely, that indicates planning. The kidnappers must have known the route and parked a car nearby where they intended to grab her.' He was speaking very quickly and becoming agitated. 'Sorry Bob, I'm getting worked up.'

'Jim, sit down and try to calm yourself.'

'OK. Sorry again.' Oldroyd sat down and took some deep breaths.

'Not at all. I think you may be on to something. I was speaking on those lines earlier when I briefed the officers conducting the search. So you think that Frances Cooper may have passed information on to the people who abducted Deborah?'

'It's possible. Can you get back to the inn and speak to her again? And talk to Reception about whether anyone asked about Deborah and where she was walking.'

'I will, Jim. Now, what are you going to do today?'

'I'm going into HQ to see if I can find something else to do – take my mind off things.'

'Good. Better not to stay at home by yourself. That's when you'd start to imagine all sorts of stuff, isn't it?'

'You're right.'

'Well, the search is underway and I'm optimistic we'll find her, so try to relax a bit. I'm going straight over to the Wharfedale Bridge Inn now to see what I can find out.'

'OK, Bob. Thanks, and good luck with the press.'

Craven laughed. 'Don't worry Jim, I can handle them.'

'Oh, by the way, I also forgot to tell you in the confusion. Hayward's wife turned up yesterday: Candida Hayward, just after you left. Said she was in the area, that means the whole of the north of England for someone like her, and she'd come over to see if she could help. I know it's a bit weak and I asked her straight out if she was involved. She denied it of course, but I think she had a motive. She was about to divorce Hayward and may have felt she'd get more as his spouse if he was dead. Anyway, I've added her to the list of suspects who had motive. But there's nothing concrete to link her to the crimes.'

'OK, Jim.'

Oldroyd ended the call and sat quietly for a while to collect his thoughts. Craven would be announcing that Deborah had been kidnapped later in the day, and before that he would have to inform people so they didn't learn about it from the media. He rang his daughter Louise but got no answer. He left a message for her to ring him. He spoke briefly to some of Deborah's friends and then called his sister Alison. She was a vicar in Kirby Underside, a picturesque village between Harrogate and Leeds. Alison was a few years older than Oldroyd and had always been a strong influence in his life and a wise mentor. She answered immediately.

'Jim! Lovely to hear from you. Isn't it a marvellous day? I thought I'd go walking later on. You could come with me. Are you working today?'

He hated to puncture her upbeat cheeriness, but he had to explain about the case and what had happened to Deborah.

'Good Lord, no! Oh Jim, that's terrible. Poor Deborah . . . what on earth is she going through? And you've no idea where she is?'

'No, but I believe she'll be safe. I don't think these people kill for the sake of it. There's a reason that Hayward was shot on that train and I'm pretty sure the second victim knew too much. I think she'll be safe as long as I stay out of it, at least in public.'

'Well, you must. I know it's not the policy of the police to give in to ransom demands but be sensible. There are other people who can solve the case; it doesn't depend on you.'

'No. Bob Craven and my two detective sergeants are on it, and they won't leave any stone unturned. But it's going to be very frustrating being away from the action just sitting in the office in Harrogate.'

'I know that's difficult. You find it hard to relinquish control in a situation like this, but you'll have to. You must come over here this evening. Don't stay in the flat by yourself.'

'That's what Bob Craven just said. It would be wonderful to see you.'

'Good. Come over at about seven o'clock. And Jim, remember that Deborah is a strong person and she'll get through this.'

'Yes,' was all Oldroyd could say as the call ended. He sat back in his chair and sighed. It was still only nine thirty. It was going to be a slow, nerve-racking day.

Steph and Andy drove up a track off the main road towards a farm. There were two barns in the fields nearby. They called at the farmhouse first, ignoring the barking dogs in the stone-flagged yard. The farmer, a portly middle-aged man, was tinkering with a tractor engine and wiped his hands on an oily rag. They presented their warrant cards and explained why they were there.

'Have you seen anything unusual or suspicious?' asked Steph.

'No ah haven't, but you're welcome to have look in t' barns. They're empty now. All t' cows are grazing in t' fields. There's nowt in there but birds: pigeons and house martins; mind they don't crap on yer 'eads.' He laughed uproariously at this prospect.

The two detectives walked through the field, carefully avoiding piles of cow muck even though they were wearing stout shoes. Andy had learned very early after his move to Yorkshire from London that any investigations involving visits to rural locations demanded a certain type of footwear. Steph pushed open the door of the first barn. It was dark inside and she switched on her torch. She was startled as a pigeon flew past her and out of the door. Andy laughed. 'That farmer was right.' He also switched on his torch, and together they examined every corner of the barn, even the wooden rafters. There appeared to be nothing but a few empty fertiliser bags, but suddenly something stood up in one of the stalls, surprising Steph for a second time. Her eyes were now adjusting to the light, and after a moment she could see it was a calf. The cow was still lying on the ground. The farmer had clearly forgotten about these two.

'Aw, look at that! Isn't it so cute?' she cooed. 'Maybe it's been a bit sickly, so he's brought it in here with its mother. It must have been suckling, aww.' She reached out to try to stroke the calf but there was a threatening moo from the cow that made her draw back.

'Yes, lovely,' replied Andy. 'But it would look even better grilled on my plate with pepper sauce, chips and onion rings.'

Steph tried to hit him with her torch. 'Oh, you're such a brute sometimes, no feelings at all! All you think about is your stomach.'

'At least I'm not a hypocrite like you.' He laughed as he caught her arm to prevent the attack. 'It's no good sentimentalising over animals when you're prepared to eat them after they've been slaughtered by someone else.'

'Hmm.' Steph looked at the calf again. 'When I see something like this it's enough to make me vegetarian.' She shook her head.

171

'Anyway, there's no one in here, is there? Or any sign that anyone has been in here recently.'

'No, let's try the other one. I think this could be a long day.'

'OK,' began Craven. He was speaking to Christine Gray, and Lauren and Amy, the reception staff, in Gray's office. He'd driven quickly down to the Wharfedale Bridge after speaking to Oldroyd. 'You're aware that DCI Oldroyd and myself are investigating the murders at the railway. You also know that DCI Oldroyd and his partner, Deborah Fingleton, are staying here with you.' The rather frightened-looking staff nodded. 'What I'm about to tell you is in confidence, although it will become public knowledge this afternoon. You will have probably noticed that they are not around at the moment. That's because, sometime yesterday, probably in the late morning or early afternoon while on a walk, Ms Fingleton was abducted.'

There were some gasps from the small audience.

'There are a number of things I want to ask you about this. First of all, can you tell me what her movements were before she left the hotel?'

'They had breakfast together,' said Amy. 'I was on duty, and I saw them come into the restaurant and come out again. Then I saw the chief inspector leave here and a bit later, she came down in her walking stuff and said she was going up on to Barden Moor. I wrote down the route she was planning to take. She's a really nice friendly person.' The woman looked close to tears.

'Oh my God!' said Lauren. 'I was here last night, and DCI Oldroyd asked me if I'd seen her. I told him she'd gone walking; I gave him the note Amy had written. We write down where people say they're going. The poor man.'

'Indeed,' said Craven, and he turned back to Amy. 'Now, think carefully. Could anyone have overheard her telling you where she was going?'

She looked up at Craven. 'Yes, someone was hovering behind her while she was talking to me and they could have heard what she said. They had a quick word with each other before Ms Fingleton left. It was Ms Cooper.'

'I see. Did you hear what they said?'

'I think Ms Cooper was suggesting they went into Leeds, I heard Leeds mentioned, but Ms Fingleton said she couldn't . . . or something like that.'

'OK.' Craven turned to the others. 'Did anyone see anything suspicious or unusual yesterday morning? Were there any people around you didn't recognise, inside or outside the inn?'

'Yes,' replied Amy. 'Another woman appeared at Reception just after Ms Fingleton left. Ms Cooper was still there, and they had a big row. I didn't say anything.'

'What was the row about?'

Amy was now enjoying herself, as she was about to become gossipy. She'd already told Lauren all about it when they changed shifts. 'The new woman, that's Mrs Hayward, accused Ms Cooper of sleeping with her husband, you know, the actor who was murdered. She even said that that was one of the reasons she was going to divorce him. Mrs Hayward was shouting, and I thought they might start to attack each other, but Ms Cooper walked away. Then Mrs Hayward booked a room here for a couple of nights.'

'I see. Do you know where Ms Cooper is now?'

'She's probably in her room, Inspector, I've noticed her coming down quite late in the mornings,' said Christine Gray.

'Could you give her a call, please? And tell her to meet me here as soon as possible.'

Amy got up, but Christine Gray moved to the door. 'Sit down, Amy, I'll do it.'

Craven smiled as he noticed the two receptionists exchange a glance and then suppress a giggle.

∽

Frances Cooper appeared in a rather dishevelled state; she had obviously got dressed hastily and she looked angry. Craven took her into Gray's office, which had been vacated by all the staff, and they sat down.

'What is it, Inspector? I've told the police all I know about everything. Why do you keep harassing me?'

'Deborah Fingleton has been kidnapped,' announced Craven abruptly. He watched her response very carefully.

Her face fell. 'What?'

'She was abducted while walking on Barden Moor. This is confidential until I announce it at a press conference later today.'

'But . . . that's terrible.'

'It is indeed. Did you know where she was going for her walk?'

'Up on to the moor. I . . . I saw her here as she was leaving. I was hoping we could go into Leeds together, but she was set on walking.' She looked genuinely agonised. 'Oh, I wish I'd gone with her now, but I've no proper walking shoes. I spent another boring day mooching about here. I thought it was odd that I didn't see her or the chief inspector at dinner.' She put her hand to her mouth. 'The poor man!'

'So you didn't pass on any information about where she was going to anyone else?'

Cooper's mouth dropped open. 'What? Of course not! Are you still suggesting that I'm involved in all these dreadful things that are happening?' Craven thought she seemed genuinely outraged, but it could be her acting skills coming in to play. He hated having to interview actors, especially the good ones.

'We believe someone did, which was why her assailant knew where she was going. The only people, besides her partner, who knew the route she was going to take were the reception staff here and, by your own admission, you.'

'Well, I certainly didn't tell anyone. Surely someone could have spied on her and then followed her on to the moor. I hope you find whoever's responsible for all this, but will you please leave me alone? I've got enough problems with my husband.'

Craven looked at her long and hard. 'I've also had a report that you were involved in an argument with Candida Hayward.'

Cooper shook her head. 'Yes. I don't know why she's here. She found out a while ago that I'd had an affair with her husband. I can understand how she feels, but it's unfair to blame me and they were separated. Dan was a womaniser on a grand scale. Is she still here?'

'I think she booked in.'

'Oh, I'll keep out of her way. She can be vicious.'

Craven was on the alert. 'Did you ever hear her threaten her husband because of his behaviour?'

'No. I've never had much to do with her, Inspector. She knows who I am, and on the few occasions we've met, she's frozen me out. "If looks could kill" sort of thing.'

'Very well. We'll stop there. But you must stay at the hotel, and not leave the area until we've investigated further.'

'I'm not leaving here until Gerry does. He spent most of yesterday trying to sort out the future of the film. He's very busy but I'm hoping that I can persuade him to have me back.'

Craven nodded but didn't say anything. To be honest, the private lives of all these theatrical types was the least of his worries.

~

Deborah awoke feeling stiff everywhere. Her arms and mouth were numb. The sunlight was pouring in through the windows and cracks in the door. She could hear the sheep again outside, and it appeared to be a fine day. But she felt shivery and miserable, cut off from the world outside and in a dismal place of discomfort and anxiety.

She'd had to use the bucket earlier. Now it stank, and she was thirsty and hungry. If she didn't get water soon, she would become dehydrated. Despite her own perilous situation, she worried about Jim and the others and how they were doing. They would have got her route from the receptionist and there would be a huge police search of the area; it was only a matter of time. Keeping this thought in her head was calming. She knew Jim would be in a very anxious state. If only she could communicate with him. It felt terrible to be alone with no one to talk to. She was beginning to understand why hostages who had been held in isolation were forced deep into themselves and, after they were released, found communication difficult.

Suddenly she heard the noise of footsteps and the door swung open. Her captor appeared and pulled off her gag. She winced with the pain. He took another bottle of water from a plastic bag and some slices of buttered bread.

'Eat and drink that quickly,' he said. 'I'm moving you from here. The fields are crawling with police looking for you and we can't let them find you, can we?'

Deborah was pleased to hear the news that a search for her was going on, which confirmed what she'd hoped, but was alarmed that her kidnapper seemed to be a step ahead of the police, and of Jim.

She said nothing, however, as she knew this might incite her abductor to violence. She drank the water and ate the bread, then he replaced the gag and put on a blindfold. He unlocked the chain from her waist, pulled it out of the metal ring and dragged her to her feet, then he pushed her stumbling out of the door and she was bundled again into the boot of a car. Her legs felt numb and her back ached. She lay there as the car drove off, fighting the feeling of despair that her potential rescue had been thwarted.

At Oldthwaite station, the media were gathered around the station entrance in keen anticipation and there was a buzz of conversation. Craven came to the top of the steps that led up to the door. This provoked an immediate response.

'Inspector, where's DCI Oldroyd? Are you standing in for him?'

'OK.' Craven had to raise his voice. 'Could you all listen carefully? I have some important announcements.' He was carrying a sheet of notes in case he forgot something. 'I've arranged this conference to give you an update on the case and to inform you that there has been a development. Yesterday another crime was committed in relation to the case we are currently investigating, that of the murders of Daniel Hayward and Brian Evans. A woman, Deborah Fingleton, was abducted on a path near here leading up to Barden Moor. Her whereabouts are currently unknown. She is DCI Oldroyd's partner.'

There were cries of surprise from Craven's audience and he had to call for quiet again.

'We have received a message from the kidnapper stating that Ms Fingleton's safety can only be guaranteed if DCI Oldroyd removes himself from the case.'

'A ransom demand!' shouted someone, and there was a terrific hum of conversation.

'Quiet, please! Quiet!' shouted Craven, and the noise subsided. 'Yes, it is. And the team involved in this case has met and decided to take the precaution of DCI Oldroyd standing down from this investigation for the moment, which is why he is not here today.'

'Does that mean you're giving in to the kidnappers?'

'No, the investigation will continue.' Craven was having to fight for attention. They were excited by this announcement, as Oldroyd had said they would be.

'Do they believe that Inspector Oldroyd was close to discovering their identity?'

'I believe you are right, and we are still confident that we can make progress in solving the case even if DCI Oldroyd is not here in the field, as it were. We are currently undertaking a search of the area, as we believe Ms Fingleton is being held in a field barn or some kind of farm building. I would welcome your help in disseminating details of Ms Fingleton's appearance and to appeal for anyone who has seen anything suspicious, or has any knowledge of her whereabouts, to come forward. These details will be in a press release, copies of which will be available after this briefing.' Craven gave a brief description of Deborah and the approximate location and time of her kidnap.

'Will DCI Oldroyd still be helping from behind the scenes?'

Craven frowned; it was not a helpful question in the circumstances. 'I'm sure you can see why it is essential that the message goes out that DCI Oldroyd has withdrawn from the case. I have no further comment on that.' This caused further excited mumblings.

'How is DCI Oldroyd?'

Craven flinched a little as he could see a dramatic headline: 'Heartbroken Chief Inspector Forced to Juggle with his Partner's Life'. The press loved to personalise things.

'He's as well as can be expected. It has obviously come as a shock to him.'

'Why was Ms Fingleton here, Inspector? Isn't it dangerous round here at the moment?'

Craven considered this carefully. It was another hard question, and he knew Oldroyd would be reproaching himself about having brought Deborah here.

'None of us considered that there was any danger to Ms Fingleton when she arrived in the area. She was simply staying at the Wharfedale Bridge Inn and taking no part in the investigation. She is an innocent person who has been ruthlessly targeted by the perpetrators of these crimes. I would ask you not to make judgements about this in any of your reporting. It will only add to Chief Inspector Oldroyd's anguish at this time and maybe increase the danger to Ms Fingleton. Let's concentrate on finding her, and bringing the criminals involved to justice.'

'Do you think you'll be making an arrest anytime soon?'

'I can't make any kind of prediction on that at the moment, but the investigation is progressing.' Craven wasn't sure that this was actually true. The whole thing had been seriously derailed by this latest development which, of course, was exactly what the kidnapper intended.

'Is this going to prevent the railway from reopening tomorrow?'

Craven's heart sank as he was reminded of yet another issue. 'I shall shortly be talking to Janice Green, the railway manager, and a decision will be made then. The railway will only reopen if it can be done without disrupting the investigation and if we are sure that the public will be safe.'

'Do you think this person or persons will strike again?'

Craven paused; another difficult one. 'The only thing I have to say is that there are dangerous people around. We remain convinced that this is not the work of one person and that the public should be vigilant until we catch them.'

It was a relief to Craven when he was able to draw things to a close. He had managed to conceal the feeling of crisis that everyone on the team felt. They could only carry on and hope for the best.

Andy and Steph had searched a number of barns and outhouses in the area that Craven had assigned to them, without success. The barns were all similar: empty except for a few animals, nesting birds and rusting farm machinery, though it was easy to see the attraction of these remote structures as hiding places.

It was late in the afternoon when they turned on to yet another winding farm track. The car bounced up the uneven surface towards the farm. There was no sign of anyone at work and when they reached the farmyard, they found it deserted and the farmhouse looked neglected. Andy knocked on the door but there was no answer. He peered in through the dusty windows and saw that the interior was devoid of furniture.

'There's clearly nobody running this farm at the moment,' he said. 'It's either closed for good or waiting for another tenant. This could be the ideal place; nobody around and it's well off the road.'

'There don't seem to be any public footpaths near here either,' said Steph, looking around. 'Come on, let's have a look.'

They wandered around the outbuildings which were in various states of disrepair. All were empty inside and echoing. The corrugated iron on the roofs of some was rusting away. The whole place was quite eerie. Steph stumbled on the skeleton of a dead rabbit. An old tractor with no headlights was parked off the track, grass growing through its wheel arches.

'OK, let's investigate the fields. There's at least one barn over there,' said Andy. They made their way to the building and forced a rather rickety door open. Steph shone her torch around and immediately saw something different.

'Yes, Andy, look! Someone must have been here. There's a toilet bucket, some water bottles and an iron ring like the one in the picture.' They both had the picture sent to Oldroyd on their phones. 'It all looks as if it's been used recently. The chain is still looped through. This must be where Deborah was being kept.' She shone her torch on the ground. 'There's a hair grip that must have fallen off her head.'

Andy nodded. 'You're right. It's her style, I think. It looks as if she was here until not that long ago. At least we know she's probably still alive. The problem is: where is she now?'

Steph shook her head and went outside the barn to get better reception on her phone. She called Craven.

'Sir, I think we've found where Ms Fingleton was being held, but she's not here now. It's a barn near Mooredge; the farm is unoccupied so it would be an ideal hiding place.' She explained the evidence they'd seen.

Craven was in their incident room at the railway station.

'Well done,' he said. 'It's sounds as if you're right. I was hoping we'd get to Deborah before the blasted kidnappers got wind of our search. It's hard to hide a lot of police officers when they descend on an area however discreet they try to be. My guess is they've taken her to somewhere more secure, but maybe a little riskier for them or they would have taken her there in the first place. Take plenty of photographs and come back here. I won't call the search off yet in case you're wrong. Anyway, I think most places will have been examined by now.'

'Are you going to contact DCI Oldroyd, sir?'

'Yes. I think we need to keep him up to date. OK, I'll see you back here.'

Steph shuddered as she got back into the car, imagining what it must be like to be tied up and left in a remote barn like that, not knowing what was going to happen to you.

'It's a bit creepy knowing that they're watching us, isn't it?' said Andy.

'Yes. I wonder who the hell they are?'

Oldroyd was sitting in his office trying to relax when his phone went. He was expecting a call from Craven on the progress they were making, but it wasn't Craven, it was his boss Detective Chief Superintendent Tom Walker.

'Jim, what the bloody hell's going on? Two murders and now Deborah kidnapped! Are you OK?'

Oldroyd and Walker had worked with each other for many years. They were both diehard Yorkshiremen and were on first-name terms in private. They were united in their dislike of the tabloid press and of managerialism in the police. Oldroyd agreed with Walker that policing was all about what happened in the field, and it was the active police officers who were important.

'As well as can be expected I suppose, Tom. But it's a shock.'

'It must be. Why didn't you call me?'

'Well, you're on leave, and I didn't want to disturb you.'

'Don't worry about that, it's awful weather over here: drizzling, cold, with that blasted sea fret covering everything. It's like bloody November. There's nothing to do except watch telly and I saw it all on the lunchtime news. They showed Bob Craven talking to reporters. He used to work with us at Harrogate, didn't he? Good bloke. Anyway, I nearly fell off my chair when he said that Deborah had been kidnapped! What a nasty bloody trick! But it shows you're on to them and they want to keep you out of it.'

'I thought about that, Tom. The problem is, I have to tread carefully. I can't risk anything happening to Deborah. I was thinking that maybe I should call you and ask if you think I should formally relinquish the case completely and then you can appoint someone else.'

'Hmm. Well, I don't know. It would take a new person quite some time to get up to speed on the case and things are urgent now, aren't they? I would suggest that you lie low but monitor how things are going. Then you can help them. Has Craven got Steph and Carter working with him?'

'He has.'

'Well, they're a capable bunch of officers and you can help them discreetly, can't you? I'd say just proceed as I've suggested and keep me informed. If the weather doesn't pick up, we'll be coming home a few days early, and then I'll be straight into the office. I'm off for a drink soon; at least they've got a decent bar on site. OK, bye for now.'

Oldroyd smiled. Walker always seemed to prefer his work to anything except his golfing. He probably wouldn't go away on holiday at all if it wasn't for his wife. His phone went again and this time it was Craven.

'Any news, Bob?' asked Oldroyd anxiously.

Craven explained what Steph and Andy had found.

'Good for them, well done,' said Oldroyd, trying hard to keep his voice strong and conceal his disappointment. 'Have we got any leads about where they might have moved her?'

'Not really Jim, but I think somewhere more secure; concealed in a house I would think, in an attic or cellar.'

'Yes, you're probably right.' He felt extremely deflated, but tried to pull himself together. 'Pass on my thanks to Steph and Andy. I'm going to do some research myself. There's something we're missing in this case. If we can find out what it is it might unlock the whole thing.'

The call ended. Oldroyd sat alone in the office staring ahead, trying to work out whether it was good news or bad. At least there was good evidence that she was alive. On the other hand, she would probably now be taken to somewhere more sequestered. He was desperate to do something practical: he wanted to be searching for her himself. Working from a distance like this was very hard.

Five

In another Agatha Christie railway mystery, 4.50 from Paddington, 1957, a passenger on a train from London witnesses a murder taking place in a compartment on another train running parallel to hers. She reports this to her friend Miss Marple, the famous private detective, who devises a plan to locate the body and investigate the crime. The action moves to Rutherford Hall where a classic cast of English country-house characters plays out the rest of the story, carefully monitored by Miss Marple who, of course, succeeds in identifying the guilty person.

'I really do need some answers from you both if that's not too much to ask. I have to know what's happening in terms of the filming and the reopening of the railway.'

Janice Green had decided that the time had come to be assertive, even if the people she was confronting were a police inspector and a film director. She'd asked Craven and Blake to meet her in her office and they were now assembled around her desk.

Blake looked exhausted. He'd spent most of the last two days talking to the cast and crew, explaining that the film was still alive, but that they had to finish all the location shots within two weeks. This included not only the action at the railway, but also scenes at the exterior of a local manor house and in a village nearby. He'd had to have intensive discussions with the production team to examine how they could modify the schedule and reduce the number of outdoor shots.

'As far as our work here is concerned,' he said, 'we've got a big problem. We don't have time to repeat the same station scenes; I've been given two weeks to finish all our location shots up here. Also, I take it we wouldn't be able to use the same carriage.'

He looked at Craven, who shook his head. 'No, we're still investigating that carriage, to work out how the murder was committed.'

'OK, so what we're likely to do then is use the footage of that scene which we already have of the train coming in, and then fiddle about with it so we can fit the new actor in. All we'll need to do is take some fresh shots of the platform with the new person and I think we've got someone. He should be here by tomorrow.'

'So does that mean you won't need the engine and the carriages any more?'

'Yes. I think we can manage with what we've got in the can. The scene won't be exactly as I'd envisaged it, but we'll make it adequate. To be honest we need to get on from here; we have other locations to visit and not much time.'

'Right, so from your point of view there's nothing to stop us opening tomorrow as planned?'

'No, that's fine. We'll do what we need to on Monday and then we'll be off.'

Green turned to Craven. 'I appreciate there's been another serious development in the case, Inspector. What's the situation in relation to the railway opening?'

'The kidnapping has no direct connection to the railway. I know you're desperate to get back to something like normal, but I don't think that will be entirely possible. We'll still need you to tape off those parts of the platform where the murders took place, and of course you can't use that carriage, but other than that, I think you can go ahead tomorrow.'

'Good.'

'You can help us by displaying a missing person poster at the station tomorrow. It might produce a useful lead.'

'Of course.' Green looked extremely relieved; it was a better outcome than she'd hoped for. 'Good, that's wonderful to hear, thank you Inspector. We'll operate trains from platform two. It will be a bit tricky, but we'll manage.' She turned to Blake. 'You're fine to use the station during the week. We only operate trains on weekdays except on bank holidays and during the summer school holidays. By the way, I have a request to make.'

'Yes?'

'Would it be possible to get some of the actors down tomorrow and mingle with the public for a bit? It would be great publicity for us, especially now as the film is definitely going ahead.'

'Yes, I'll ask them. I think they're so fed up with waiting around that they'll be pleased to do it.'

'That's great.' She sighed and sat back in her chair. 'Thank you both again.'

Blake and Craven nodded and got up to go. They were both quite envious of Green, whose problems were beginning to resolve themselves. In contrast, their difficulties in filming and in the crime investigation were as formidable as ever.

Deborah's second dark journey in the boot of the car was similar to her first. It wasn't very long, but again she had no idea in which direction the car was heading. She lay on the duvet which the kidnapper had thrown into the back of the car with her, and there was also her rucksack, which she managed to get her head on and use as a pillow. It felt like a link with normal life and happy walks in the countryside with Jim.

The car stopped and she was pulled out of the boot. It was warm and she briefly felt the sun on her skin as she was led, stumbling, across a paved area that she thought was probably a yard. She could hear dogs barking. They entered a building, and then she was being helped down some stone stairs. The temperature dropped and sounds were muffled.

She was pushed to the floor, and the blindfold was pulled off once again. She saw that she was in a cellar with a stone floor and whitewashed walls that were crumbling in places. It was lit by one bare light bulb dangling on a cord from the ceiling. It was dry but cold, and full of the kind of detritus that finds its way into a cellar: old bikes, tins of paint, some planks of wood and a pile of tiles left over from some job. Dust covered everything, but one corner had been prepared for her. There was another toilet bucket, another duvet and a carton of water bottles still covered in plastic and a bag containing some food. She could see supermarket-bought sandwiches in their plastic wrappers and some fruit. The kidnapper pulled off the gag and untied her wrists.

'So, I'm going to leave these off. Don't bother shouting, no one is going to hear you. Keep away from that door.' He pointed to the top of the stone steps where there was presumably a door on to the ground floor. 'If you don't behave, we'll put the gag back on and tie you up again. Here are a few things to keep you amused.' He dropped another plastic bag next to her and then went off quickly up the stairs two at a time. There was the rattle of a key in a lock.

She looked around her. Was it worse or better? She wasn't gagged and could move around, but she was in semi darkness with no sounds of animals and birds. She looked in the bag of stuff. There were some magazines and a copy of a cheap thriller. The irony made her smile. There was a book of puzzles but no pen or pencil.

Suddenly she heard raised voices. She listened carefully but couldn't make out anything except maybe the word 'choice'.

At least it meant the house was probably inhabited. Was the kidnapper arguing with an accomplice? Were they arguing about her? Maybe the other person didn't want her there.

The idea that there might be discord between them gave her a glimmer of hope on which to survive; perhaps this other person would regret what they were doing and let her out. It didn't sound as if their scheme was going according to plan, and it suggested that they were genuinely afraid that they were going to be tracked down. This could be another hopeful sign, but on the other hand, when people get desperate, they do rash things.

She took the risk of climbing to the top of the steps; the voices became clearer. It appeared that the police had somehow worked out that she was being held in a barn and had been searching the area, wherever that was. How were they ever going to find out where she was now? It was a depressing thought, but how many times had she talked about the power of positive thinking with clients? She forced herself to concentrate on the comfort of being able to move around easily and do some exercises to stop her muscles from seizing up entirely.

Back at the Wharfedale Bridge, Gerard Blake was meeting in the bar with his principal actors and explaining the situation regarding the film.

'I'm just glad to get any kind of news,' said Sheila Jenkins, sipping a gin and tonic. 'I've been going out of my mind here waiting for something to happen. At least now we can get on with it and then get away. It's beautiful round here, but it's going to be forever tainted for me after all this.'

'You've got someone to replace Dan?' asked Anna Whiteman.

'Yes. Desmond Hammond. He's possibly a bit too old for the part, but I'm sure make-up will do wonders. And he's available. He'll be here tomorrow, so we can get on and do some filming on Monday. The railway people are happy for us to go ahead. We've altered the sequence a little. We'll just do the scene on the station where you all meet him. We can't use the train any more, so we'll have to use the scenes we've shot and edit them so that Desmond appears on the platform as if he's got out of the train. I don't think there'll be any serious continuity problems. Luckily we hadn't done many indoor scenes with Dan and what we have done we'll just have to do again.'

'So, we've got to do that and then all the other location stuff within the next fortnight,' observed Christopher North, sceptically.

'Yep. It's going to be very demanding, I know, but I've spoken to all the crew and they would much rather carry on than lose everything we've done so far. It's a mess. We've lost time, we've got to give a contract to a new actor and we're paying you all to do nothing at the moment. The finance people won't like it; they're losing money as we speak, and we've got to make it back somehow. I honestly think Henrietta did a good job persuading them to let us carry on. It wouldn't have surprised me if they'd pulled the plug. But we can save this thing, I'm sure. It can still be a great film.'

'I'm with you,' said Anna. 'It would be awful if it was all abandoned. I agree that it could be a really good film. Let's go for it! We'll just have to work extra hard, but it will be worth it.'

'I agree,' said Jenkins. 'I'm just desperate to start work again. We've nothing to lose, have we? But if we give up now, our contracts will be terminated and that will be hard for me. I'm not rolling in cash, I can tell you.'

'I presume you've notified the house where we're filming, what's it called?' asked North.

'Barden Manor, it's Bolton Gill Manor in the film.'

'Yes. We weren't due to go there until next week, were we?'

'No, but they've been very good. They've obviously heard about what's happened and they want to help. They said we can go there whenever we want.'

'Well, they don't want to miss an opportunity for their place to be filmed, do they?' said Whiteman.

'No.'

North shrugged. 'OK, well of course I don't want to let the side down, but I just want to say that I'm not as young as I was, and I can't really deal with marathon filming sessions these days.'

'Don't worry, Chris, we won't overwork you,' Blake promised with a smile.

'By the way, have you checked with the police?' asked Jenkins. 'There's been another development, hasn't there? That chief inspector's partner, you know, the woman we saw him with in the dining room, she's been kidnapped.'

'Kidnapped!' exclaimed Whiteman. 'How do you know that?'

'It was on the news. The other detective held a press conference. It seems like the killers want DCI Oldroyd off the case and they're holding her hostage.'

'Oh no! That's terrible! She seemed such a nice woman. She was helping Frances, wasn't she? Oops, sorry.' Whiteman put her hand to her mouth as she remembered that Blake was there.

'Don't worry,' he said. 'My wife needs some help. Maybe that woman was able to knock some sense into her.'

Whiteman cast a disapproving look at Blake.

'Anyway,' Blake continued, 'I had a meeting with the police and Janice Green, and the inspector was happy for us to carry on, although there will be bits of the station taped off. We can work round that.'

North shook his head. 'Whatever next? Kidnapping an innocent woman like that and threatening violence. She must be terrified wherever she is. I'm happy to get on and complete this film because I don't want to let any of you down, but it does seem to be somewhat cursed. I'll be quite glad when we've finished it.'

'Don't worry, Chris,' said Jenkins. 'You know the saying: "there's no such thing as bad publicity". The public have an appetite for such things; who won't want to see the notorious film made in such gruesome circumstances?'

North grimaced. Although he was actually inclined to agree, he thought the way Jenkins had put this was in rather bad taste.

'There's one more thing,' said Blake. 'Green has asked if you will attend the reopening of the railway tomorrow and talk to the public, you know, for a bit of publicity.'

The actors looked at each other. 'Fine,' said North. 'We've brought them so much trouble that I think it's the least we can do. Why don't we put our costumes on?'

'That's a good idea, Chris, and it will add to the vintage atmosphere,' observed Jenkins. Whiteman agreed. Blake was right: they were only too happy to do something useful after all the tense days of waiting.

The detectives met in their office. Craven had made some tea, which was badly needed by all of them. They'd had a difficult day so far, especially Craven who was feeling the weight of responsibility in the absence of Oldroyd. In a case like this, difficult decisions had to be made all the time.

Craven began. 'I've got the report from Tim Groves, the two victims were definitely shot by firearms matching the ones which were stolen. I think that's what we expected, and it confirms that the killer had local knowledge of where to steal those weapons. Well done again, you two, for finding that barn. The forensic team's out and I'm sure they'll confirm what you saw as evidence that she was being held there. The question is, where is she now?'

'She'll have been taken inside a house or something, won't she sir?' asked Steph. 'They know we're on to them and they won't risk leaving her outside again.'

'I think you're probably right, but it means we've got a harder job finding her. We have no clues at all as to where she is.'

'What we do know, sir, is that someone is watching us, so they must still be nearby.'

'Yes, more than one person. These crimes only make sense if you assume that there are a number of people involved and that they are still alert to what is going on in the investigation. We've found people with a motive for the first murder, but none of those people could have actually done it. Which means that there is at least one person with a knowledge of the railway who had a motive for killing Hayward.' He shook his head. 'When you narrow it down like that, it shouldn't be too difficult to find out who. I've got my team going through the list of everyone who worked on the engines and carriages in that engine shed. The answer lies there somewhere. I'd like you two to help. It will speed up the process and we're really under pressure now to get results. I gave details of the kidnapping at the press conference, so the profile of the case is going to soar.'

'OK, sir.'

'The problem is: what is the connection between a London actor and a local person who spends their spare time helping to maintain locomotives and carriages at a local vintage railway?'

'There must be a link, sir,' said Steph optimistically. 'And we'll find it. How's the chief inspector, sir?'

'I spoke to him this morning. He seemed much better than last night. I imagine he's deeply frustrated at not being able to be with us out in the field, but he'll find something useful to do in the office.'

'You can be sure of that, sir,' said Andy.

∾

'Granville, where've you been?' Hardy's wife went into the kitchen as she heard her husband coming in through the back door.

'I've been walking; it's a beautiful day.'

'Why don't you tell me instead of just going off like that? It's dangerous round here at the moment. Do you know what's happened now?'

'No, what?'

'The partner of the detective in charge of the investigation has been kidnapped. It's just been on the local news.'

'Really?' Hardy seemed unperturbed.

She frowned at his apparent lack of concern. 'Yes, what's the matter with you? Don't you think that's awful? The poor woman. And that detective must be frantic.'

'Yes, but there's also some good news. I called at the railway and it's going to open again tomorrow. So, I'd better get my uniform ready. I said I'd go up to the shed later on today and help to get the locos and carriages ready.'

She looked at him with disgust. 'Sometimes I think the only things you're interested in are railways; the one upstairs and the one up the road. It's as if you've never grown up. You're like a little boy.'

Hardy looked away. 'No need to be like that. What's wrong with having a hobby?'

'Nothing, but since you retired it's become an obsession. You're either up at the station or upstairs playing with your toy trains. We hardly spend any time together.'

'We never have spent much time together, have we?' he said darkly, before he went upstairs. He ducked under the lines to his control centre, switched on the panel, rubbed his hands together and turned the switch to set off the express pulled by an A4 Pacific class Lord Faringdon. He looked at the timetable behind him. There was just time for it to get to the station without being late. He grinned and completely forgot about the conversation with his wife. The railway was going to reopen and things were going his way. Those ridiculous film makers would not be using the engines and carriages and contaminating them any more. The Wharfedale Railway would be a proper railway again.

Deborah was trying to read one of the magazines that had been left for her, but it was difficult in the poor light afforded by the single bulb. It was a lifestyle magazine full of attractive people practising 'self-care' by doing yoga, eating Mediterranean-style food and ironically, chilling out in luxury spas much like that one she had been enjoying so recently. She'd lost track of time; it seemed an age since she was lying out with a novel by the side of the pool, her skin silky smooth and glowing after a very indulgent massage. At least looking at the magazine helped to pass the time.

She had no idea what time it actually was, but she heard the door at the top of the steps being unlocked and then a figure with its face covered with a scarf came down. It was not the person who'd kidnapped her.

'Sit down and don't move,' he said. It was an older man with a stronger local accent. He seemed nervous and hesitant. 'Are you all right?' It was the first time she'd been asked anything about how she was.

'Not brilliant,' she said. 'How can I be?'

'Well, hopefully it won't be for much longer. If that partner of yours does as he's told.'

This gaoler seemed less hard and ruthless than the one who had abducted her on the fell. 'What's the point? The other police will still be investigating. They'll track you down eventually.'

He looked away and she sensed he was uncomfortable. 'We all know Oldroyd's the main man. He's famous round here. They won't do as well without him. Anyway, I've brought some more food and some more stuff to read. I'll take this away and empty it.' He indicated the toilet bucket.

'Can you bring me some hot water, soap and a towel? I haven't had a wash for two days.'

'Aye, OK. Just wait here, don't cause any trouble and we'll look after you.'

He went off up the stairs carrying the bucket. His reactions and attitudes are curious, thought Deborah. She remembered the raised voices she'd heard. Was there indeed a dispute about holding her here? The second man was markedly more sympathetic towards her and almost apologetic. She was probably being held in the second man's house and he was not happy about it. She heard the door again and he came down the steps with a brown washing up bowl filled with steaming water. He had a towel over his arm and a bar of soap in a small plastic bag. He set the bowl down on the floor.

'Right, there we are then.' He almost seemed embarrassed. 'I'll . . . I'll leave you to it. And I'll be back later.'

Deborah said nothing. He went up the steps again, leaving her thoughtful. She was beginning to build up a picture of her two captors and an idea was developing about how she might be able to influence her situation.

~

Candida Hayward was lying on her bed in her room at the Wharfedale speaking on the phone to a friend in London.

'It's absolutely true, darling. I can't believe it; he's dead. I had to come all the way over here from Manchester to hear it from the police – I know, it's just amazing!' After a pause, she shrieked with laughter. 'How dare you? What on earth do you mean: "It was almost as if you'd arranged it"?! Of course I didn't, but whoever did, I'd like to shake them by the hand, they've done me a good turn – oh I've no idea, but do you wonder that it's happened? There must be so many people who'd like to see the back of him. I know he owed money all over the place, to say nothing of the cheated husbands and boyfriends – oh yes, we're still married. I'll get the lot – no, not a fortune because he spent money like water . . . but there's the London flat and that will be worth a bit. I'm surprised he never sold it; nowhere else to go I suppose – some artworks that he wouldn't part with and that sports car he never used. When I've paid off his debts, I'll still make a tidy sum, don't worry – yes, I'll be back soon, I'm just revelling in the fact that I'm getting back at him.' She laughed again. 'Yes, I know he's dead, darling, but it's still sweet; anyway, toodle-pip for now.'

She ended the call, and her expression became more serious. She went to the window and opened it. Then she lit a cigarette, blowing the smoke out of the window as she stared out at the garden. When she'd finished the cigarette, she rearranged her hair, reapplied her lipstick and went downstairs to get a drink.

~

Gerard Blake was once again in the bar at the Wharfedale. He knew he was drinking too much, but he felt that he needed it in this stressful time. The last two days had exhausted him, but at least he was now feeling a measure of relief. There seemed to be a way forward even if it was going to be hectic and extremely tight in terms of the time available. The railway and the manor house had been very accommodating, and he had managed to replace Hayward. He looked at his watch. Desmond Hammond would be arriving soon. Desmond was a reliable old pro who would do a good job. He wasn't as recognisable a figure as Dan Hayward, but the part was relatively small. They would have dinner together at the inn and talk through the role.

He was just beginning to relax into his chair when his wife walked in. He didn't feel like talking to her and having a heavy discussion about their feelings for each other. He was still feeling badly stung by her recent behaviour. She ordered a gin and tonic, looked around the bar, saw him and came over.

'Gerry, there you are.' She sat down and put her drink on the table. 'Can we talk?'

Blake sighed. 'What about?'

'Well, you know . . . us.'

Blake sipped his whisky. 'Do you think this is the right time? I'm worn out with working to save the film.'

'I bet you are. How did the technical people respond?'

They had a conversation about how Blake had managed to placate everyone including the actors and had engaged a replacement for Hayward.

'Oh, Desmond! What a good idea. He'll be excellent. Well done you!'

'I thought he would be the right person and luckily he was available.'

He finished his whisky and felt more relaxed. His wife was knowledgeable and interested in his work. They shared the same values on many things.

'Let me get you another drink,' he said. 'I've just got time for another before Desmond arrives. We're going to have dinner and talk things over. Do you want to join us?'

'Oh, Gerry, that would be lovely, yes.'

He wasn't just being kind to her for no reason. She was a very charming woman, and he knew that Desmond Hammond would respond well to her presence. It would ease his way into the company of people who were making the film. He was beginning to see why he'd missed her. Maybe this could be a new start for them. Especially now that Hayward was out of the way.

While he was at the bar, Candida Hayward walked in through a door just by their table. It was impossible for the two women to avoid each other.

'Oh, not you again!' said Hayward in disgust. Cooper looked at her angrily. She didn't want her conversation with Gerry to be interrupted.

'Just go away, Candida. I don't want to talk to you.'

'Oh dear, is it too embarrassing? The marriage breaker can't face her victims.'

'Candida! That's preposterous. There's no point blaming me for Dan's behaviour and the breakdown of your marriage. He was all over the place and you know it.'

'How does that make the way you carried on with him any better, you little slut?' shouted Hayward, and everyone in the bar was now looking towards them.

'Well, maybe if he'd been happier with you, he might not have strayed so often.'

Hayward seemed literally speechless. Wide-eyed, she stuttered something inaudible and then she picked up the remainder of Cooper's drink, threw it over her and stomped out of the room.

Cooper was in tears as Blake returned from the bar.

'Good Lord! What was all that about?'

A waiter came over with a cloth and Cooper tried to dry herself.

'Nothing, it's all my fault. Can we just go up to our room, Gerry?'

'Of course. We'll take the drinks with us.'

It was a gorgeous evening as Oldroyd turned into the drive of what he called the Jane Austen vicarage in Kirby Underside. He was met by his sister Alison who gave him a big hug and ushered him inside into the large kitchen that overlooked a yard and the rather overgrown and neglected back of the garden, which nevertheless looked attractive at this time of year when the large rhododendrons were in flower.

They sat at the table and Alison poured them each a glass of wine. 'I don't know what to say to you, Jim. I can't imagine what you're going through.'

Oldroyd smiled weakly. 'It's not good. I can't pretend I'm not beside myself with worry. But I'm much better here with you; it's terrible by myself – almost impossible not to start catastrophising about all kinds of things that could happen.'

'Knowing Deborah, I'd say she'd cope with it much better than many people. She's got resources both in her personality and in her knowledge of psychology.'

'Yes. I take a bit of comfort from that.' He put his elbows on the table and his hands over his face. 'The worst thing is feeling powerless. I want to run around checking everywhere until I find her, but I know it would be pointless.' He looked at Alison. 'Steph and Andy found the barn high above the Skipton Road on a deserted farm where she was probably being kept, but she's been moved. They must have realised we were on to them.'

'Well, that's good, isn't it? Your colleagues are on the trail.'

'Not necessarily. We've no idea where they've taken her now and it's most likely to a more secure location. I thought it was better to put the pressure on by publicising that she's been kidnapped. I just hope it hasn't angered them and made it more difficult for Deborah.' He took a deep breath. 'It's probably better if we change the subject, otherwise I'll just talk about it all night and we'll get nowhere.'

'Let's eat,' said Alison. 'I've made a fish curry. I know you like that.'

'I do, though I must warn you, my appetite is not what it normally is.'

'Never mind. It won't do you any harm to eat a bit less.'

'That's just the kind of thing she would say to me.' Oldroyd shook his head and wiped away a tear.

Alison served the curry with a bowl of white rice and some chapatis. She told Oldroyd all about the events in the parish.

'There was a climate action demonstration in Leeds last week, they occupied a road and closed it off. I'd normally expect people here to complain about that kind of protest, but do you know, three members of our congregation were there and were cautioned by the police. I was so proud of them.'

'Good Lord! Well, the world must be changing if Kirby Underside is becoming a hotbed of protest.'

Alison laughed. 'Indeed! It's all due to my influence of course. Anyway, how's Louise getting on?'

'I rang her today briefly to tell her what had happened to Deborah. I don't like people finding out things like that from the media. Obviously we spent a lot of time talking about that, but she did tell me that she's nearly finished her master's and she's applied for a job. It's in London, but then I think she'll come back up to Yorkshire at some point. I know she misses it. Good news is she has a boyfriend. It's taken her a long time to get over that business in Whitby, but she's finally got there.' He paused. 'I was telling Deborah this only a couple of days ago.' He looked downcast again, but Alison ignored this and continued the discussion about Louise.

'I'm pleased to hear that. It will have taken some courage to trust a man again. Shall we go into the living room for coffee? I've got a few Indian sweets as well.'

In the spacious living room, they sat in large armchairs opposite each other. Alison had inherited a lot of furniture in the vicarage. Large pieces like a grandfather clock and a large oak sideboard stayed in place and were handed down to successive vicars. Bookcases lined two walls from floor to ceiling and contained a collection of classical texts of the type sold in old antiquarian bookshops.

Oldroyd sat feeling drained but more relaxed than when he'd arrived. He looked up and down the bookcases as he munched a barfi. 'That's a very impressive collection of old tomes. I imagine they would be worth a bob or two.'

'Yes, they've been there since the eighteen-nineties from the time of the Rev Herbert Livingstone. He was a bachelor vicar with quite a bit of private money.'

'He probably came from an upper-crust family. You know how they used to say that the third son in the family went into the church.'

'You're probably right. Anyway, he was an antiquarian book collector and built up a considerable collection. In his will he left everything to the parish including quite a bit of the furniture you see around here. The only problem is that the parish is now stuck with it all. They want to sell this building, it's absurdly too big even for a vicar with a family, but where would they put all that?' She waved her hand at the bookcase. 'Some would be prepared to sell them off, but others think that would be against Rev Livingstone's wishes.' She smiled and shook her head. 'There's a good example of a First World problem, as they say nowadays. We're destroying the world, and the church argues about some mouldy old books.'

'But not everyone, as you were telling me earlier.'

'No, that's true. Oh.' She looked up. 'I've never shown you this, have I?'

She got up and went to one of the bookcases and pulled out what seemed to be a batch of about six books all at once.

'What on earth?!' said Oldroyd.

Alison laughed. 'Don't worry, I'm not a magician. They're false, you see, and behind them is a safe. Nifty, isn't it?'

Oldroyd stood up and went over to examine the contrivance. A block of books, which were fastened together, had the same type of cover as the others on the shelf, but behind the cover they were hollow so that they could fit over the safe. Oldroyd put them back in place. They fitted perfectly. It was a superb piece of craftsmanship.

'Marvellous, what skill! I expect Rev Livingstone kept his large stash of money in there.'

'He may well have done.'

'And from the front they look just . . . the same.' His voice trailed off and he stared at the bookcase.

'Jim? Are you all right? Come and sit down.'

'I'm fine. Don't worry. Those books have actually given me an idea.'

'Really?'

'Yes. I think I know how the murderer concealed himself in that railway carriage.'

Desmond Hammond was an actor somewhat older than Hayward, but he had the same build, a similar voice and a confident bearing. As Blake looked at him in the dining room of the Wharfedale, he felt sure that the actor could slot into the part well. They would have to put in some work refilming certain scenes that they'd already shot in the studio, but it could be done.

Hammond looked tired after his journey from London but was responding to the welcome and warmth being extended to him by Frances, who had recovered from the attack by Candida Hayward. As she'd changed out of her wet clothes, she'd blamed herself for the incident and again asked Blake to forgive her for the encounter with Daniel Hayward. Now she was playing an important role for him.

'It's so good to see you again, Desmond; it's been too long.'

'It was that comedy at the Eastern Playhouse, wasn't it? *Over the Hill.*'

'Oh yes, and the director was over the hill, wasn't he?' she laughed. 'He wheezed his way up the steps every morning for rehearsals and he was so deaf he couldn't hear a thing. "Speak up, can't you?"' She mimicked the old director very accurately and Hammond was in fits of laughter. Blake smiled. When Hammond had arrived, he was still in a little doubt as to whether he would agree to go ahead. Frances was helping to make Hammond feel at home.

'I'd recommend the braised lamb shoulder with rosemary jus, it's excellent,' said Frances as Hammond was consulting the menu. 'Gerry, let's have some of that Pinot Noir. It goes so well with the lamb.'

At the end of the evening, Hammond looked relaxed, well fed and well oiled with good wine.

'Wonderful evening, thank you both,' he said as he bid them goodnight. 'I'm so looking forward to getting started tomorrow.'

'Well done,' Blake said to his wife as Hammond went off to his room. 'I think he's well and truly secured. Thank you.'

She smiled at him. He gave her a kiss and they went back up together to their room.

The next day was Sunday and Janice Green arrived early at the railway to check everything before the reopening, which was scheduled for ten o'clock. The weather was a little overcast but dry and warm, ideal for a family ride on the railway.

She went first to the platform. The area where the carriage carrying Hayward had stopped and his body had been brought out was neatly cordoned off, as was the place where Brian Evans had fallen. Because of this they were using platform 2. She walked over the bridge. It was wide, but half of it had also been cordoned off to protect the place from which the sniper had shot Brian Evans. It was still possible to get across in single file. Volunteers were going to be stationed by the cordoned-off areas to make sure no one wandered into them.

Across on platform 2, Green was pleased to see that a steam locomotive was already in position and fired up ready for the first trip. It was a shiny black engine known to trainspotters as a Black Five and it was coupled to another vintage carriage. She walked up to speak to the driver who was leaning out of the cab wearing oily overalls and a cap. Andrews was not on duty today. The driver was called Ted Drake.

'Well done, Ted, you look as if you're all ready to go.'

'Yes, I thought I'd get here early with it being such an important day, like. She had to be fired up from scratch,' he said, patting the engine. 'None of them have been used for a bit, they're completely cold. I had to clear all th' ash out of t' firebox. That's a long job 'cos when—'

'Excellent,' said Green, rather abruptly. She knew little about the technicalities of running steam locomotives and didn't have time for a long account of them now. 'Sorry, but I must be off to see how everyone else is doing.'

When she got back over the bridge to platform 1, she saw Granville Hardy dressed in his immaculate Edwardian railway company uniform. 'Hello, Granville,' she said. 'You must be a happy man today. You're doing guard duty, aren't you?'

Hardy was beaming. 'Yes, it's a great day for the railway; we're getting back to what we're here for. People getting to see the trains and ride on them.'

It was on Green's mind to say that she couldn't see why a short break for the filming really threatened any of that, but she hadn't time to engage in another fruitless discussion with him.

'Yes, well thank you for turning up as ever,' was all she said, and then moved on.

She spoke to people in the ticket office and in the café and was pleased to find everyone enthusiastic about the day to come. Someone had even designed a poster welcoming people back that was hung over the station entrance, along with bunting. The ice-cream vendor who parked by the entrance was just arriving in his van. She looked around and everything was clean, bright and tidy in its cute Edwardian tweeness. It was as if nothing violent had happened until you saw the cordoned-off areas and realised that there were blood stains on the platform.

She went past the room being used by the police for their office. It was empty today. Were the detectives taking a well-earned rest, or were they hard at work elsewhere? Whichever it was, she didn't envy them trying to find the killers and dealing with an innocent person being kidnapped and held to ransom. Her job, hectic though it could be, suddenly seemed very easy in comparison.

Deborah was no longer aware of day and night. No glimmer of light from the outside world penetrated her prison. She knew she'd been brought into the cellar in the daytime, but she had no idea how many hours had passed since then. She seemed to be sleeping intermittently in short spells that disrupted her sense of time even more.

She'd done some exercises – running on the spot, mostly – and had read as much of the magazine content as she could manage. It was important to distract herself from catastrophising thoughts that could lead to rising levels of anxiety and panic if they were focused on too intensively. She'd also been working on a strategy to deal with her captor.

The door opened and someone came down the steps. Was it the first kidnapper or the second man?

'Hello, wake up.' It was the second man. The other seemed to have disappeared, at least for now, so she was even more convinced that she was in the second man's house, or at least very nearby and that he was now looking after her.

'I'm not asleep.'

'Oh, good, well I've brought you some breakfast.' He was carrying a tray with a plate containing toast and a hardboiled egg. There was also a cup of tea. He set the tray down.

'Thank you for bringing this.' She looked at him pleadingly. 'You seem like a kind person. Do you think it's right that I should be held captive like this? What have I done wrong?'

Because of the face covering she couldn't really gauge his response, except his eyes looked rather restless.

'He told me . . . I can't talk to you about this.'

'Who's "he"? Is he the man who kidnapped me? The killer? Is he telling you what to do? If anything happens to me, it will make everything much worse for you. You do realise that?'

He looked extremely uncomfortable and shifted around nervously. 'OK, just stop it. I'm not listening to any more of this. Eat your food and I'll come back later.' He started up the stairs.

'There's just one thing.'

'What?'

'Can you get me a pen or pencil? I can't do these puzzles without one.'

'Oh, right.'

Deborah smiled as he shut the door and locked it. She was definitely getting to him.

Oldroyd woke early but he waited a while before calling Craven as it was Sunday morning. He made tea, ate a bit of toast and paced up and down like a caged animal. After a while he couldn't stand it any longer.

'Bob, sorry to disturb you. I think you'll be taking today off. If you're not, you should be.'

'I am, Jim . . . but go on.'

'I've got a good idea about how the killer was able to disappear from the compartment and I want to share it with you.'

'Fine, go ahead.'

'The answer is the luggage on the racks above the seats. In the compartment where the murder took place, you remember there was luggage on both sides on those racks. There were probably two or three large vintage suitcases on each side, would you say?'

'Yes . . . about that.'

'So, I think one of those sets of luggage was false. The suitcases were fastened together and cut away to form a space someone could lie in. The ends of each case were left intact, as they were visible. It looked like three suitcases placed end to end, but they were hollow inside.

'The killer, having got from the next compartment through the hole, climbed into that hiding place well before the train set off. Almost straight away they would have emerged and shot Hayward, so Tim Groves was right: he was shot from inside the compartment. Then they would have worked fast. They drew the curtains and removed the panel to get access back to the next compartment. Then they swapped the luggage so that the fake luggage was in the compartment next to Hayward's. The killer then got back up into that fake luggage after they had replaced the panels. Of course, you came along and subjected Hayward's carriage to a meticulous examination but found nothing.'

'Because they weren't there. You're saying they were in the next compartment.'

'Yes.'

'Bloody hell; the damned cheek of it!' said Craven. 'We did look in the next compartment and all the others which didn't have anyone in, but not as thoroughly as Hayward's. I never considered that the murderer might be hiding in there.'

'Which is exactly what they were relying on. It must have been a heart-stopping moment when you came in and they could hear you knocking around below them. If you'd pulled the luggage down as you did in Hayward's compartment the game would have been up. But why would you? At that stage, there was no reason to think that the killer was there. How would they have even got into that compartment, never mind hiding in there? It was more logical to think they had somehow left the train, which was the idea we stuck with for a long time. But we could never quite accept that they could have got off without being seen.'

'So are you saying they were still there when you arrived?'

'Yes, all the time we were looking at that carriage. I imagine they stayed there until the middle of the night, until their accomplice came to tell them the coast was clear. And this theory explains a number of other things: the fact that that compartment next to Hayward's was locked. They couldn't risk anyone going in there when the train set off; it would have ruined the whole thing.'

'But it was open when we started to investigate?'

'Yes. I think the accomplice must have opened it to draw suspicion away, otherwise you might have wondered why that compartment was locked. Had the murderer locked themselves in? And so on. Then you might have undertaken a more detailed search.'

'True. So, the accomplice was around on the platform?'

'Probably. It was a very audacious scheme, and it might have worked. It certainly fooled us for a while. It was the unfortunate Brian Evans who first suspected something. I think he noticed that the fasteners holding those pictures on the walls of the compartment were different and worked out that someone might have made an escape route into the next compartment. He probably asked the killer, someone he knew – and he didn't realise that they were the killer – to come and have a look with him. That's how the killer knew he was at the station. They must have quickly decided that they had to kill Evans. Poor man, he was too naive and trusting. He never suspected that someone he knew at the railway could be the killer. I'm sure they never intended to kill anyone other than Hayward, but we still don't know what their motive was.'

'Then they killed Evans and also realised we were getting too close for comfort when we came to examine the carriage again.'

'Exactly, which is why they panicked and kidnapped Deborah. Their whole plan is in ruins, and they must know it's only a matter of time before we get to them.'

'So, Jim, this must narrow things down a bit. One of the people working in that shed must be involved because they knew we'd been looking at the carriage.'

'Unless one of them told someone else about us being there.'

'And what about the driver? Could he have slowed the train down in the tunnel so that the killer had more time to do whatever they had to do?'

'Yes, I've been suspicious about that from the beginning, but we can't prove anything. But there was definitely at least one other person at the station that day who was an accomplice.'

'The people on the platform were mostly the cast plus a few railway officials.'

'Yes, but that's quite a lot of people. No one is going to notice someone discreetly unlocking that door. Anyway, Bob, there's plenty to think about. First thing tomorrow, get down to that shed again and have a look, but don't go alone. These people are desperate now. Take some officers with you. And, Bob?'

'Yes?'

'Take things easy, we can't risk anything, you know.'

'I do, Jim. You try to relax, too. We'll take it all very steadily and I'll let you know if we have any leads about where Deborah might be.'

'OK.'

When Oldroyd ended the call, he was shaking. They were getting closer to finding Deborah but that meant that the danger was intensifying too. It was absolute agony to be here away from the action and be unable to do anything to help the search.

He got dressed and decided that the best thing to do was to go out for a walk. He made his way to the Valley Gardens. He usually found this a soothing place. It was Sunday morning, and the gardens were full of people strolling on the paths and walking their dogs. The playground was heaving with noisy children playing on the swings. Lots of people were on the tennis courts and the pitch and putt course. It was reassuring to be with other people, to watch what was happening around him and to escape from his dark thoughts. He went to the Magnesia Well Café, a favourite haunt, and had coffee. He sat for a while thinking about Deborah. He didn't believe in telepathy, but he found himself trying to communicate with her: trying to tell her he loved her; that they would find her; that she must hang on and try not to despair. After a while he realised that there were tears running down his face. He paid his bill and walked back through the gardens.

Back at the Wharfedale Railway things were going well at the reopening. The weather was good, the car park was filling up as lots of families arrived to go for a ride on the famous steam trains. The ice-cream vendor was doing a good trade and there was a long queue for tickets. On one corner of platform 1 a jazz band was playing, and this distracted the visitors from the cordoned-off areas. Over on platform 2, Ted Drake was still waiting in the cab of the Black Five to drive the first train up the line towards Skipton. He gave an occasional toot of the whistle and released some noisy steam to add to the atmosphere.

As planned, North, Jenkins and Whiteman had put on their Edwardian costumes and were greeting the visitors as they came on to the platform. This was unexpected and, as the three actors were fairly well known from their television work, caused a minor sensation. Autograph requests were frequent, and children were being told that they could go to see a film with these ladies and this man in it, and then they would see the trains again. It was another feature of the day that bolstered the cheery atmosphere.

Janice Green was very pleased and relieved. She wandered around outside, near the ticket office and on the platform, smiling as she greeted people. It was so good to see the station bustling again. She popped into the café and saw that there were plenty of tables occupied. Elaborate, lacy table coverings and black uniforms for the waiting staff continued the Edwardian theme. She stopped to speak to a volunteer guard who was punching the little cardboard tickets using an antique ticket punch, much to the amusement of regular rail users who used electronic tickets on their phones.

There was an announcement that the train on platform 2 was going to depart in ten minutes, so adults and their whooping, excited children opened the heavy slam-doors and climbed into the old compartments. The carriages were similar to the one in which Hayward had been murdered, but all that was forgotten on this happy day.

Soon, the rituals surrounding the train's departure took place. The guard on the platform checked that all the doors were closed and then blew a whistle and signalled to the train guard, who waved a flag back to indicate that everything was ready for departure. It was a marvellous bit of noisy and gesticulating theatre. The whistle tooted loudly, and the engine began a slow deep chuff as Drake pulled the regulator over. Smoke and steam were thrust out of the funnel and the carriages began to move slowly along the platform, much to the glee of small children who were peering through the windows and waving to people watching the train leave.

Green observed the train's departure with a smile. What was it about a steam train that people found so appealing? Was it because the locomotive seemed to have a face? Or because it had so many moving parts and made such a variety of noises? Was it redolent of a different age that some people perceived to have been more peaceful and less complicated? Whatever it is, people seem to love them, she thought as she watched the train disappear slowly down the line.

It was only when the train had finally gone and the station was quiet that she noticed the first signs that something wasn't right. She heard shouting from the direction of the shed and walked quickly down the platform so she could see the building. Smoke was rising from one of the sidings near the shed; something was on fire. Two of the platform guards, one of them Granville Hardy, ran down the platform to join her, and they all made their way across the tracks towards the source.

When they reached the scene, it was clear that one of the vintage carriages was on fire. Two engineers from the shed were trying to douse the flames with buckets. One of them was Terry Hopkins, and he shouted to Green to call the fire brigade. She immediately pulled out her phone. Then she heard a cry of alarm from behind her.

'No! We must save it!'

It was Hardy whose face was white with shock and his eyes wide with alarm. The carriage was one of the prize possessions of the railway: it was an original carriage from 1905 that had been extensively refurbished. And it was the carriage in which Hayward had been murdered. Hardy picked up a bucket of water and ran towards the carriage. Smoke was coming out of the windows.

'Granville, stop! You can't go inside, it's too dangerous!' shouted Green, but Hardy was already at the door of one of the compartments. Hopkins tried to pull him back, but Hardy pushed him away. At that moment Jack Smith appeared. He was dressed in ordinary clothes and holding a bag as if he'd just arrived to do some work but hadn't yet changed into his overalls.

'What the hell's going on?' he said.

'It's on fire!' cried Hopkins.

'I can see that! How did it happen?'

'No idea. Stand back, everybody!' The fire was spreading rapidly through the wooden carriage and the heat was growing rapidly. They caught a glimpse of Hardy inside the compartment trying to beat the flames back with a piece of carpet that he'd wrenched from the floor.

'Granville! Get out of there!' screamed Green, but there was no response. The man ignored all their calls to get him to leave.

Shortly after, they saw him fall to the floor. The heat was now so intense that no one could get anywhere near the inferno, and they had to move back. They all stood helplessly watching the flames climb higher and the carriage slowly disintegrate.

At that moment they heard the siren of the fire engine that turned into the yard at great speed. The crew emerged and got their hoses working remarkably quickly, but it was too late; by the time the fire had been put out, there was little left of the carriage apart from a blackened framework. Hardy's face was unrecognisable and the uniform of which he'd been so proud had been burned away.

It was another disaster for the railway. One of their most dedicated helpers had died trying to save one of their most valued assets. It would have been cruel at any time, but that it had happened on the very day they had reopened seemed a nasty extra twist of the knife.

When the fire brigade arrived, Janice Green ran back to the station to give news of what had happened to the other staff and to announce over the public address system that, due to the fire and to the injury to a person, there would be no more trains today. Back on the platform, she found a crowd of people looking over toward the engine shed from which black smoke was billowing. There was the sound of an ambulance arriving.

People were given refunds for the tickets they'd bought. The café stayed open for a while, but everyone started to slowly drift away, looking sombre. The fun atmosphere of earlier in the day had been destroyed. Green was so devastated she had to sit on one of the benches on the platform and try to compose herself. She was joined by Christopher North still in his Edwardian solicitor's costume. Jenkins and Whiteman had gone to sit in the café.

'What exactly happened?' he asked gently as he sat by her.

'One of the old carriages caught fire, but I've no idea how. It was the one you'd been using for the filming.' She put her hands over her face. 'One of our volunteers went in to try to save it. The ambulance came but he must have died in the heat and smoke.'

'Why did he do that, the poor man? Sounds a bit reckless.'

Green shook her head. 'I can understand it. Granville was very keen on everything to do with the railway. He wasn't just a volunteer; it was his life. I suppose he couldn't bear to see that carriage destroyed. It was before I came here, but I know the railway organised a big fundraising effort to buy that carriage; it was an original. He would have been heavily involved with the efforts.'

'That's tragic,' said North, and looked at her. 'This is very hard for you after everything that's happened. You must have been relieved to get the railway back in action today.'

Green gave him a wan smile. 'I was. I don't know whether we'll get through this now.'

'Of course you will, don't despair. Things aren't as bad as they seem. You're running a popular attraction and people will rally round. This filming is the thing that seems to be bringing you bad luck, but we'll be off soon and then later when the film's released, you should get a bonanza because people will want to see the location. I've seen the effect before with other films.'

'I hope you're right. Oh, here's the inspector.'

When Craven had received the news about the fire, he'd decided to drive over to Oldthwaite immediately, even though he was supposed to be taking a break. He'd already had reports from the fire and ambulance crews.

'I'm glad I've found you,' he said to Green. 'The fire's out and the body has been recovered. I'm sorry to say that he's dead. I'm sure you were expecting that.'

Green nodded. 'The fire could have been accidental,' continued Craven, 'but I strongly suspect that we're looking at arson. That carriage was evidence in the murder of Daniel Hayward, and it was in someone's interest to get rid of it.'

'Of course,' said Green. 'I never thought of that.'

'It's not your job to,' said Craven with a smile. 'Officers will be coming round to take statements. If you saw any suspicious activity around the station or shed, please let us know.'

'I didn't see anything, Inspector, I don't know if the engineers in the shed did. They were much nearer.'

'Quite,' said Craven. 'We'll be asking them. In the meantime, unfortunately you'll have to shut down again until the forensic teams have searched the area.' He turned to North. 'I understand you were going to do some filming just on the platform tomorrow?'

'I think you're right.'

'Mr Blake is not here, but can you tell him that it's OK to continue with that as long as everyone stays on the platform. The whole of the shed area will be cordoned off.'

'I will. I understand we're not using the train, just filming on the platform.'

'OK. Well, that should be fine.'

Craven turned and walked back to the station entrance feeling angry and frustrated. Damn! Why hadn't he thought of keeping a guard on that carriage? He felt he was letting down Oldroyd and the investigation. It was even more abundantly clear to him now that the killers were desperate, prepared to do risky things, and determined to stay a few steps ahead of the police for as long as they could. He decided not to contact Oldroyd until the morning. The man needed to rest.

When he finally left the café, Oldroyd wandered aimlessly around the Valley Gardens for a while watching people playing tennis, crazy golf and pitch and putt. He eventually walked into town and into Riverstones Bookshop where he browsed for a while. The problem was that this was the place where he'd met Deborah on their first date. They'd found each other on a dating site. He went upstairs to the café and ordered a sandwich and another coffee. From his seat, he could see the table where they'd sat during that first meeting. He felt terrible, but he hoped that they might sit there together again one day.

After this, he walked back to the Valley Gardens and through the Pinewoods all the way to the Harlow Carr RHS Garden where he paid his admission and walked around the borders and into the wooded area where the rhododendrons and azaleas were at their best. He reached the big Alpine House with its collection of tiny colourful plants. Everywhere he went, things reminded him of Deborah, but at least he felt some peace through being in contact with nature.

He returned home to the flat late in the afternoon and spent most of the evening listening to music. He chose pieces that took him into deep spiritual places: the late string quartets of Beethoven. He listened to Opus 132 which took him on a journey into pain and suffering and out again into acceptance and a measure of joy. The quartet had just ended, and he was contemplating the silence in the dark room, when his phone went.

He was slow to respond and when he looked at the phone, he was surprised to see that it was Tom Walker.

'Hello, Tom.'

'Jim! Thought I'd give you a quick call to see how you are. It can't be any fun in your position. No developments, I take it? I haven't heard anything over here.'

'No. But thanks for ringing, Tom, I appreciate it.'

'Not at all. People don't always understand that we're on the front line in policing, there's always danger lurking. I want you to know that the force appreciates all that you do and that it's sometimes at personal risk or even at risk to your family, as it's proved to be now.'

'Well, thanks again Tom, I—'

'Of course, I can't say we all have the same attitude. I don't think Watkins has a damn clue about the hazards of police work, mainly because he's hardly done any.'

Oldroyd's heart sank. Matthew Watkins was the trendy, managerial chief constable of West Riding Police, and Walker loathed him. Oldroyd frequently had to listen to Walker's rants against the man. But this evening, at least, Oldroyd was saved from yet another tirade.

'Anyway,' continued Walker. 'I won't go on about him tonight. He's the last person you want to think about.'

'What's the weather like over there, Tom?' said Oldroyd, adroitly changing the subject. 'Any better?'

'Not much. We'll probably come back tomorrow. I managed to get a round of golf in earlier but it's raining again now. I'm sick of the inside of this caravan. Anyway, I won't keep you. All this over Daniel Hayward, eh? I've seen him in a lot of films and in stuff on telly, those costume drama things. Did you know he came from Yorkshire originally?'

'I think Bob Craven might have mentioned it.'

'Aye, he's not lived up here since his film career took off and after that accident.'

Oldroyd sat up. 'What accident, Tom?'

'Oh, it was a long time ago, in the nineties. It would have been before you came to Harrogate. He was in a car crash; three people were killed; he escaped with minor injuries, lucky bugger.'

'Where was this?'

'Out towards Skipton from Addingham on one of the back roads. It was late at night . . . June, I think it was. His sports car collided head-on with another car. The driver of the other car and the passenger were killed instantly, and the driver of Hayward's car – a woman, presumably his girlfriend at the time – died later.'

'I see.'

'And it was controversial.'

'Why?'

'The woman who died was an inexperienced driver and her family said there was no way she would have driven a powerful car like that and taken risks. They believed that Hayward was driving and had pulled her over into the driving seat after the crash, when she was unconscious. There were no witnesses to support this, but apparently he was well over the alcohol limit for driving. The officers and ambulance people who attended could even smell it on his breath and he was unsteady. It suggested he could have been protecting himself. The worst thing was that if he had put her in the driver's seat, he'd wasted time and not called the ambulance straight away. Not many mobile phones in those days, he had to go up to a farmhouse to make the call. But if he'd called earlier, she might have lived.'

'Bloody hell!'

'Yes, but there was no proof that he'd done it. It meant that he left the area under a bit of a cloud. I'll bet he didn't like driving after that.'

'Can you remember the names of any of the other people involved, Tom?'

'Why's that? You don't think it has anything to do with the case, do you? It was a long time ago.'

'But we've been looking for a motive and I have an idea it's about something from the past.'

'Oh right, well . . . can't remember any details, but you could search the records.'

'But we have, Tom, and we've not come up with anything from Hayward's early life round here.'

'That's probably because you were searching under Daniel Hayward. That's his stage name and we all call him that now, but I remember his real name was Alan Ross. Try that.'

'Thanks Tom, I certainly will.'

When he rang off, Oldroyd was so excited that he even forgot briefly about Deborah. Steph had been right! At the beginning of the investigation, she'd suggested that 'Daniel Hayward' might have been a stage name, but with things turning so dramatic, they hadn't pursued that idea.

Oldroyd thanked God for modern technology that meant he could log straight on to his profile at work from his home computer and start the search. After all, he needed to do something even if it was unofficial. Deborah's kidnappers would never know.

Now that he had the right name, it didn't take long to locate the incident. He found police reports and local newspaper stories, and some vague memories came back to him although he'd had nothing to do with the case at the time. It was June 1995. The accident happened at 2 a.m. The cars were virtually write-offs. Officers estimated that the sports car must have been doing in excess of seventy miles an hour on the winding lanes. Ross had called the services; officers found him tearful and somewhat inebriated, as Walker had described. He said he didn't know why Sally was driving so fast.

She was taken to Airedale Hospital but died later from her injuries. When Oldroyd saw her surname, he knew he was on to something. The couple in the other car who died at the scene were Gary and Anne Spencer. Their surname didn't resonate, but one newspaper reporting on the terrible tragedy recorded that the victims had two small children who had now lost both their parents.

Janice Green took the responsibility for informing Granville Hardy's wife of the death of her husband. She sat with her in the little kitchen. The woman seemed stunned, but not hysterical.

'Would he have suffered a lot?' she eventually asked.

'The fire brigade people said not. He would have been overcome by the fumes and lack of oxygen before the fire got to him.'

'Good.' She paused for a few seconds. 'Well, at least he died doing something he enjoyed and trying to save something he cared about.'

'Yes, that's a positive way of looking at it.'

She looked up at Green. 'Thank you for coming to tell me. It must have been difficult.'

'That's fine,' said Green. 'There was one thing I wanted to talk to you about. The police have said that the film crew can continue filming tomorrow. Apparently, they're only going to do one more day and then they'll leave. I wanted to check that that was all right with you the day after Granville has died. I'm also aware that he was opposed to the filming, and you might think that it's an insult to him for the crew to be there.'

'Oh no, Janice, please go ahead. Granville was wrong about the filming. I argued with him about it. It's good for the railway and it should continue.'

Green was rather surprised at this response, but she thanked Hardy and left.

The new widow sat for a while thinking. She was quite calm and felt no terrible sense of loss. In fact, there was a sense of release. She and Granville had grown further apart as his railway obsession had intensified, to the point where they'd had no real relationship any more and he'd been a terrible restriction on her life. The truth was she had given the go-ahead for the filming in order to spite him.

She got up and went upstairs to the loft. There was the enormous and intricate train set all silent and still. How much money had he spent acquiring all this stuff? And they'd never gone out much together and enjoyed themselves because he said they couldn't afford it. Oh dear, she thought with a twisted smile, the five-fifteen express will be late! It would never leave the station; no trains ever would again, at least not in this house. She smiled again as she wondered how much it must all be worth. She knew that some of the models were rare, and found that she looked forward to selling them. With the money she got, she would be able to go travelling and who knows? She might meet someone who would give her a good time. How many years had she'd stayed in Oldthwaite because Granville wouldn't go anywhere?

Granville had installed a master switch for all the circuits that operated the railway. Symbolically, she switched it and the lights off, then went back down the stairs. She felt a lightness in her step.

As the public slowly drained away from the station, the three actors, realising that they were of no further use, left the platform and changed out of their Edwardian costumes in the wardrobe area and made their way back to the hotel together.

'How was that poor woman?' Jenkins asked North, whom she'd seen consoling Janice Green after the fire.

'Shocked; it's another blow for her, but I think she's resilient and she'll bounce back. And I told her the railway will too, especially after the publicity they'll get from the film.'

'Once they get over the awful things that have happened,' remarked Whiteman. 'Though to be honest, it might work in their favour. The ghoulish public like to see where gruesome things have taken place.'

'Well, I've seen enough. I hope we can do the filming tomorrow after this because I'm heartily sick of it all and just want to get away,' said Jenkins.

When they arrived at the inn, they were met at Reception by a worried-looking Gerard Blake.

'What's going on down there?' Blake asked. 'There's smoke in the sky above the station and we heard the sound of sirens.'

'There was a fire; one of the old carriages was burnt out; apparently it was the one we used in the film,' said North.

'Bloody hell! Whatever next?' replied Blake.

'But the worst thing was that someone was killed,' added Jenkins. 'One of the volunteers went inside to try to save the carriage. The fire brigade couldn't get to him before it was too late.'

'Oh God no!' Blake slumped on to a nearby chair with his head in his hands. 'I just wish we'd never come here. The people at the railway must be cursing us. We've brought them nothing but terrible trouble.'

'I don't think they blame us,' said Whiteman. 'I was just saying that they'll benefit in the long run. There's no such thing as bad publicity. We don't know that this fire is anything to do with the other things that have happened.'

Blake sighed. 'Sounds to me like someone was trying to get rid of evidence.'

North looked at him curiously. 'I never thought of it like that. I suppose you may be right. But what kind of evidence?'

'I don't know, but that murder was committed somehow. There was probably something in that carriage that someone didn't want the police to see. It's a bit of a coincidence, isn't it?'

Blake's phone went off and he answered it. It was Janice Green.

'Yes, I've heard,' said Blake. 'I'm really sorry. I don't know what you want to do about tomorrow – are you sure? I mean, someone's been killed – I see, well that's very generous of her – we will; we're desperate to get it all finished and then we can be out of your way. Thanks.' The call ended.

'Well,' he said to the others, 'that was Janice Green. It seems they want us to film tomorrow despite everything and the poor bloke's widow has given her approval.'

'On that subject,' said North, 'the inspector asked me to tell you it was OK to film as long we don't move off the platform.'

Blake was surprised. 'Oh, OK then. I suppose we should just get on with it tomorrow and then get off.'

'Gerry, I think the general feeling will be that people are being generous and accommodating and that we should do exactly what you've just said,' said North, wisely and succinctly capturing the mood.

Six

In Strangers on a Train, *1951, directed by Alfred Hitchcock, a tennis star and a charming but sinister psychopathic character meet on a train. On learning that each of them wants to get rid of another person, the psychopath suggests that they exchange murders. They will each kill a total stranger and will thus never be caught. The film was based on the novel by Patricia Highsmith.*

Deborah's mind was foggy, and time was passing in a strange way. Sometimes a few minutes seemed an eternity; sometimes she drifted off to sleep and it felt like a long time went by quickly. She'd almost given up trying to read because the weak light from the single bulb made her eyes hurt. It was almost impossible to lie in a position that was completely comfortable, and her back was still painful. She'd walked around the cellar exploring every bit of it for possible escape routes. She found a part where it was clear that coal had been kept, but the hole down which the coal had been tipped was now sealed.

The silence was rarely broken by any noise. The cellar must be deep and the walls thick. Occasionally there was the sound of a particularly noisy vehicle passing in the distance. Once an RAF jet thundered past overhead. She was more and more having to turn inwards to sustain herself. She sang songs softly and she recalled good times she'd had in great detail. She set herself mental tasks like recalling the names of as many rivers in Yorkshire as she could.

There was again the sound of raised voices on the ground floor and then her gaoler came down the steps.

'What day is it?' she asked. Her voice sounded strange. It felt weak with lack of use.

'It's Monday morning,' he replied.

That meant she'd been in captivity for three days.

'Who were you arguing with?' She felt she could challenge him like this, and he wouldn't be violent towards her like the other man had been.

'None of your business.' He put down the food and water he'd brought and then turned to her. 'Look, I'll be honest. I'm not happy with keeping you here.'

'Let me go then. I'll tell the police you were kind to me, whoever you are. What are you gaining by keeping me here?'

'It's not that easy. Things are bad. It was all about getting rid of that bastard Hayward, and now it's all got out of hand. He's doing more and more reckless stuff.'

'Who's he?'

'I can't tell you. Just stay here and wait. When I've got a chance, I'll see what I can manage, but I'm not promising anything. If he finds out, I don't know what he'll do.'

'Call the police. You're only making it worse for yourself by carrying on. They'll find you eventually.'

'It's not that easy. He's always got a gun or a knife.'

'You're frightened of him.'

He looked at her and she saw the fear in his eyes. 'I didn't expect all this. They made it sound simple. I didn't do much and now I . . .' Realising that he was saying too much, he stopped and abruptly went back up the stairs, slamming the door behind him.

Deborah lay on the grubby duvet trying to make sense of all he'd said. He'd referred to 'they', so there must be at least three people involved in this. What did he mean when he said he'd not done much? He was clearly very unhappy with keeping her there, which gave her hope, but she sensed that things were moving to a climax and how would that work out for her?

The desperate need to communicate came back to her; she wished she could tell Jim what she'd found out. And she felt frightened: maybe she wouldn't be kept in captivity for much longer, but how was this all going to resolve itself? She began to shake a little and felt tears in her eyes again.

As Deborah was talking to her captor, Craven was back at the railway getting the investigation into the carriage fire underway, and also looking at the false luggage cases that Oldroyd had suggested as the hiding place in the two compartments. He conducted a search of the shed with a couple of officers and one of the engineers who opened up every storage area for them. There were boxes of tools, metal trolleys, engine parts and piles of overalls and uniforms. It took a while but eventually one of the officers called to Craven.

'Sir, I think I've found something in here.'

The officer was searching in a skip and had pulled out exactly what Oldroyd had predicted: three large vintage cases cut away on one side and hollowed out. They'd been ripped apart, but it was easy to see how they'd recently been fastened together to effectively make one large case that looked like three separate ones from the front.

'Well done!' said Craven. He laid the cases side by side and it was clear that the space inside was big enough to conceal someone.

When he got back to Skipton station, he rang Oldroyd and explained what they'd found and to tell him about the fire.

'You were right, Jim, we've found those false cases. It's a very clever trick. The killer must have practised getting in and out and lifting them into the other compartment. I still can't believe they were in that carriage lying just above my head when I had a look in.'

Oldroyd laughed. 'Well, me too, remember. But as I said before, we had no real reason to think that anyone would be hiding in there any more than in any of the other compartments because we thought they would have had to get out of the one where Hayward was killed and open the door to another. We didn't know they could get through the wall.'

Craven told Oldroyd about the destruction of the carriage.

'I'm sure you're right. It's an attempt to destroy the evidence,' said Oldroyd. 'What state is the carriage in?'

'It's pretty much a blackened shell. It burnt easily being made of wood.'

'We may still be able to see where the hole was constructed between the compartments, but we'll get them on some other evidence if not that. Now listen, I've had a major breakthrough here and it came from Tom Walker of all people.' He explained about the car crash. 'The thing I've picked up on is that the woman who died in Hayward's car was called Sally Andrews. That's the same surname as the driver of the train in which Hayward was murdered: Philip Andrews. I suspect it could have been his sister. If he's involved, it would explain why he slowed the train down in that tunnel: it would have been to ensure that the killer had enough time to do all they needed to do with those panels and the false suitcases.'

'Right, I'll get out there. He lives off the road between here and Oldthwaite, doesn't he?'

'Yes. Take Steph with you, she interviewed him with me last time. She'll show you where it is. You can easily miss the track up from the main road. You'll need to take some armed officers with you. We've seen how handy at least one of them is with firearms.'

'OK.'

'And Bob?'

'Yes?'

'Go easy, because if Andrews is involved, Deborah could be there; it's a suitable place out of the way. She might be hidden away in an attic or somewhere.'

'OK, Jim. I understand.'

Oldroyd felt better after the call, but still extremely tense. At last, they seemed to be getting somewhere, though crucial questions remained: who else was involved and what was their motive? And more important: would they find Deborah there?

At the station, the actors and technical crew were preparing to film again after a break of four tumultuous days. The atmosphere was downbeat. Some thought that what they were doing was disrespectful even though Hardy's widow had said that the filming could go ahead. Everyone was determined to get on and finish what they had to do as soon as possible.

No one felt this more keenly than Whiteman, North and Jenkins after their second bad experience at Oldthwaite station. They were sitting on the platform benches waiting patiently for things to start to happen. All the actors were used to this. Making a film involved far more sitting around than people thought. North was reading a newspaper. Neither Jenkins nor Whiteman were in the best of moods. They said little to each other and spent most of their time reading messages on their phones.

'I've told Neil I might be back tonight,' said Jenkins at last.

'That's a bit optimistic,' replied Whiteman, without looking up from her phone.

'OK! Scene three: arrival; everyone in position,' called an assistant director. North looked up. All the technical stuff: cameras, lighting, sound equipment was in position. It reminded him of the fateful day when Dan had been killed, though this time there was no steam train approaching the station, they were only filming on the platform itself.

North, Whiteman and Jenkins, as Edward Wilding, Victoria Branwell and Mrs Wilson respectively, stood together to welcome Desmond Hammond as Montagu Lloyd to the village of Hartlington and his inheritance at Bolton Gill Manor. And suddenly the scene took place as it was meant to have done that fateful day, as if the cameras had frozen at that point and were now rolling again.

Wilding approached Montagu Lloyd as he descended from the carriage on to the platform.

'Welcome to Hartlington, sir. My name is Wilding and it's been my privilege to act as the solicitor for the Bolton Gill Manor estate for many years. I would welcome an opportunity to acquaint you with some legal aspects of the estate at your earliest convenience.'

'Thank you, Wilding, very nice of you to be here. I will contact you in due course.'

Wilding nodded. Lloyd turned to Victoria.

'Welcome, sir,' she said, curtseying and looking down as she blushed with embarrassment.

'And you, my dear, must be Victoria.' He reached forward, lifted up her chin and his eyes roved over her face. 'Very pleased to meet you, I must say.'

He moved along the line to Mrs Wilson who also bobbed a curtsey. 'Mrs Wilson, sir, housekeeper at Bolton Gill.' She curtseyed again.

'You're very welcome, sir, I'm sure. Everything is ready for you up at the manor, sir.'

'Splendid!' declared Lloyd, and walked out of the station to where a horse and carriage were waiting to take him up to the manor house.

Blake finally had the scene he wanted in the can.

Steph drove the police car out of Skipton station with Craven in the passenger seat and Andy in the back. A second car followed containing two armed officers. She knew the way to Andrews' remote cottage. Craven had briefed them on Oldroyd's discovery of the possible link between Andrews and the fatal car crash.

'If DCI Oldroyd is right, sir, this will be a massive leap forward,' said Andy.

'Yes, but we'll have to be really careful because if Ms Fingleton is being held there, then things could get tricky.'

'In a way let's hope she is, sir, then we can get her out.'

'Yes,' replied Craven, and things went quiet. The officers knew that this could be a difficult and dangerous encounter.

Steph drove up the overgrown track to Andrews' cottage. It was quiet in the yard. They got out of the car and looked around. The second car drew up and the armed officers got out. There was no sign of anyone.

Craven addressed the armed officers. 'We need to go carefully. The hostage may well be here. Stay close to me.'

'Sir.'

Craven hammered on the door and shouted, 'Mr Andrews, open the door. We have reason to believe that you are holding a person captive against their will. I repeat: open the door. We have armed officers with us.' There was the sound of a key turning and a bolt being drawn back. The officers trained their guns on the door, which opened, revealing Andrews standing there, white-faced and haggard. When he saw the guns, he raised his hands. The officers piled into the house. Andrews said nothing; he just pointed to the door that led down to the cellar. Steph opened it and went down the steps. Immediately she heard the sound of Deborah's voice.

'Oh, thank God!' she said, before she burst into tears. 'I heard a car coming so I made a noise, I . . .'

'Don't try to speak,' said Steph. 'We're going to call the ambulance. I'll help you up the stairs.'

With Steph's help, Deborah staggered up the stairs and lay on the kitchen floor, sobbing. Steph got cushions to support her head while Andy called for the ambulance. Craven had handcuffed Andrews, who sat in a chair, his head drooped over. He looked at Deborah and blurted out, 'I'm sorry!'

'It seems you've got quite a bit to be sorry about,' said Craven sternly.

Andrews nodded. 'I'll tell you everything. I'm sorry it turned out like this, but—'

Andrews stopped and everyone looked towards the door. There was the sound of another car turning into the yard.

'That'll be him,' cried Andrews. 'Be careful, he's always armed. He might have a gun.'

'Who is he?' asked Andy.

'Jack Spencer.'

'Who?'

There was no time for Andrews to answer. Craven went to the door with the armed officer and shouted, 'We're armed police officers. Throw down any weapons you have and raise your hands.'

The masked figure who had just emerged from the car immediately got back in, started the engine and drove off at high speed, raising a cloud of dust as the vehicle shot back down the track.

'Shall I chase him, sir?' asked Andy.

'No, we're closing in. I've got the reg. I'll put a call out and we'll track him down. I think the game's up. There's another call I need to make first though.' He got out his phone and dialled a number. 'Jim, it's over, we've got her and she's fine – yes, absolutely fine. You were right, she was in the cellar at Andrews' house – yes we've got Andrews – the ambulance will take her to Airedale Hospital – yes go over now and then come over to Skipton and we'll see what Andrews has to say – that's fine Jim, Andy and Steph are both here . . . yes, I will thank them. OK, bye.' He ended the call and smiled. 'He says thank you,' he said to Steph and Andy, 'and he really sounded as if he meant it. I've never heard him cry before.'

Oldroyd sat by Deborah's bed in Airedale General Hospital. She had bandages on her wrists, a plaster on her head and ointment around her lips and mouth. She'd had a much-needed bath and lots of tests that had revealed nothing serious. Despite tiredness and general aches and pains in her back caused by lying in awkward positions, she was in good shape after her ordeal.

Oldroyd had sped to the hospital after Craven's call and arrived not long after the ambulance that brought her from Andrews' house. He sat at her bedside holding her hand and anxiously scanning her face.

'I'm fine, Jim,' she said. 'Honestly, nobody assaulted me in any way . . . apart from a few minor blows to the head. Nothing really hard, but just to keep me in order. It's sore but nothing serious.'

'Good, well you'll have to stay in here for a little while so that they can make sure everything's OK.'

'OK, that's fine. I definitely need to rest, and I ache all over.'

Oldroyd looked at her for a moment and found tears coming to his eyes again.

'I'm sorry,' he said.

'What on earth for? What are you sorry about?'

'For bringing you over to Oldthwaite and putting you at risk.'

'You weren't to know that I was in danger.'

He shook his head. 'It was unprofessional. I should never have brought you near a crime scene where violent people were at large. I was trying to make it more pleasurable for me, having you there in the evenings. It was selfish.'

'It's OK saying that in hindsight but I didn't feel it was dangerous. If they were so set on kidnapping me to get you off the case, they could have tracked me down in Harrogate and taken me there.'

'Well, I don't know,' said Oldroyd. 'And then I couldn't save you, I couldn't get to you, and it was . . . was terrible.'

'What did you expect to be able to do, you daft thing? Ride up on a white charger and throw the prison door wide open?'

He laughed. Her sense of humour was one of the things he most loved about her. 'I don't know, but anyway . . . you're here and that's all that counts.' He leaned over and gave her a kiss. 'Hurry up and get better and then we'll get you home.'

'Sally was my little sister and I adored her,' said Andrews, facing Oldroyd and Craven in an interview room at Skipton station. In his face there was guilt and regret but also deep sadness which had been there for many years. A police officer sat on a chair at the side. 'We grew up together in Skipton. We weren't well off, my dad worked on the railway, and I followed him when I left school. Sally was always a lively, daring kind of lass; she passed her driving test at seventeen and borrowed my dad's car to drive over to Bradford or Leeds to see her friends. She promised him she wouldn't drink and drive and she never did. That's one of the reasons why we didn't believe Ross's account of what happened because the post-mortem said she was well over the limit for driving. Sally would never have driven if she'd drunk that much.

'She was a lot cleverer than me. She stayed on at school and went to university. She was training to be a solicitor when she died.' Andrews stopped and his head went down for a moment.

Oldroyd prompted him to continue. 'So how did she meet Alan Ross?'

'I don't remember exactly. He was part of a group of her friends from school. He must have gone to acting school or something after that, but he was knocking around here when she came home from university in the holidays. This was before he became famous. I think he was playing small parts in local theatres. My dad didn't like him: thought he was too full of himself, but Sally wouldn't hear anything against him. He had a flashy sports car, and he was very charming. I'm sure she found it all very exciting.'

'What happened that night?' asked Craven.

Andrews shut his eyes. The memories were still painful. 'You'll have to read the reports. It was Saturday, a lovely day in June, Sally and Ross went into Leeds to a club or something and they must have stayed 'til very late. They crashed on the back roads near Addingham on their way back to Skipton.'

'And you don't believe Sally was driving?'

Andrews' eyes flashed with anger. 'No, never – I'll never believe it. I think that bastard framed her to save his skin and that delay before he called the ambulance probably killed her.

'I was married then and living in Skipton not far from my parents. The police knocked them up at four a.m. to tell them. My mum went into hysterics and Dad rang me to tell me what had happened. He was crying his eyes out and he begged me to come round. It was a nightmare. They never got over it. They were both quite happy people, always laughing and smiling, but after Sally died, they became quiet and moody. All the joy in life had been knocked out of them. Dad started to drink quite heavily, and Mum was on medication. I suppose they were both deeply depressed, and they died younger than they should have.'

'I take it you always nursed a desire to get revenge on Ross?'

Andrews' lip curled with contempt. 'He didn't even attend the funeral. He knew he was guilty and he daren't face us. He caused that crash and he put Sally in the driving seat, and she took the blame. Then he buggered off to London and started calling himself Daniel Hayward, the bastard!' Andrews was shaking with anger. 'He wanted to become someone else and forget who he really was and what had happened.'

'Tell us how you got involved in the plot to kill him.'

'I've lost a lot in my life. After Sally and Mum and Dad, my wife died a few years ago from cancer and we had no children. Maybe it made me bitter. Somehow I blamed him; everything seemed to go wrong after Sally died. He cursed our family.'

'And it wasn't just your family, was it?' asked Oldroyd.

Andrews looked at Oldroyd. 'No, it wasn't. Two people were killed in the other car: Gary and Anne Spencer. They were a nice couple apparently. They were on their way back to Ilkley after they'd been for dinner at a friend's house in Skipton.'

'They had two children, didn't they?'

'Yes. I often wondered what had happened to them. It must have been bloody awful to lose your parents like that.'

'And then suddenly they returned.'

Andrews sighed. 'Yes. There was a new volunteer at the railway, an engineer called Jack Smith. He came to me one day a few months ago after I'd finished driving and had taken the engine to the shed. He said he knew who I was and that my sister had been killed. I was shocked; it brought everything back. We went into a little room at the back of the shed, and he told me that his real name was Jack Spencer. It was his mother and father who had been killed in that crash. I didn't believe it at first, but he knew so much about it. He said that when he and his sister were children, they were just told that their parents had been killed in an accident. As an adult he was curious about what had happened and had been finding out about it. He now believed that Ross was guilty and had caused his parents' deaths and my sister's.'

'He had a plan to get revenge.'

'Yes. We knew that there was a film crew coming to the railway. He said that Daniel Hayward was going to be in the film, and I knew who that was. He had a plan to kill Ross and get away with it and did I want to help.

'At last, I saw a chance to make Ross pay for what he'd done, and I agreed. Spencer told me about his scheme, which was ingenious. He learned which carriage they were going to use in the film, and he knew which compartment Ross would be in because he helped to get it ready. He did the work on that compartment wall himself during the night. My job was simply to slow the train down in the tunnel so that he had enough time to get out of it and into the other. Later that night I distracted the PC guarding the carriage so that Spencer's sister could get him out of the compartment.'

Oldroyd nodded. 'We thought that's what had happened. But you mentioned his sister. Was she involved too?'

'Yes, you see she was in the film and was able to monitor what was happening.'

'What's her name?'

'Her real name is Lesley Spencer. But she has a stage name, too: Anna Whiteman.'

237

The scene on the platform had been completed and the actors were sitting on the benches again when Anna Whiteman's phone bleeped to say that she had received a text. She read: *It's over they've found her. Andrews must have been arrested. He'll tell them everything. Get back to the Wharfedale and I'll pick you up.*

It was a shocking blow, but she'd known deep down that this was going to happen as soon as everything had started to unravel with Brian Evans.

She turned to Jenkins. 'You know, I'm not feeling well,' she said, putting her hand to her brow. Her face was indeed white. 'I think Gerry's finished with us. I'm going to go back for a lie down. Tell him where I've gone, will you?'

'OK,' replied Jenkins, looking concerned. 'Shall I come with you?'

'No, no, that's fine.'

She got up and left the platform. She didn't change out of her costume but ran frantically up the path back to the inn, trying to control her feelings of utter panic. What would they do now? Jack had become desperate and out of control. She was frightened of him. The whole thing had blown up in their faces and now there was no escape.

She made an outlandish figure as she arrived at the inn in her Edwardian dress and ran past Reception, leaving Amy the receptionist open-mouthed. Up in her room she hastily changed out of her costume and threw her clothes and belongings into a case. Tears were streaming down her face. It was utterly hopeless.

She went out of the hotel by a back entrance in order to avoid Reception, just as a car drove quickly up towards her and skidded round. She got in without a word and the car shot back down the drive.

～

'So, the plan to murder Alan Ross succeeded?' asked Oldroyd as he continued interviewing Andrews. All officers involved in the case had been informed that the two suspects still at large were Jack Spencer alias Smith and Lesley Spencer alias Anna Whiteman. Descriptions had been issued along with the registration number of Jack Spencer's car. It seemed as if it would only be a matter of time before they were caught.

'Up to a point. It was a clever plan, but not quite clever enough to fool everybody.'

'Brian Evans noticed something.'

'He did. There are too many people around like him and Granville Hardy who know the railways inside out. He must have noticed that the fixings on those panels with the pictures were different in those two compartments. It was such a minor detail and the only thing which gave anything away, but he noticed. His knowledge did for him, poor sod.'

'What happened?'

'He rang Jack and said he thought he might know how the murderer had managed to escape from the compartment. I suppose he never thought that Jack could actually be the killer. When he explained it, Jack knew that we'd been rumbled. He arranged to meet with Brian and then he called me.' Andrews paused and his face was tortured. 'It was then things started to go wrong. He said the only thing we could do was to get rid of Brian, otherwise it was only a matter of time before we would be caught. He said he was going to shoot Brian with the rifle he'd stolen from that gun club in Keighley. I pleaded with him not to. I'd known Brian a long time, as I told you, and he was an innocent man. But Jack wouldn't listen, and you know what happened next.'

'And how did you feel about it?' asked Craven.

'I was horrified. I wished I'd never got involved with the thing. Getting revenge on that bastard was one thing but killing an innocent man was another. But once Brian was dead, what could I do? I couldn't bring him back and it was possible that we might still get away with it all. I know Lesley felt the same.'

'It was soon clear that you were not going to escape, though, wasn't it?' said Oldroyd.

'When you two went to the shed to examine that carriage, he knew you were on to something.' He looked at Oldroyd. 'He was aware of your reputation as an expert in solving difficult mysteries and he started to panic. He began to do desperate things. He was dangerous. Me and Lesley were wary of him. He was always armed with his pistol or a knife. We were frightened he might turn on us if we didn't do what he said. Kidnapping your partner was a stupid idea. He said it would at least slow the investigation down and give us time to decide what to do. But what the hell could we do? And then his last mad thing was to set fire to the carriage.' Andrews continued to address his comments to Oldroyd, looking ashamed at having to admit to these events.

'I'm really sorry about what happened to your partner. Jack took her from the path up to Barden Moor and put her in a barn to begin with. He wasn't planning anything properly by this time. When he realised the police search of barns and outbuildings was progressing faster than he'd anticipated, he brought her to my place. We had a big row. I didn't want any part in it, but he threatened me and said it was our only hope. I had to look after her because it was too risky for him to keep driving round; the police knew the murderer was somebody who worked on the railway. Anyway, I looked after her better than he did, and I'm sure she'll be all right.' He looked at the detectives. 'I'm sorry about the whole thing. I should never have got involved. I just . . . hated that man so much.' He stopped and put his head in his hands.

Oldroyd was not sure what to say in the face of such contrition. He almost felt sorry for the man, although he had to remind

240

himself that he had played his part in a murder plot. He'd got involved with evil and found that there was no way back.

~

Steph and Andy were part of the team trying to track Spencer down. They had the make of the car and the registration number and were in communication with other police cars in the area.

'He can't have got far,' said Steph, who was driving. 'The problem is there are so many quiet minor roads round here that loop over the hillsides and cross over each other that there's always more than one route to anywhere you want to go.'

Andy consulted his phone, which had bleeped. 'Message from Craven,' he said as he read it. 'Right, the third person involved is Anna Whiteman, the actor. Apparently, she's Jack Spencer's sister. He was volunteering at the railway shed under the name of Jack Smith. Hayward, who also had a stage name, was in a crash years ago and their parents were killed. Bloody hell! So they blamed him.'

'So that means Spencer will most likely have gone to collect her from Oldthwaite and then they'll try to escape together.' She thought for a moment. 'OK, let's head for this back route towards Skipton.' She turned off on to a narrow lane. 'If I'm right we might catch them up.' She gripped the wheel and went as fast as she dared.

They'd not gone far before Andy shouted, 'Yes! Look, I'll bet that's them ahead.' He pointed to a car climbing up a hill on the road ahead. 'It's the right make; I can't see the reg yet, but they're racing along a bit.'

'I think you're right. Brace yourself.' Steph switched on the siren and sped up still more.

~

'Jack, slow down!' urged Lesley Spencer, alias the actor Anna Whiteman. She sat in the passenger seat beside her brother as he drove the car at high speed along the back roads.

Jack had a desperate expression on his face; his eyes were wild and staring above his thick beard and moustache.

'We've got to make a run for it,' he said, his voice tight and clipped.

'What do you mean? Where to? It's over, Jack, don't be stupid, we can't escape from the police. Let's just hand ourselves in and take our chance. At least we did what we aimed to do: we got revenge for Mum and Dad on that bastard.'

Spencer glanced at his sister. 'Look, if we can get to London, I know people who can hide us.'

'What then?'

'We can go abroad, get new identities; people do disappear and are never found again and . . . Oh shit!' He stopped because he had heard the sound of a police siren and then he saw the car in his rear mirror. He slammed his foot down on the accelerator.

'Jack! Stop! You'll kill us both!' shrieked Lesley.

They were now driving on a narrow country road that wound between drystone walls and the car tore round corners, veering out into the path of oncoming traffic.

'How the hell have they tracked us down so quickly? We'll shake them off I'm not—'

'Jack!!' Lesley screamed as a tractor appeared in front of them. Spencer pulled the steering wheel to the left and the car hit the bank at the side of the road. It shot into the air, narrowly missing the tractor. The passenger door sprang open, and Lesley was thrown out, landing on a grassy bank where she rolled over. The car turned over in the air and crashed down on to its roof.

The tractor stopped a little way down the road as the police car raced up, siren still blaring, and then pulled up sharply. The siren stopped; Steph and Andy got out and ran over to the crashed car. The tractor driver, grim-faced, ran back, but there was nothing he could do to help. Andy rang for the ambulance and for a team to remove the wreck, which was blocking the road. Lesley sat up moaning and looked towards the car.

'Jack!' she cried, and burst into tears. Andy peered under the wreck and looked back at Steph, shaking his head. Steph kneeled down beside Lesley and checked that she was OK. In these terrible circumstances, the formal arrest could wait.

Two days later Oldroyd and Craven faced Lesley Spencer in the interview room at Skipton station in which they'd previously spoken to Andrews. Her stage name of Anna Whiteman was unlikely to be used again. Jack Spencer had died in the crash, but Lesley had had a near-miraculous escape; virtually unscathed apart from bruises and a broken ankle. She looked at them impassively with her bruised and discoloured face.

'This story goes right back to when you and your brother were children, doesn't it?'

'Yes, Jack and I were very close as kids. He was less than two years older than me, and we spent a lot of time together.' She spoke with a calm dignity. 'We played in the garden of our house in Ilkley and down by the river. We used to go swimming by the suspension bridge.'

'I know it,' said Oldroyd. 'I've swum there myself. So it was a happy childhood until the accident?'

She sighed, showing the first sign of emotion. 'Yes. Mum was a teacher and Dad was a financial advisor. We had a comfortable life which was completely shattered.'

'How old were you and what happened that night?'

She paused and closed her eyes. 'I hate thinking about this. It's so vivid in my memory it's like it was yesterday. I was eight and Jack was ten. It was Saturday night, and Mum and Dad had gone over to Skipton for dinner with some friends. The babysitter was a sixth former at the school where Mum taught. It was all just a normal evening when Mum and Dad went out. She put us to bed, and I fell asleep. The next thing I remember was hearing a loud knock on the door. It was all dark and quiet apart from that and I knew it was very late. Francesca, that was the girl, must have opened the door. Then I heard a funny crackling sound and voices, that was the police radio, and then Francesca shouting: "What?" and "No, oh my God!" I was scared and I came out of my room to see what was happening. Jack was already at the top of the stairs looking down, but he didn't say anything. We just stayed there for a long time. I heard someone saying something about what's going to happen to them, but I didn't realise they were talking about me and Jack. I just wanted Mum and Dad to come back because I didn't like what was going on.

'Eventually Francesca's mother arrived, which was very strange, and then Francesca came upstairs and found us there. She'd been crying. I'd never seen an expression like that on her face before. Normally Jack would have asked her something, but he didn't. I think he knew something really bad had happened. Francesca said we were going to go home with her, because Mum and Dad couldn't come back tonight.' Lesley, whose voice had been breaking, started to cry at recalling this still extremely painful memory. 'She didn't tell us that they were never coming back.' A female police officer who was present gave her a tissue. 'Thank you.'

Clutching the tissue, she continued. 'We went to Francesca's house too scared and confused to say anything. We didn't even ask where Mum and Dad were because we sensed something had happened to them and no grown-up wanted to tell us anything. We went into the same bedroom together in single beds, but when I cried, Jack came over on to my bed and put his arm round me. We were so tired that we did eventually fall asleep.

'The next day when we came downstairs, we were taken into the living room and there was a woman there who smiled at us and said she worked with the police. I suppose she was a family liaison officer. She told us that our parents had been in a very bad car crash and that they were both dead.' Lesley started to cry again. 'I've never felt the same since that moment. Something hit me so hard, I was smashed up inside. It was unbelievably cruel, too much for a child to deal with. I screamed and Jack yelled "No!" He went hysterical and started to kick the furniture and they had to restrain him . . .' She stopped and shook her head. 'I buried my head in the sofa cushion to try to shut it all out.'

'And what happened to you both after that?' asked Craven.

She dried her eyes. 'We had to go into local authority care for a while, until it was decided we should go to live with my Uncle Simon and his wife in Leeds. They already had two children, our cousins, but they moved into a bigger house, I suppose they sold ours and used the money. We were never told anything about stuff like that.'

'And how was it?'

She shrugged. 'It was OK. My aunt and uncle did the best they could with two deeply traumatised kids. We lost all our friends and had to change schools. We were difficult: moody, angry, tearful. I refused to eat much for a long time and lost a lot of weight. I never felt like eating; my stomach was always tight. Jack was constantly in trouble at school which he hadn't been before. We did have counselling from some psychological service; it helped a bit and we gradually settled down.

'In the end we did well considering what we'd been through. Jack joined the army which is where he learned how to use guns, and trained as an engineer. I went to drama school. I was always in plays at school. I think I found it therapeutic to play roles; I could become someone else for a while and forget the pain that was always there in me. Jack and I were always close; there was a special bond between us because of what we'd been through.'

'So you both reached some kind of equilibrium and acceptance of what had happened?' asked Oldroyd.

She frowned. 'I wouldn't say that. Jack has always had a very short temper and got into a lot of fights. He was still very angry deep down. I still use acting as an escape. Being me isn't always pleasant: I get depressed and anxious, and it all goes back to what happened. Neither of us have found relationships easy.'

'Nevertheless, your lives were progressing reasonably well, weren't they? So what happened to change things?'

She dried her eyes again and blew her nose. 'It was Jack who started to research what had happened in the crash. You see, we were just told that there had been an accident, but no details. For years we didn't want to know any more and we had no ideas about who might have been to blame or anything like that. We didn't think of it in that way when we were kids. But Jack must have got to the point where he wanted to know more, and he was horrified by what he found. He discovered the whole controversy about who was driving the car. Here was this man, clearly drunk according to the reports, claiming this young woman had been driving, which was hotly disputed by her family who said she would never have driven after she'd been drinking. Why would she have been driving his sports car? And going so fast? It was definitely that car which smashed into my parents' car and not the other way round. Dad would have been driving sensibly; he always did. The post-mortem showed he hadn't been drinking.'

She looked at the two detectives and there was anger in her eyes. 'I know there was no proof, but the circumstantial evidence against that man was overwhelming. The police knew it at the time, and you know it now. He got into that car well over the limit. I suspect Sally didn't want to get in, but she had no other way of getting home at that time of night. He went on the back roads to avoid being stopped by the police. He drove too fast and lost control. This is what Jack told me was most likely to have happened and I believe him. That man killed our parents and his girlfriend.'

'You're right that it seems there was no hard evidence for what you're saying took place, and so the police could do nothing. Which is why I suspect you decided to take matters into your own hands,' observed Oldroyd.

She glared at him defiantly. 'How else could we get justice for ourselves and for our parents?'

'OK. So tell us what happened.'

She paused and drank some water from a glass that had been placed in front of her. 'Jack knew I'd got a part in *Take Courage* and then he found out that not only were we coming up to the Wharfedale Railway, where he was a volunteer, to do location shots, but that Dan Hayward was also in the film. Jack had found out who Dan Hayward really was. He called me and said it was fate. Things had come together in an unbelievable way, and it was our chance to get revenge. It was meant to be.'

'Is that what you thought?'

'No, I don't believe in fate like that, but I did want to get justice. Jack had gone back to live in the countryside around the Ilkley and Skipton area where we were born, and I was in London. He told me that he had a plan which would enable him to kill Ross and get away with it, but he needed help. He'd been watching the preparations for the filming and had volunteered to do extra work to help. He knew what was going to be filmed and he knew which vintage carriage they were going to use. He also told me about creating a hole through to the next compartment and creating the false luggage. I thought it was all ingenious at the time.'

Oldroyd looked at her. 'Have you changed your mind now?'

'No, I still think it was very clever, but now I can see that it was risky; things could go wrong, and something did. There was a recklessness in Jack which I didn't see because I was still angry, like he was.'

'He told you about Philip Andrews?'

She nodded. 'He did, and he saw it as further confirmation that we were meant to do it. He was the brother of the girl who was killed, and Ross probably caused her death by delaying his call to the ambulance service. And then he blamed her for it all. It made our revenge even more satisfying: relatives of all the victims were going to be involved. Jack was starting to get a gleam in his eye which should have been a warning, but I ignored it. His time in the army seemed to have made him harder and more ruthless.'

'The preparations started before the film crew and actors arrived.'

'Yes. Jack did the work secretly on the compartment wall and then he stole those guns. He knew how to use them. I was unhappy about that. I couldn't see why he needed a rifle as well as a pistol, but he said it was a useful back-up in case something went wrong. Of course, he was right but it wasn't as easy as he thought.'

'Go on.'

'Jack did everything really. Philip slowed the train down in the tunnel and my job was to monitor what was happening on the platform and text him if there were any problems.'

'And you opened the compartment next to Hayward's?'

'Yes. Jack had locked it so that none of the actors went in and we weren't sure whether to leave it locked or not. In the end we decided that it would look more suspicious if we left it locked. It might look as if the killer had hidden in there and locked the door.

Of course, Jack was hiding in there, and we didn't want you to do a thorough search. It was easy for me to open the carriage with the key Jack gave me. Everybody's attention was on Ross's body and his compartment. We thought you wouldn't look too closely at the next compartment.'

Here Craven shook his head. If only they had searched more carefully they would have found Spencer and lives would have been saved.

'Everything went well. Jack had to stay there hiding in that luggage until everyone had gone and it was dark. He had some food and water and a bottle to pee in. When the coast was clear after dark, Philip distracted the officer on duty, and I came to help Jack out of the carriage, and we removed the trick luggage.'

'So it looked as if everything had worked?'

'Yes, but not for long. The next day, Jack called me in a bit of panic saying this man Brian Evans had noticed what was different in those compartments. He said he was going to shoot him.'

'How did you feel about that?'

She sighed. 'I was appalled. He was going to kill an innocent man. I'd never have got involved if I'd known that was going to happen. But he said it was our only chance to stop the police from finding out. He rang off and before I could do anything he went down to the station and did it.' She closed her eyes. 'From that point on it all started to unravel and I then saw what a risky plan it had really been. I think Philip Andrews and I were blinded by our desire for revenge. He was shocked too, but we couldn't stop Jack.'

'Then he thought we were getting on to him.'

'Yes, I realise now that Jack was unhinged. He would stop at nothing to foil the police and make his escape and he became more and more desperate.' She looked at Oldroyd. 'He told us that you had been to the engine shed to examine the carriage. He knew your reputation and he was terrified that you were going to discover the trick.'

'So he kidnapped Deborah?'

'Yes. And I'm sorry. I'm sure Philip has said the same to you.'

'He has.'

'Jack was out of control; he was flailing around doing anything which might buy him a bit more time. He said that if we kidnapped her, he could make you withdraw from the case and that would hold up the investigation. Neither Philip nor I were convinced, but Jack now seemed dangerous. We were frightened that he might even turn on us, so I agreed to help him kidnap her as long as he assured me that it was only a bluff, that she would not be hurt even if you didn't withdraw from the case. He promised and said that you wouldn't want to take any risks. Just before she left the inn, I was hiding behind the door into the bar which was empty, and I heard her telling the receptionist where she was going. Frances Cooper was there too. Then I texted Jack the details.' She looked at Oldroyd. 'I'm sorry,' she repeated.

'What happened when he realised the kidnap hadn't worked?'

'Jack didn't trust Philip; said he was too soft. He was paying Philip a visit when he saw the police cars and knew it was all over. He texted me and picked me up at the Wharfedale. I tried to persuade him that the only thing we could do now was to give ourselves up, but he wouldn't have it. I think his rationality had gone by then. He had this crazy idea that we could go abroad and take on new identities. He was driving like a maniac.' She paused and looked at the two detectives. 'I realise how ironic it is that he crashed a car, like Ross did. Thankfully he didn't crash into another vehicle. And it was also not that far from where our parents died.' She burst into tears again. She had now lost all her family.

Oldroyd nodded and looked at her. 'I believe you when you say that you intended nobody any harm except Ross, and I understand that your brother and yourself were damaged by what happened to you. We'll have to see what the jury makes of it all.'

'Thank you,' she said, looking at Oldroyd with genuine gratitude and contrition mixed with pain. She was definitely not acting now. She'd played her final part in the world of stage and screen. Somehow it was very sad.

Oldroyd turned to the female officer. 'Take her away.'

Oldroyd and Craven went up to the latter's office.

'Well, Jim, leave all the tidying up to me,' said Craven on whose ruddy face the relief was clear, although he also looked extremely tired. It had been a whirlwind of activity since the first murder and the stress of having to take charge of the investigation had been intense. He felt that he had not got everything right, but at least it had turned out reasonably well in the end. 'We've got enough forensic evidence to link Spencer with the crimes, but it's turned out to be a strange case, hasn't it? Everything happened so quickly and now the main culprit isn't here to face justice. It's not satisfying somehow. I have a measure of sympathy for the other two, don't you?'

'Yes,' replied Oldroyd, who was also savouring the relief that it was all over and that Deborah was safe. 'Though Jack Spencer was deeply damaged too. In fact more so than anyone realised.'

'True. I suppose some people would say it was better that he didn't survive. He and Ross are both dead so maybe it's all evened out in the end. I don't know.'

'I felt the whole thing was an awful tragedy and it claimed so many lives. Spencer got into the Macbeth syndrome,' said Oldroyd. 'Once you go down the wrong road, evil is unleashed, and you can't contain it. And the other two were dragged down with him. He had to do more and more terrible things in order to try to secure his position, just like Macbeth in the play. And Richard the Third is the same: the more people he kills, the more enemies he makes until he's finally overwhelmed.'

Craven laughed. 'Well, that's all a bit too literary for me, Jim, but what I do know is that it's been a pleasure as always to work with you, though I must say it's always a roller coaster of a ride on a case when you're involved. I'll be glad to get back to obstructed paths, sheep stealing and pubs opening at illegal times.'

'That's not all you do, Bob.'

'No,' replied Craven. 'But that's what a lot of people think we do at these police stations in the country areas.'

'Well, they haven't seen the violence between the rival money-laundering gangs in Grassington.'

'No,' laughed Craven. 'Neither have I. Anyway, I know you'll want to get back, so all the best to you and Deborah, Jim. I'm sure she'll make a full recovery and I hope it's not long before you and I work together again.'

'The feeling's mutual, Bob.'

The two detectives shook hands.

When Oldroyd got back to Harrogate HQ he went up to see Tom Walker who had returned from his holiday in Scarborough. Walker was a very experienced detective who had spent many years in the field. Oldroyd always thought he looked out of place behind a desk and not particularly happy playing management games with data, money, spreadsheets and outputs.

As always, Walker was pleased to see him. 'Ah, Jim, sit down. How's Deborah? That was a nasty ordeal she went through.'

'She's fine, Tom; getting better each day. She's a tough lass.'

'Good. Well, ah'm glad tha got to t' bottom of t' case in th' end.' They liked to throw bits of dialect into their conversation, both being Yorkshire born and bred. It was almost a running joke they shared.

'Thanks. But I couldn't have done it without you, Tom. You provided the key piece of information about that car crash. It turned out that the whole thing was based on what happened that night. You were absolutely right that most people believed that Ross or Hayward was driving that car, and the relatives of the victims were determined to get revenge.'

Walker nodded. 'So I understand. It was a long time to carry around such terrible feelings, wasn't it?'

'Yes, but the Spencers were only young children when they lost their parents. That trauma went in very deep. Anyway, did you enjoy your holiday?'

Walker pulled a face. 'It was OK. The weather was poor. You've had it much better here. The east coast often gets it bad with those bloody sea frets coming in, but I got in a couple of rounds of golf and a few drinks at the bar afterwards, so it was fine for me. Gillian likes Scarborough whatever the weather, so she was happy. She takes the dog for long walks on the beach.'

'You have the satisfaction of knowing that you played a key part in solving the case from a remote position in Scarborough.'

Walker laughed. 'Well, I suppose you're right. I hadn't thought of it like that. What a genius eh? So, what about that railway? Do you think it will recover OK? I'm fond of that line. I was only a young boy at the time, but I just remember travelling on it when it was still run by British Rail.'

'I'm sure it will be fine, Tom. They lost a very devoted volunteer, but they've got a very competent person in charge, and I think people will flock back now it's all over.'

'Good, I hope you're right.'

'I'm not sure what will happen about the film though. Now they've lost another of their principal actors it will be even more difficult to continue, I expect. Who knows? The people who are financing it might decide it now has a kind of notoriety which will play well with the box office.'

'Well, theirs is a different world, isn't it? Money, glamour, media image; it wouldn't do for me.'

The two men chatted on for a while and arranged to meet one evening for a drink. Although these evenings could be tricky as Oldroyd had to steer Walker away from his pet hates, he thought it judicious to occasionally see his boss socially.

He left the office in good heart knowing that Walker was as impressed, as ever, with his work. And what was more, he hadn't had to listen to a single rant about Matthew Watkins, the press or anything else.

Everybody in Oldthwaite was trying to come to terms with the shock of the latest drama and the revelations that followed. The atmosphere at the Wharfedale Inn and the Wharfedale Railway was sombre. People whispered to each other and shook their heads as they talked about what had happened and hoped that the terrible series of events was now over.

After calling the producer, Blake gathered the remaining principal actors, including the newly arrived Desmond Hammond, together in the bar. Frances was there too. Candida Hayward had disappeared back to London, much to Frances's relief.

'I won't go over everything that's happened,' said a very serious pale-faced Blake. 'I've spoken to Harriet and basically it's all over. There's no way we can continue. We can't replace Anna at this stage and reshoot all her scenes. The company will be in touch about final payments. I just wanted to thank you all for your efforts and to apologise to you, Desmond, for bringing you all that way just for one day's filming.'

'Not at all,' said Hammond. 'It's not your fault, Gerry.'

Sheila Jenkins was sitting next to Christopher North, and she burst into tears. North was not far from tears himself, but managed a reply to Blake.

'Thank you for all you've done, Gerry. Desmond's right: it's not your fault.' He put his arm round Jenkins' shoulders. They were all thinking about Anna, but nobody could bring themselves to say anything. They were too shocked.

There was nothing left to do. They all shook hands. Jenkins hugged Blake and then they all left to pack up and return home. The whole experience was the most traumatic of their acting careers.

Blake sat with his head in his hands. It was devastating to lose the film after so much work, and in such appalling circumstances.

'Can I get you a drink, darling?' asked Cooper.

'Yes,' he replied with a sigh. 'You know,' he said bitterly. 'The terrible irony is: what a good film you could make out of what's happened here. It's got everything, hasn't it: revenge, romance, suspense, drama? It would be much more exciting than *Take Courage* would have been.'

Cooper put her hand on his arm. 'That's how you feel now. It's very disappointing. But you'll come back from it. No one's going to hold this against you, you'll get more work as a director.'

He looked at her. 'Do you really think so?'

'Yes. You'll come back from this difficult time.' She looked him in the eyes. 'Just like we have.' He held her hand. North came back into the room.

'Gerry, I fear I owe you an apology.'

Blake looked up. 'What for, Chris?'

'I feel I should have warned you that Dan was bad news. If I had, maybe you wouldn't have cast him in that role. Then this whole wretched business would not have happened.'

Blake shook his head. 'No, Chris, no one could have foreseen all this and anyway, Dan was a good actor despite the kind of person he was, and he was right for that part. In that sense I don't regret it. I was making the correct professional decision. None of us could have known what a terrible series of events would be triggered by my choice.'

North put his hand on Blake's shoulder. 'That's a very sensible way to look at it and you'll recover from this; you've got the talent.'

'That's what I've told him,' added Cooper.

Blake smiled, thankful that two people who were important to him still had faith in his future.

Later that day Andy and Steph were relaxing in their flat in Leeds. It was a fine evening, and they were out on their balcony with glasses of wine overlooking the river. The waterside bars were busy with drinkers sitting out and enjoying the warm June weather.

Both detectives, having worked with Oldroyd for some time, were familiar with the pattern of involvement in one of his mysterious and dramatic investigations: puzzlement; the urgency of finding a solution as more victims appeared; the breakthrough; the hectic pursuit of the perpetrators and finally the relief as everything was wound up, relief that almost shaded into a sense of anticlimax. They had now reached the final stage and this case had left Steph in a thoughtful mood. She sat quietly for a moment, twirling her glass and thinking while Andy read a message on his phone.

'Andy,' she said finally.

'Yeah?'

'Do you ever think about that man who killed your father?'

When Andy was eleven, his father, who had also been a police officer, had been shot dead in the street by a drug runner whose car he was investigating.

He looked up sharply. 'Whoa! That's out of the blue, where's it come from?'

'It's just that this case has made me think about some stuff. I mean, those three were motivated by a need for revenge which was so strong that they were prepared to kill. Did you ever think that you'd like to kill that man?'

Andy nodded. 'The answer is yes, when I was a kid. I think I was about the same age as Jack Spencer when he lost his parents. I think it's a natural reaction isn't it, to want revenge? But I don't believe it does any good. If you don't let those feelings go, they just eat you up and that's what happened in this case, particularly with him.'

'I know you can't take justice into your own hands and stuff, but it must have been awful to lose both parents like those two did and they were so young. I sometimes wonder what would have happened if my dad had killed my mum that time, you know; how would I have felt? Also, that man Andrews lost his sister, and I think about Lisa. All I'm saying is, I can understand that it must have been really difficult for them all to ever forgive Ross and they wanted him to pay for what he'd done.'

'Yes, but what's made you think about all this?'

She told him about her father wanting to contact her and her sister again and how she felt very ambiguous about it. 'I didn't want to tell you until the case was over. We had too much going on and we couldn't discuss it properly. But now, do you think I should contact him? I hate him and so on, and I have a strong instinct to ignore him or even call him and tell him what a bastard he is to treat my mum like he did, to try to get revenge on him like they did with Ross but not as extreme, obviously.'

'What would that achieve?'

She sighed. 'I know. It sounds very childish, doesn't it? This case has made me see how destructive revenge can be. Another part of me wants to find out if he is really sorry and genuinely wants to find out about me and Lisa.'

Andy took a sip of wine and thought for a moment.

'I'd go with that. What have you got to lose? You'll soon find out if he's trying to tap you for money or something. When I first joined the force, I thought policing was all about retribution and revenge and stuff. That's probably because I was still angry about Dad. I wanted justice for everyone who'd been wronged. Well, I still want justice, but I also believe that people can be really sorry for what they've done, so why not give him a chance?'

Steph looked at him sideways and smiled. 'Wow, that's very thoughtful coming from you!'

'Hey! Cheeky beggar, you're talking about me as if I'm some brainless operative. I do have a mind and values as well as this hunky physique.'

'Oh really,' she laughed.

'It's working with the boss that makes you stop and think. He makes you consider everything deeply and see that crimes are not only mysteries where you have to use your powers of reason, but they're also about people who are all complicated and that's when you have to use your knowledge of human nature.'

Steph clapped. 'Bravo! I think you're staking your claim to be his successor.'

'Not much chance of that, I'm not sure anyone could succeed him, but anyway do you feel any clearer about what to do?'

'I do, and thank you.' She took a drink, and thought for a while before changing the subject. 'Do you think he and Deborah will be OK?'

'I'm sure they will, given a little time to recover.'

She looked at him. 'Have you ever thought that in some ways he's like a substitute father to us? We both lost our real fathers, after all.'

'Wow! That's very deep. I'd never really thought of it that way, but I suppose you're right. I certainly look up to him a lot.'

'Me too. And I think you're right about Dad. I think I'm going to suggest to Lisa that we at least see him.'

They were quiet for a while and then she looked at him mischievously from behind her wine glass. 'You know, I think it's time we went in.'

'It's still quite warm out here.'

'Whatever happened to romance! I didn't mean I was cold, you twit.'

'Oh, I see, sorry! Well, I'll raise my glass to that,' he said, drinking the rest of his wine.

A week later the weather was still fine, and a sunny afternoon found Oldroyd and Deborah by the Wharfe at Barden Tower a few miles to the north of Oldthwaite and the Wharfedale Bridge Inn. After her incarceration, Deborah had a great urge to spend time out of doors in the sunshine and fresh air, although Oldroyd had to go with her. She felt it would be some time before she could go for a walk by herself, and maybe she would never again feel secure alone on the more remote parts of the moors and fells.

They crossed the narrow road bridge and walked through the woods on the west side of the river. Oldroyd smiled at Deborah and looked around.

'Isn't it wonderful to be here on a beautiful day like this after what's happened?' said Oldroyd.

Deborah linked arms with him. 'Yes, it is. There were times in that barn and cellar when I thought I would never see all this again but, paradoxically, one of the things that sustained me was thinking about places like this and trying to meditate on them. It gave me a sort of peace. It also makes you value them more.'

Oldroyd shook his head. 'You're amazing. I think it would have driven me mad.'

'It was only for a few days. Hostages have been kept for years in isolation not knowing what was going to happen to them and fearing they would be killed.'

'It must have been hard when Spencer paid you visits, and you didn't know if he was coming to finish you off.'

'Yes. He was always hard and rough. He hit me a couple of times, but I kept reminding myself that a dead hostage is useless, and I didn't believe in the end that they would kill me. Because I wasn't a threat to them. It was much better with Andrews because I knew he was really on my side, and he felt guilty about my being there. I was able to talk to him and it's strange, but any human connection you make feels good when you're by yourself all the time. It reminds you that you're still a person. I think that's also why captors don't talk to their captives or only in an abrupt, aggressive way. If they were warmer, they might start making a human connection with their victims. It would be more difficult to keep them there if they started to see them as people.'

'That's interesting.'

'Yes, do you know what else kept me going?'

'What?'

She smiled at him. 'You. I had faith that you would take care in order to protect me, but also you would work out what was going on and catch the people involved.'

'Oh, that's lovely!' Oldroyd pulled her round and kissed her.

'And you did,' continued Deborah. 'And here we are.'

They had reached an ornate Victorian pipe bridge constructed over the river, and they crossed over in order to enter Bolton Woods on the east side. Oldroyd paused on top of the bridge, stood by one of the parapets and looked down at the river. He saw the usual birds and heard their calls close by and further away in the fields. Trout were swimming in the water. 'This is one of my favourite places in the world,' he said. 'Do you know the poet, Edward Thomas? He wrote that famous poem "Adlestrop" about a timeless moment of beauty and peace.'

'Yes, I've read that one, it's beautiful.'

'It's set in the Midlands but I've been having a go at writing a Yorkshire version of it. You know, the same sentiments but in a Yorkshire setting.'

'Have you got it with you?'

'Yes.'

'Let's hear it then.'

He pulled a notebook out of his jacket and read the following:

> Barden: the Yorkshire 'Adlestrop' (after
>   Edward Thomas)
>
>
> Yes. I remember Barden—
> The name, because one day
> In spring I stood there by
> the Wharfe. It was late May.
>
> There was no one on the path.
> Trout swam near the river bed.
> Over the clear water,
> Wrens fluttered and dippers sped.

And flowers in the woods,
And smooth green grass,
Grazing sheep and distant hills
A wild and rugged mass.

And for that minute a curlew called
Nearby, and round him, mistier,
Farther and farther, all the birds
On the moors and fells of Yorkshire.

'Wonderful,' said Deborah.

Without a word Oldroyd gazed again at the river, the banks, the fields with their barns and the distant hills. And he heard a curlew calling as he'd described in his poem. Then he put the notebook back into his jacket and they continued over the bridge, turning right to follow the path into the woods.

Acknowledgements

I would like to thank my family, friends and members of the Otley Writers' Group for their help and support and the many people around the world who buy my books.

The fictional Wharfedale Railway is based on Yorkshire's heritage railways, some of which have been used as settings in films and television series: the Keighley and Worth Valley Railway, the Wensleydale Railway, the North Yorkshire Moors Railway and the Embsay and Bolton Abbey Steam Railway. I had the setting and route of the latter in mind when describing the railway in the story. I would like to thank all the volunteers whose efforts keep these wonderful railways running.

Granville Hardy's model railway layout was inspired by the one at the Buffers Coffee Shop at Back O' Th' Hill Farm near Bolton Abbey, sadly now closed. I would like to thank the former owners for running such a lovely and unusual café for so many years.

The dramatic Strid is a real feature in the glorious Bolton Woods in Wharfedale. If you visit it, be careful; it really has claimed lives.

The West Riding Police is a fictional force based on the old riding boundary. Harrogate was part of the old West Riding, although it is in today's North Yorkshire.

About the Author

John R. Ellis has lived in Yorkshire for most of his life and has spent many years exploring Yorkshire's diverse landscapes, history, language and communities. He recently retired after a career in teaching, mostly in further education in the Leeds area. In addition to the Yorkshire Murder Mystery series, he writes poetry, ghost stories and biography. He has completed a screenplay about the last years of the poet Edward Thomas and a work of faction about the extraordinary life of his Irish mother-in-law. He is currently working (slowly!) on his memoirs of growing up in a working-class area of Huddersfield in the 1950s and 1960s.